**Praise for the Novels
of Jo Davis**

Hidden Fire

"Surprisingly sweet and super hot. . . . One of the best heroes I've read in a long time. If you want a hot firefighter in your room for the night, grab a copy and tuck right in with no regrets. Four hearts."
—*The Romance Reader*

"A fast-paced romantic-suspense thriller."
—The Best Reviews

Under Fire

"Four stars! A totally entertaining experience."
—*Romantic Times*

"Scorching hot kisses, smoldering sex, and explosive passion make *Under Fire* a must read! Experience the flames of *Under Fire!*" —Joyfully Reviewed

"Exhilarating [with] a 200-proof heat duet . . . a strong entry [and] a terrific, action-packed thriller."
—*Midwest Book Review*

continued . . .

Trial by Fire

"A five-alarm read . . . riveting, sensual."
—*Publishers Weekly* Beyond Her Book Blog

"Jo Davis turns up the heat full blast. Romantic suspense that has it all: a sizzling firefighter hero, a heroine you'll love, and a story that crackles and pops with sensuality and action. Keep the fire extinguisher handy or risk spontaneous combustion!"
—Linda Castillo, national bestselling author of
Pray for Silence

"Jo Davis . . . completely reeled me in. . . . Heady sexual tension, heartwarming romance, and combustible love scenes."　　　　　　　—Joyfully Reviewed

"One of the most exciting 'band of brothers' series since J. R. Ward's Black Dagger Brotherhood. It's sweet and sexy, tense and suspenseful."　　—myLifetime.com

"For a poignant and steamy romance with a great dose of suspense, be sure to pick up a copy of *Trial by Fire* as soon as it hits the bookstores! Five Bookmarks!"
—Wild on Books

"Hot, sizzling sex and edge-of-your-seat terror will have you glued to this fantastic romantic-suspense story from the first page to the final word. Do not miss the heart-stopping, breath-stealing, incredibly well-written *Trial by Fire*."　　　　　　　　　—Romance Novel TV

ALSO BY JO DAVIS

The Firefighters of Station Five Novels

Line of Fire
Hidden Fire
Under Fire
Trial by Fire

I Spy a Naughty Game
I Spy a Wicked Sin
When Alex Was Bad

RIDE THE FIRE

THE FIREFIGHTERS OF STATION FIVE

JO DAVIS

A SIGNET ECLIPSE BOOK

SIGNET ECLIPSE
Published by New American Library, a division of
Penguin Group (USA) Inc., 375 Hudson Street,
New York, New York 10014, USA
Penguin Group (Canada), 90 Eglinton Avenue East, Suite 700, Toronto,
Ontario M4P 2Y3, Canada (a division of Pearson Penguin Canada Inc.)
Penguin Books Ltd., 80 Strand, London WC2R 0RL, England
Penguin Ireland, 25 St. Stephen's Green, Dublin 2,
Ireland (a division of Penguin Books Ltd.)
Penguin Group (Australia), 250 Camberwell Road, Camberwell, Victoria 3124,
Australia (a division of Pearson Australia Group Pty. Ltd.)
Penguin Books India Pvt. Ltd., 11 Community Centre, Panchsheel Park,
New Delhi - 110 017, India
Penguin Group (NZ), 67 Apollo Drive, Rosedale, North Shore 0632,
New Zealand (a division of Pearson New Zealand Ltd.)
Penguin Books (South Africa) (Pty.) Ltd., 24 Sturdee Avenue,
Rosebank, Johannesburg 2196, South Africa

Penguin Books Ltd., Registered Offices:
80 Strand, London WC2R 0RL, England

First published by Signet Eclipse, an imprint of New American Library,
a division of Penguin Group (USA) Inc.

First Printing, December 2010
10 9 8 7 6 5 4 3 2 1

To my beautiful children, Kayla and Bryan.

Let nothing stand in the way of your dreams. Push on and go for it, no matter what anyone says. The world is yours for the taking. Be a better person than I ever was. Fly higher than I ever did. Embrace life with all the joy you've brought to me.

You two are my greatest work, my proudest achievement. You are good, fine people who I'm honored to know and love. Because of you, my happiness is complete.

I love you,

Mom

ACKNOWLEDGMENTS

With heartfelt thanks to . . .

My family for encouraging me to keep writing, even when life refuses to cooperate.

My agent and friend, Roberta Brown, for her unfailing support.

My editor, Tracy Bernstein, for her faith in me and for keeping me wonderfully busy.

The Foxes, for keeping me sane. Or maybe we're all just insane together and don't know it.

My friend Brad Craghead, for naming Detective Taylor Kayne when I absolutely couldn't think of what to call him! Great name, buddy.

And to you, the readers, for loving my Station Five boys as much as I do. It's been a great ride, with new adventures to come. Thank you.

PROLOGUE

On the night the world ended, Blair Tanner had told her husband to go to hell.

The argument had been stupid. Just one of many they'd had lately, going at each other like scalded cats in a sack. Sean leaned his back against the grille of Engine 171, arms crossed over his chest, and stared out the open door of the fire station's bay, watching brown leaves drift from the trees to litter the ground outside.

Everyone assumed he and Blair were blissfully happy, the quintessential Barbie-and-Ken couple with their two gorgeous children, not to mention a pair of nice vehicles, living on a spread they'd never be able to afford if not for Blair's fancy job. Sean snorted, figuring at least one of those points was spot-on.

His teenage son and six-year-old daughter were perfect. Even more than the job he loved so much, he breathed for his children. Not, however, according to his pissed-off wife when they'd had it out over the phone earlier.

Your son is going to be so let down. How can you do this to him, Sean?

Bobby understands. I can't leave my men in a bind—

Oh, save it! Always with the excuses, and they're getting

old. You know, if you can't appreciate what you have here, someone else might.

What the fuck is that supposed to mean? Blair?

"Hey, Cap. What's with the long face? In the doghouse again?"

Sean turned to see Clay Montana swagger toward him, grinning like a fool. "Is my name Sean Tanner and do I have a pulse?" He couldn't help but smile back at their resident cowboy.

"Ouch." Clay grimaced in sympathy. "That's what happens when you break the first rule of bachelorhood."

"What's that?"

"Never sleep with the same woman twice. Unless a man wants to end up like you—pussy-whupped and with couple of rug rats biting at your ankles."

Sean laughed, shaking his head at the cowboy's earnest expression. The guy wasn't joking. "Yeah? At least I know where my woman's been, and I happen to like my rug rats just fine, thanks."

Clay shrugged. "Whatever, it's your blood pressure, not mine. So, what happened?"

"Blair ripped me a new one for working overtime tonight instead of going with her and Mia to watch Bobby's football game. He's the starting quarterback again, and he's doing really well since he took over for the first-string kid who got injured. He's even been approached by a couple of college scouts." His chest puffed out with pride at that.

"Hey, that's great! For Bobby, anyhow. We can probably swing it if you want to take off and catch the last half. If nothing else, we can try to call in the lieutenant to cover."

For a long moment, he was tempted. "Nah, that's

okay. I already asked Six-Pack. He couldn't make it in and I don't want to leave you short a man. Besides, there's a couple of games left in the regular season and I promised Bobby I'd make those."

"Sucks being the boss, huh?"

"Only when I have to disappoint my kids to come ride roughshod over you bozos," he said, shooting the other man a grin. "Someday you'll understand."

Clay shuddered. "Not me, man. No freaking way will you see me stick my head through the golden noose."

Sean snickered as Clay strode back inside, presumably to make himself useful doing something. Sean thought his friend protested too much. Firefighters were family people, nurturers at heart. They all fell eventually, and he'd bet Clay would be no different.

The evening crawled at a snail's pace with only a couple of minor calls, and Sean began to think he'd given up his day off for nothing. But if he hadn't come in, the station would've gotten called to some real disaster and he would've ended up here all the same. Murphy's Law.

It was almost a relief when dispatch sent them out to an accident—except this one was major, with two possible fatalities and a third person, a screaming child, trapped in the burning car. In the front passenger's seat of the quint, Sean stared intently down the highway, knowing time wasn't on their side. They weren't going to make it before the fire consumed the vehicle, and he hoped the police or bystanders were able to free the child and anyone else involved.

Behind the wheel, Clay gestured to the blaze in the distance, growing closer. "Is that what I think it is?"

"Sure as hell is," John "Val" Valentine said grimly

from the back. "We've got a car bred to an eighteen-wheeler, folks."

The police hadn't yet arrived. The eighteen-wheeler was parked on the shoulder, as though it had some sort of engine trouble. The car that had hit the rig from behind was fully involved with flames, too, the blaze beginning to engulf the back end of the big semi. Clay pulled the quint as close as they dared, the ambulance on their tail, and they all jumped out. Clay and another man scrambled to grab hoses, while Sean and the others went to assess the situation, check on survivors and their injuries. Other cars had pulled onto the shoulder, and shocked witnesses stared at the spectacle, a couple of women sobbing.

One older woman grabbed the sleeve of Val's heavy coat. "They c-couldn't get the little g-girl out! The older boy, who was driving the car, a-and the woman, they were dead. But the little one was screaming for her daddy to put out the fire and—and . . ." The woman clapped a hand over her mouth, overcome by recounting the horrifying events.

Sweet Jesus. Her words made Sean's blood run cold. "Ma'am, are there any other survivors you know of?"

"The driver of the big truck says he's fine. He's over there," she said in a wobbly voice, and pointed. Sean followed the gesture to a distraught man sitting on the shoulder of the highway, his face in his hands, and doubted the man was fine at all.

"Val, check on the driver while I go talk to the witnesses."

"Got it, Cap."

Pushing his fire hat back on his head, Sean turned and began to walk toward the inferno and the agitated witnesses. Three men were pacing too close to the fire, hopeless expressions on their faces. There was nothing they could have done, and Sean felt sorry for the poor bastards. Nobody should have to encounter something as sad as this.

He opened his mouth to yell at the three men to move back—

And that's when he saw the license plate on the back end of the car, curling and blackening from the intense heat. Saw the letters and numbers rapidly being overcome by the flames.

Blair's car.

An older boy and a woman.

A little girl screaming for Daddy to put out the fire.

"No." He stopped, rooted in place, his mind resisting the truth. Unwilling to make the final connection, to make it real.

Because if it was real, he had nothing. *Was* nothing. Not without his family.

His children.

"Oh, God . . ."

His knees buckled, hit the asphalt. He struggled to draw in a breath, to scream, but his lungs were frozen.

"Cap! Cap, what's wrong? Talk to me!" Someone crouched beside him and a gloved hand grabbed his arm.

"That car," he whispered. "That's my wife's car. My family . . ."

"What? No, no, I'm sure you're mistaken. Sean?"

The truth swept in, as black and bitter as the stench of gasoline and burning bodies, and he couldn't stop the images.

Blair. Bobby. Mia, his sweet baby.

Blair had been right to damn him to hell. He'd put work above his family and they'd paid the ultimate price. He hadn't deserved them, and now . . . *No, please, God. Please.*

He slumped sideways, falling into darkness.

"Sean? Oh, Jesus. Somebody help me over here!"

But there was no help for him.

Not ever again.

1

Laughter and celebration carried on the warm spring breeze, and with the sounds of merriment, the swell of excitement reflected in so many young faces. This day truly marked the first day of the rest of their lives.

Bouncing on his feet, Sean Tanner impatiently searched the sea of caps and gowns for the one person who mattered most. The one who always had his back, no matter what. Finally, he spotted a familiar blond head weaving through the crowd, headed straight for him and rapidly closing the distance.

Jesse Rose's smile lit his handsome face as he wrapped Sean in a manly hug, slapping him on the back. "Dude, was that boring or what? Thought they'd never stop preaching about us being the future of mankind and shit."

Sean drew back, playfully ruffling his best friend's hair. "Scary thought, huh?"

"You know it! So tell me, what's the plan? Made up your mind yet?" Still smiling, Jesse arched a blond brow. As if he knew damned well that hearing the words was a mere formality.

Sean sucked in a deep breath, and forced down the flutter of fear in his heart. It was just the thrill of the unknown, *that was all. "You and me, the few and the proud. We're gonna see the world, man!"*

His friend slung his arm about his shoulders. "I knew I could count on you."

"Always, Jesse. Always."

Sean Tanner leaned against the porch railing and wrapped his hands around his coffee mug, relishing the warmth. The fall morning was crisp and cool, sporting enough of a bite to justify the light jacket he wore over his navy fire department polo shirt. As he watched the horses graze, his thoughts tumbled one after another, a lengthy, confusing list of things to do.

Amends to make.

Emotions assailed him, a cacophony of trepidation, anxiety, amazement. And hope.

Hope, because as terrifying as the tasks laid before him were, the miles left to travel, all these intimidating thoughts and emotions had one important thing in common.

They were those of a sober man.

But for how long? Would he screw up tomorrow, next week? Even now his hands trembled as he clutched the mug, longing to skip the much-anticipated reunion with his team. To jump into the Tahoe and make tracks to the liquor store outside of town, grab a bottle of bourbon to add some kick to his coffee. Replace the raw pain of reality with the comforting haze of oblivion.

Closing his eyes, he clamped down hard on the temptation and beat it into submission. If he went down that road again, he might as well be dead. *No.* When he finally joined his family on the other side, he'd go to them as a man they could be proud of, not the mean, drunken wretch of the past two years. The man who'd became so sloppy and inattentive at work, he'd cost Tommy Skyler his firefighting career and nearly his life.

That man isn't me. Never again.

Heading inside, he rinsed out the mug and placed it in the dishwasher. Turned off the coffeepot. Wiped down the counter. Watered the ivy on the windowsill. Anything to keep him busy and his mind off another drink, not to mention his dubious reception in—he glanced at the kitchen wall clock—forty minutes.

A deep sigh escaped his lips. No sense in putting off the inevitable. Even if he'd rather get caught in a backdraft with no hope of escape than face five of the people he'd let down time and again.

"Jesus, grow a pair and get going, Tanner." End of pep talk.

Before he could change his mind and do something truly idiotic, like call in sick, Sean snatched his keys off the counter and headed out the door.

The drive into Sugarland had never seemed so long, and singing country music along with the radio hadn't provide much of a distraction. Then suddenly he was at the station, parked in his usual spot around back, almost frozen in place by the difficulty of taking the next few steps.

If they'd strung up banners and shit, he was going straight home.

He slid out of the Tahoe, locked up, and pocketed his keys. Walking around the side of the building, he steeled himself for whatever was to come. Awkwardness? Or, worse, sympathy?

Taking a deep breath, he stepped into the bay and found . . . complete normalcy.

Zack Knight, their FAO—fire apparatus operator—
had his back to Sean and was busy buffing the quint to
a candy-apple shine. A couple of guys just getting off
C-shift were standing around, bullshitting with Julian
Salvatore and Sean's best friend, Lieutenant Howard
"Six-Pack" Paxton. Clay Montana, who'd moved to
A-shift and taken Tommy Skyler's vacated spot, was
fishing around in the back of the ambulance. Sean
scanned the group for Eve Marshall, Station Five's
only female firefighter, but didn't see her, and figured
she was inside, maybe manning breakfast. A day just
like any other.

Thank fuck.

Sean cleared his throat. "Is that all you lazy bone-
heads have to do, stand around and jaw like a bunch
of old fishermen?"

A bead of sweat rolled down his temple, the only
outward sign of the knot in his stomach. Conversation
halted and all eyes swung his way, wary and uncertain—
until he gave them a tentative smile.

"Hey, Cap!"

"How's it hangin'?"

"Damn, you look good! Don't he look good?"

The general explosion of heartfelt well-wishing
wrapped around him like a blanket, eased a sore place
in his gut as the guys migrated toward him. No cheesy
banners, but he had to admit the backslapping that
ensued was all right because it meant his boys still
gave a fuck about him. This was their way, he realized,
of making sure he knew they respected him—or at
least were willing to forgive. Even after the crap he'd
put them through.

And, yeah, he must have gotten some dirt in his
eyes, making them sting.

Dammit.

"Let the man breathe," Six-Pack boomed, pushing the others aside and promptly ignoring his own dictate. He scooped Sean into a bone-crunching bear hug that lifted him off his feet with no effort whatsoever, which was saying a lot, since Sean wasn't a small guy.

Sean laughed, the sound strange and rough to his own ears. "Put me down, you big ox!"

Six-Pack did, and Sean had to look up at him, standing this close. His best friend was six feet six inches and two hundred fifty pounds of solid, intimidating muscle, if one didn't know the man was a teddy bear. Sean was no shrimp at just over six feet and two hundred pounds, but he was much leaner in build. Hell, everyone was smaller next to the lieutenant.

Six-Pack grinned at him, brown eyes dancing. "Man, it's great to have you back. Trying to keep these guys in line is like trying to herd baby ducklings." This prompted a round of good-natured protests.

"Then it's a good thing Captain Hard-ass is back to save the day, right?"

A couple of them grimaced and Julian coughed, and Sean took perverse pleasure in their discomfort. "What, you didn't think I knew? There's nothing wrong with my hearing, you know. But hey, all's fair. I'll just have to work on earning a different nickname."

Clay smirked. "Like Captain Candy-pants?"

"Smart-ass," Julian said, punching his arm.

"How about Captain Cool?" Sean suggested, which elicited more laughs and a few ribald comments. He loved this. How long had it been since they'd felt comfortable enough to stand around and joke with him instead of running in the other direction when they saw him coming?

Out of sheer self-preservation, his brain slammed the door on the answer.

The lieutenant waved a hand. "Come on, slackers. Get to work and let Sean get his bearings."

The two men from C-shift said their good-byes and left. Zack went back to buffing the quint, Clay to whatever he was doing in the ambulance, probably stocking the meds. Yep, a normal day. Except for one thing.

"Where's Eve?" Sean asked Six-Pack. He'd be damned if he'd admit how much it stung that she hadn't come out to say hello.

"Inside, making your favorite breakfast, though you're not supposed to know. Act surprised."

"Oh." Pancakes and bacon? Especially for him? Well, that sure went a long way toward soothing his remaining unease. In fact, it caused a weird little bubble of something in his chest that he couldn't define. Something different from how relieved the guys' greeting made him feel. "Damn, that's really thoughtful of her."

None of *them* had made his favorite breakfast.

"Ain't it? Why don't you go inside and say hey. I'm gonna go call Wendy Burgess back about the charity thing."

"What charity thing?"

"You know, the auction and calendar deal."

"No, I don't." A sneaking suspicion crept over him that he wasn't going to like this.

"Jeez, I didn't tell you when you came to the barbecue? Could've sworn I did. The City of Sugarland is holding a firemen's auction in about three weeks, and also choosing twelve of our guys to do a calendar shoot, all for charity. Wendy and some of the other department brass are taking care of the bigger details."

Sean eyed him warily. "That doesn't sound too bad. What are we auctioning?"

His friend smiled, his expression a bit too mischievous. "Ourselves."

He snorted. "Get outta here! No way."

"Yep. Us in front of a bunch of squealing ladies, wearing nothing but our fire pants and red suspenders."

"Hold on. Us? There is no *us* in the equation," he said firmly. "Have fun living your Chippendales fantasy."

"Oh, we will, all of us. I already signed you up, my friend." Six-Pack clapped him on the shoulder.

"Well, you can just scratch my name off the list, *friend*. There's absolutely no way in hell I'm going to stand around half-naked in front of a bunch of screeching women."

The other man arched a dark brow. "Even when I tell you the event will benefit the families of fallen firefighters?"

Sean groaned. "Don't do this to me."

"Even if your participation could add hundreds or even thousands of dollars that will go to a grieving widow and her children? That you could singlehandedly ease someone's burden long enough to let them get back on their feet?" Six-Pack speared him with a pointed look.

"You suck," he declared in defeat.

"I knew we could count on you! Think how much better about yourself you'll feel, doing a good thing for someone less fortunate." His friend beamed as they started inside together. "Besides, it'll be a blast, you'll see."

"Yeah, yeah. I'm a regular Mother Teresa and party animal, all rolled into one." Christ, he was forty-three years old, his brown hair turning silver at the temples. What if he looked like the Pillsbury Doughboy next to the department's young studs? What if nobody bid on him? Now, *that* would be embarrassing. Maybe he should plant someone in the audience to step forward just in case. Problem was, he had no idea whom to ask.

The issue was put on hold as they walked into the kitchen and were greeted by the smoky aroma of frying bacon. Sean's stomach rumbled in approval. He marveled, not for the first time in the past few weeks, how good it felt to be hungry without alcohol killing his appetite. Now he'd have to watch his weight on top of everything else.

"God, it smells good in here," he said. At his declaration, Eve turned from the stove to face him, and his stomach did a funny lurch that had nothing to do with hunger pains.

"Well, if it isn't our fearless leader."

A broad, dazzling smile transformed her angular face, bright against her smooth coffee-with-cream skin. The smile reached all the way to her big blue eyes, warm and welcoming. Dark hair shot with reddish highlights fell in gentle curls to her shoulders.

Holy shit, she's beautiful. Why haven't I noticed before?

Or perhaps he had sometime in the past few months . . . but he didn't want to dwell on those fuzzy memories at the moment. He didn't have time to, because Eve was striding toward him while he stared like a witless fool.

She wrapped him in a fierce hug, and he found himself noting how wonderful her taut, sleek body felt pressed against his. How well she fit in his arms, her chin resting on his shoulder, soft, curly hair tickling his nose. Her fresh scent, not floral, but clean and herbal.

"It's so good to have you back." She drew away some to hold his gaze. "I mean *really* back."

"Thanks," he said quietly. "I've got a ways to go, but I'm right where I belong. Just don't give up on me." Hell, that last part just slipped out. God, could he sound more needy?

An odd flash of emotion crossed her expression, there and gone. "Are you kidding? We haven't so far, and we won't. You're going to be fine." Releasing him, she went back to tending breakfast.

"From your lips," he said softly, but she didn't hear him.

The way she said that, he almost believed her. Immediately, he missed her heat pressed to his body, the soft words just for him. *Why? What's wrong with me? I'm her captain, for God's sake. Hopefully her friend. To entertain anything more is highly inappropriate.*

He'd tested the department's goodwill and stretched it to a microscopic filament. Fooling around with a female firefighter under his watch after they'd all stuck out their necks to save him and his career? That would be the end.

The others drifted in from the bay, saving him from getting too maudlin. Leaning against the counter, he watched them horse around like a litter of goofy puppies, razzing each other and cracking jokes. Julian attempted to steal a piece of bacon from the platter only to get his hand smacked by Eve.

Sean spent a few private moments thanking God he hadn't lost this, his second family, in the wake of trying to drown his grief. All along, he should've been seeking the comfort and strength his friends had had to offer, not pushing them away. Time and counseling were finally getting that through his head.

"Let's eat!"

Eve's announcement was met with hearty approval and they all settled around the table, digging in. Sean took a bite of fluffy pancakes and listened to the chatter around him, content to soak in the scene. Okay, so this was good but a little weird. Like he was a guest in his own body, watching everything from a perspective that was suddenly too close-up and bright.

And it frightened him, too, the idea of living up to their faith in him. There would be no third chance. If he failed—

"Right, Cap?"

He blinked at the group, caught Eve and Six-Pack exchanging concerned glances. "I'm sorry. What?"

"I said we've decided to wear red G-strings for the auction instead," Clay drawled, grinning. "Across the front they'll say 'Firemen have big hoses.'"

"Shut up, moron," Julian said, pelting the cowboy in the face with a balled-up napkin. "Half the women in the county have already seen you in less, so where would be the surprise?"

Clay snorted. "There's still the *other* half to conquer. You could get a piece of the action, too, except, wait— you're neutered now."

"I've got your 'neutered' hangin' low, cowboy, and Grace has no complaints. Don't you have an 'off' switch?"

"Jules finally has to put up with someone more annoying than he is," Eve whispered in Sean's ear, good-natured humor lacing her words. "Sweet, huh?"

Sean laughed, the sound not quite as alien as before. "True justice."

No sooner had they finished their breakfast than the intercom emitted three loud tones and the computerized voice dispatched them to a traffic accident with a major injury out on I-49. Those calls were the worst in Sean's opinion, the ones that made his blood run cold and threatened his sanity. The victims' faces would haunt him for days, and now he had no buffer to place between himself and the nightmares.

They reached the scene to find a single car in a gully. The driver's door was buckled inward just enough to prove impossible to open, a long scratch running down the side of the vehicle. An elderly gentleman sat slumped behind the wheel, unconscious and bleeding profusely from a long gash in his head.

The lieutenant and Zack brought out the Jaws of Life and went to work on the door, prying apart the stubborn metal. Moments later, Clay and Eve had the man stretched out on even ground, working feverishly to save him. The man's face, the unmarred half, was parchment white. Slack. Shaking her head, Eve began CPR.

"Sideswiped," an officer told Sean grimly. "Some bastard cut off the old guy, ran him right off the damn road, and didn't stop to help."

"Road rage?"

"Shapin' up that way according to the witnesses. Helluva way to start the mornin', if ya ask me."

Sean nodded, unsure whether the cop was referring to them or the victim. He crossed his arms over his chest, watching the futile attempt to revive the man, who might have been in his eighties. Hard to tell.

Whoever he was, he didn't make it.

Sean and his team stayed out of the way after that, using their vehicles to block the far right lane, routing traffic around the police and emergency vehicles so the officers could take photos, make reports. A mound of paperwork always followed a traffic death, particularly one now labeled a possible vehicular homicide.

Welcome back, Tanner. The day can only improve. Right?

He'd repeat that to himself over and over, until he believed it.

A knock sounded on Sean's office door a second before Eve popped her head in.

"You got a minute?"

Sean swiveled his chair away from the computer screen and the report he'd been typing, gesturing her inside. "I've got several if it means putting off my paperwork. Come in."

Eve closed the door behind her and sprawled in the chair across from his desk, all sleekly muscled limbs, like a cat. Strong enough to hold her own in a male-dominated profession, yet no less womanly. A combination Sean found intriguing. Sexy.

An observation he had no business making.

"Funny how most stuff is done online nowadays, but it's still called paperwork," she said, giving him a guarded smile. As though he might find an excuse to bark at her like he would've done a few short weeks ago.

He leaned back in his chair, linking his fingers over his flat stomach. "And it's still a pain in the ass, too. How did we ever cope without computers and e-mail?"

A mischievous twinkle lit her blue eyes as she relaxed. "Some of us are too young to remember not having them."

"Ouch! Third-degree burns on my first day back," he joked. "And here I am, caught without my protective gear."

"Just making sure you're reinitiated properly."

"Why do I get the feeling this is only the beginning?"

"Because it is. Don't be fooled by the pancakes— they were merely an evil ploy to lull you into complacency."

"Hmm. I'll consider myself warned. So, what's on your mind?"

Humor fading, she hesitated before getting to the point. "I want to clear the air between us once and for all, and to do that, I need to apologize."

He stared at her in surprise. "What for?"

"For not being more supportive these past few months," she said, guilt coloring her voice. She held his gaze, though, unflinching. "I've bucked you at every turn and even been a real bitch, at times in front of the others, when I *knew* I wasn't helping the situation. For that, I'm deeply sorry."

"You're kidding, right? I was an unbearable, drunken, self-pitying son of a bitch, and you're apologizing?" Pushing out of his chair, he stalked to the small window behind his desk and looked out at the view of the field beyond the parking lot where the guys sometimes played football. But he didn't appreciate the scenery, as he hadn't appreciated so many good things in his life when he'd had them.

"Yes, I am. You don't kick someone when they're down, especially when they're no longer in control of their own actions, and that's exactly what I did."

He shook his head. "No, you didn't. You had the best interests of this team at heart every single time we butted heads. You and the guys were afraid I'd do something to seriously fuck up and I did, so badly I can't believe I still have a job, much less that I'm still alive. I understand that and I'm trying to make peace with what I've done."

The words were horribly familiar, as though the movie reel of his life had rewound twenty years. They left him shaken.

He could never atone for what he'd cost Tommy, any more than he'd been able to atone for that other mistake so long ago. But he could try really hard to live a good life for the rest of his days—a life denied to so many he'd loved and lost.

A soft hand gripped his arm, and Eve's sweet voice whispered next to his ear. "Everything is going to be okay, Sean. I believe in you."

Startled, he turned to find her practically in his arms. Right where he wanted her to be, and damn him to hell for feeling this way. They stared into each other's eyes, the moment stretching into a thin wire, supercharged, and he forgot where he was. His responsibilities, his reputation, his position as her captain. Gone, with the first brush of his lips against hers as his palm slid down her arm. Lost, with the need in her eyes and her beautiful face tilted up to his, her taut body pressed close, warm and safe.

Heaven. *Oh, God, it's been so long. Need this, need you . . .*

The cell phone on his desk shrilled a rude interruption and they sprang apart as though the fire chief himself had walked in unannounced. Off balance from his lapse in judgment, lips tingling in pleasure, Sean grabbed for the phone.

"Hello?"

A man's voice responded, quiet and amused. "Did you ever ask yourself . . . what if it wasn't an accident?"

Click.

A couple of heartbeats passed before Sean frowned

and lowered the phone from his ear, his brain scrambling to assimilate the caller's meaning. Weird. What could that possibly . . .

"Oh . . . oh, God, no."

"Sean? Sean, what's wrong?" Eve's voice called to him from miles away.

And the phone slipped unnoticed from his frozen fingers. Clattered to the desktop.

"Talk to me!" Strong fingers wrapped around his upper arm, shook him.

Blinking, he gazed into Eve's worried face and cleared his throat, suddenly gone dry. "Prank call. Had to be."

"What did he say? Or was it a woman?"

His voice trembled, betraying his upset. "No, it was a man. He asked if I'd ever considered whether 'it wasn't an accident.' Then he hung up."

"What accident?" She frowned. "That wreck we worked earlier? Somebody sideswiped the guy and he was killed. Could that be what he was talking about?"

"I don't know. That's all he said. But I got the feeling it was meant to be more personal." Leaning his rear against his desk, he ran a shaking hand through his hair and studied the floor.

"Why? Did you recognize his voice?"

"No, it was too low. And there was some background noise, like a radio or something. His tone was almost like a smirk, though. Like he was enjoying every second of jerking me around." He raised his eyes to meet hers. "I have a feeling he was referring to the wreck that took my family."

God, he'd said the words without falling to pieces. A first. But his chest still burned as though he'd been shot.

Eve gasped. "I can't believe anyone would be so cruel! Who would do something so horrible, and just when you're beginning to heal?"

He thought *heal* was a pretty strong word, but didn't point it out. Considering the answer to her question, he gave a harsh laugh and spread his hands as though indicating the whole city. "Pick a contestant. There's bound to be a couple of guys in the department who are less than thrilled to have me back. My actions killed Skyler's career, remember?"

"Tommy is still your friend," she said softly. "Everyone knows that."

The kind reminder helped, but not much. "Yeah. Doesn't mean everyone likes it, though."

"True, but I can't honestly think of anyone who'd go that far. Can you?"

The three loud call tones interrupted further speculation, for the time being. Sean almost breathed a sigh of relief, but experience had taught him better. A firefighter should never let his guard down, never take a call for granted as simple or easy.

And this one was anything but.

"A water rescue." Eve groaned as she pushed out the door ahead of him, and broke into a jog. "Shit, we haven't had one of those in ages."

"Be glad I had Six-Pack take all of you through that drill on the Cumberland last week," he said, hurrying after her into the bay. A quick check showed the others were already there, pulling on their gear, two of them hitching the rescue boats to the smaller red truck.

"Which you conveniently missed because you weren't back at work yet."

At her raised brow, he just shot her a grin and said, "I'll pull the boat. You ride with me."

Her eyes widened and she opened her mouth, but the order had surprised her into silence. As they prepared to leave, he couldn't help but gloat a little. Catching Eve off guard wasn't easy.

And for some reason, he looked forward to doing it a whole lot more in the future.

2

1983

"One hundred push-ups, motherfuckers!" The big drill sergeant strolled down the line of new recruits, square face hard. Unsympathetic. "I own your asses! I will push you, work you, fuck you over, until you fall down on your knees thanking God that the marines made you a better man! What do you think of that?"

The question required only a loud, "Sir, yes, sir!" from the entire group.

But not from Jesse. Into the stillness afterward, he muttered, "I think God's a joke, asshole."

Sean's eyes widened, but he kept doing his push-ups. What the hell was his friend doing?

The drill sergeant apparently wanted to know the same thing. "Private Rose! Do you have something to say to me?"

Jesse leaped to stand at attention, and saluted. "Yes, sir! I said that God loves the U.S. Marines, sir!"

This prompted a few muffled snickers from the other recruits, but not from Sean. As the drill sergeant allowed his friend to fall back into place and resume his exercises, adding fifty more to everyone's count, Sean frowned.

The comment, and Jesse's lie, stayed with him for days.

*   *   *

Eve slid into the passenger seat of the truck and buckled her seat belt, trying like hell not to stare at the man who made her heart pound. Made her palms sweat, her stomach flutter with nerves. After all, she'd lived with the attraction for Sean—and no little heartbreak as a result—for years. Wasn't anything she hadn't endured many times in the past on his account.

Except back then, he hadn't been available.

Idiot! He's not available now, either.

But that kiss! Oh, God. Her body still hummed from the press of his hard, muscled form against hers. The soft touch of his lips, his warmth, expression filled with raw need. A need she wanted nothing more than to satisfy.

Reality, however, was a bitch. Of course he had needs. What man wouldn't on the heels of coming out of a two-year fog? It likely had less to do with her specifically and more to do with a man simply learning to walk among the living again.

Being his rebound fuck would tear her to pieces.

But someone else being his rebound fuck would kill her.

Despite her resolve, she sneaked a peek at his profile as he pulled out of the bay, following the quint. No one could call his a classically handsome face. His looks were rugged, some might say harsh and intimidating with that wide, unsmiling mouth and that bottle green gaze that could cut the strongest of men off at the knees. Dark brows arched over those amazing eyes, accenting what her mother would call a "Roman nose." The beginnings of crow's-feet crept toward temples liberally laced with silver in an otherwise dark brown head of short, silky hair barely covering his ears.

Taking each feature into account, she supposed Sean should've been an average-looking man.

Until he smiled.

Until he laughed, cracked a joke, or praised one of his team for a job well-done. Until he made you feel like the most special person in the universe, because while he was a hard-ass bastard much of the time, his approval meant that much more to those having earned it.

That strong, confident leader had been missing for far too long, and today he'd returned. Not quite whole, still battle-scarred and hurting, but on his way back. He was clean, sober, and determined.

That man, she would follow into hell. What sort of asshole would want to ruin the progress he'd made?

"You're giving me a complex."

She blinked, feeling her cheeks heat at being caught. "Why?"

"You're staring." He shot her a sideways glance. "Do I have a pimple or something?"

"No, I was just thinking."

"About?"

"How much progress you've made," she said, opting for a simple explanation.

He was silent for a moment, the wail of their sirens piercing the quiet. His hands tightened on the wheel. "I really am trying. It's harder than I ever imagined."

The candid admission from this private man, not to mention the conversation in his office, surprised and pleased her. Few, except Six-Pack and his dad, Fire Chief Bentley Mitchell, were ever included in his inner circle of confidence. She hoped this meant he was offering the same to her—friendship, if nothing else.

"If you ever need anyone to talk to . . ." She shrugged and let the invite hang.

"Thanks, Eve. That means a lot to me." Flashing her a quick smile, he squeezed her shoulder before turning his attention back to the road.

She did the same, staring at the trees whizzing by and trying not to get her hopes up too much. That made twice in one day that he'd touched her voluntarily—three if you counted the hug when he returned to duty this morning—something she couldn't ever remember happening before outside of what was required for the job.

Didn't necessarily mean a thing, though. Best to remember that.

As Sean started across the Cumberland bridge, Eve suppressed a shiver. They were almost on top of the spot where Zack, her best friend, had damn near lost his life on a call last winter. Since then, she hadn't been able to cross without remembering that horrible day.

"Holy shit." Sean pointed out her window. "There's our problem. One of those looks like a tour boat."

She followed his gesture and gasped, personal problems taking a backseat. "Oh, God. What a disaster."

About fifty yards upriver, one of the tour boats with a blue canvas top was on fire and listing badly to one side. Some people were on board and some were in the water. No other boats had yet gone to their rescue, but that was no surprise. This end of the Cumberland was primarily commercial, not residential, which meant fewer personal watercraft.

Sean got on the radio and requested another engine company. "Christ, I hope we're not pulling out bodies."

"Me, too."

Zack pulled the quint down the road leading to the Riverview Restaurant, which was precisely what the name implied. Next to the popular seafood place was a boat ramp where they could launch and get to the accident victims by the fastest route.

Once they reached the parking lot, the quint and the ambulance pulled out of the way and parked off to the side. The other four team members jumped out of their vehicles and jogged toward the ramp, while Sean whipped the truck around and backed the boats down the incline, into the water.

"Whoa, you've got it," the lieutenant called to Sean, waving a hand. To the others, he yelled, "Let's move it!"

The men grabbed the rubber boat and flipped it over, Zack and Clay climbing inside. The bottom of this boat had a slit for hauling up victims who were incapacitated and unable to climb the ladder of the larger boat.

Eve and Julian manned the larger boat, steering it toward a knot of victims who were treading water, faces panicked, teeth chattering from the cold. They helped several people aboard, who were sputtering about what had happened.

"Damned g-guy on the Jet Ski plowed right into us."

"Didn't mean to," another said. "He fell off and the thing kept coming at us. He must not have had his safety rope attached to the kill switch."

"Still makes it his fault."

Eve eyed the scene as they drove people to the shore. If she wasn't mistaken, these tour boats had a gas tank located in the center of the craft that was designed to prevent fire from breaking out. The fire must have spread from the Jet Ski's impact.

Zack and Clay called that they had the other three victims aboard, including the driver of the Jet Ski and one unconscious woman. To their knowledge, that was everyone.

But not quite.

A cry sounded. That of a man. About forty yards out, a dark head bobbed, the figure desperately treading water. With the noise from the boats' engines and the fire, people yelling, no one had noticed the guy, who was obviously injured and unable to get to safety. Before anyone could react, Sean stripped off his coat and ran. Dove into the water and swam for the man with strong, sure strokes.

As he reached the guy, placed him in a rescue hold, and began to swim back toward shore, Eve breathed a sigh of relief and began to interview victims about their injuries. Treated those with minor scrapes and bruises while the others dealt with the more serious cases. Station Two arrived to assist and provide transport for the unconscious woman.

Later, Eve yanked off her hat and wiped her face, exhausted. Her clothes were soaked, her feet freezing. She knew her buddies weren't in better shape, and the race would be on for a hot shower. Thank God she didn't have to share a bathroom facility with the guys, a perk not every man in the fire department was happy about regarding female firefighters. Her team was cool, though. She wouldn't trade them for anything. Most days.

She turned to yell at Julian that he'd forgotten to hook the boat to the trailer and the words died in her throat.

Sean was crouched on the grass next to the dark-haired man he'd pulled from the water, speaking in soothing tones while tending a gash that ran from the man's shoulder downward, across his chest.

"Relax, buddy. You're gonna be okay."

"I saw the guy on the ski, but I couldn't swing the boat out of the way," he said, voice breaking. "Oh, God. My passengers."

Eve moved closer, noting that the boat captain's head and face were bloodied as well. Probably concussed and in shock.

"They're being taken care of. Don't worry. What's your name?" Sean asked as he worked.

"Huh?" Unfocused eyes searched Sean's face.

"I'm Sean. What's your name?"

"Oh. Uh, Andy."

"You married, Andy? Kids?"

The man gave a lopsided smile. "Yeah. Me and Sandra have a little girl."

Though Andy didn't notice, Eve saw the way Sean's smile tightened. Became forced. Every time he was reminded of his loss, the pain must have been unbearable.

"Cool. You're gonna go for a ride to the hospital, where they'll fix you up, and then you'll get to go home with them. Sound good?"

"Can't I go home now?"

"Not a good idea. You've got a concussion and this cut might need some stitches. Rest easy."

A woman's frantic voice called out. "Andy? Andy!" The lady and a little girl dashed across the parking lot toward Sean and the man. The girl, who was apparently the man's daughter, bolted straight for him.

"Daddy!"

Andy sat up despite Sean's order for him to lie still, enfolding his daughter in a careful hug. "Jenny, baby. Daddy's a little dirty." He groaned, releasing her and holding a hand to his head.

The woman crouched next to him. "Oh, honey," she whispered. "Lie back down."

As he did, Jenny pulled back, small face scrunched into a worried frown. "You're bleeding! Mommy said you had a boat wreck."

"Yeah, I did, sweetheart. But I'm going to get patched up and go home with you and Mommy, okay?" He looked up at his wife, who wiped tears off her cheeks and tried to smile at her husband.

Sean stared at the family with undisguised longing etched on his face, fathomless pain swimming in his green eyes.

"Your daddy is going to be fine," Sean told Jenny in a soothing tone.

"Promith?" Two huge eyes filled with tears and her little chin trembled.

"Promise." Sean snapped his fingers, face suddenly animated as he smiled at her. "Say, there's someone I want you to meet. Can you wait here for a minute?"

"O-kay."

Rooted to the spot, Eve watched him jog a few feet to the truck. She knew what he was after and her heart melted into a puddle at her feet as he leaned into the cab and fished around. When he emerged holding a small, fuzzy purple teddy bear, her larynx shrank to the size of a pinhole.

Flashing the little girl a brilliant smile, he hurried back to her and knelt, holding out the gift. "This is my friend Violet. She's a little scared, too, and—"

"He." The girl sniffled. "Violet's a 'he,' I can tell."

Sean's lips quirked and he made a great show of peering into Violet's fuzzy face. "Well, right you are! It's a good thing for Violet that you came along, huh? He's scared, too, and he needs a friend just like you. Can you give him a hug, make him feel better?"

"Yeah." The girl held out her arms, took the bear, and held him close, a slow grin brightening her expression. "Hey, I think he's better already!"

"I think he is, sweetheart," Sean said hoarsely, glancing away as he pushed to his feet again.

Eve knew he was no longer referring to the bear.

Sandra touched Sean's sleeve. "Thank you. For taking care of Andy, and for how you handled Jenny. Though thanks don't seem nearly adequate."

"Believe me, it's more than enough." Sean briefly patted her back in a gesture of comfort.

The ambulance from Station Two returned and the guys offered to transport Andy, an offer Sean gratefully accepted. Andy shook Sean's hand as the stretcher was wheeled away, and Sandra herded Jenny toward their waiting car to follow the ambulance.

The little girl turned and waved at Sean, blew him a kiss. The captain sent her one in return and slowly lowered his hand to his side. Watched until the car was gone. Then he walked around to the driver's side of the truck and braced his forearm above the window, resting his head on his sleeve. He didn't move.

The lieutenant was talking to Captain Holliday and didn't notice his best friend having a small crisis. Julian and Clay did, though, and made themselves real "busy" checking the boats and the trailer. Zack caught Eve's gaze and jerked his head toward Sean, urging her to talk to him.

Wimps, all three of them.

Walking over to him, she laid a hand on his back. His shirt was soaked and she could feel the chill radiating off him even through the material. "You okay?"

"Christ, she looked so much like Mia." Heaving a sigh, he straightened and turned, but didn't meet her eyes. "I'm fine."

"You don't have to say you are if you're not. This is me you're talking to," she said softly.

"I know." He looked at her then, eyes sad. "Maybe I'm not, but I will be. That's what matters, right? Tell me there's an end in sight, Eve. 'Cause if there's not, I can't do this anymore. Not one more second."

Oh, God. "There is, and you're making it through. We're all here for you and we're not going to fucking let you quit when you're so close," she said, keeping her voice and expression stern. Sean needed that right now more than pretty words. "You quit. That's the same as telling all your friends they can throw in the towel, too. Is that what you want?"

"Jesus, no." He pushed his fingers through his damp hair.

"You told Jenny's mom that the thanks you get for saving a life is enough. Did you mean that?"

He stared at her. "Of course I did."

"Then *let* it be enough. You can't save everyone, but you saved that little girl's father. You impacted lives today, and a family is safe because of you. Own it, and let it be enough."

He returned her gaze steadily for a long moment. Then a slow smile lit his face, made her breath leave her lungs. The sadness still lurked, but it was diminished.

"Thanks. I guess I needed to hear that."

God, she wanted to take him into her arms, love

him the way he deserved. She settled for a friendly
punch on the shoulder. "Jeez, you guys are a lot of
work. It's enough to drive a girl crazy. Can we get out
of here?"

"You bet." He gave her a wink and climbed into the
truck.

Climbing in her side of the vehicle, it struck her
suddenly that he'd never again be the man he'd been
before.

Whether that was good or bad remained to be seen,
miles down the road.

On the drive back to the station, Sean did his best to
keep from putting the truck—boats, trailer, and all—
into a ditch.

That was damned hard to do when all he could see
was Eve the way she'd looked on the riverbank after
the rescue—wet and bedraggled, wet clothes clinging to
every lean muscle on her body.

Never in all his years in the department had he seen
those fugly navy blue pants look so goddamned fine
on anybody. There ought to be a law. Probably was.

The woman was poetry in motion this afternoon,
pulling people out of the water left and right. Braving
gas, flames, and smoke, saving lives just as every one
of them was trained to do. Nothing he hadn't watched
her—hell, the whole team—perform countless times
before.

But he'd never *watched* Eve, fully appreciated the
sheer beauty of her in motion, before today. Like for
years he'd had on blinders that allowed him to view
her only as one of the boys and they'd been abruptly
stripped away. Okay, if he was honest, the blinders

had been peeling away for months—it was just that now he was sober and able to realize it.

He tried to picture Blair jumping in a freezing river to save total strangers and was disturbed to find he couldn't. The thought seemed somehow unfair and disloyal. Blair had been a completely different person from Eve.

He was starting to see just how different. As if a basket case like himself had a chance with a woman like Eve. God, that sweet little girl, Jenny, looked so much like his Mia it had torn out his heart. If he hadn't been able to get to her, he didn't know what he would've—

"You coming to the Waterin' Hole tomorrow night?" Eve asked, breaking into his thoughts.

"I guess so." He shrugged a shoulder, covering his surprise. "No one told me about it." That hurt more than he cared to admit.

"Well, that didn't sound defensive or anything."

"What am I supposed to say? The guys haven't breathed a word," he muttered. "Maybe they don't want me there." Glancing over, he found her giving him an irritable glare.

"What do you want, an engraved invitation? I'm telling you now, ding-dong. Wasn't like it was planned in advance or anything. Jules and Clay cooked up the idea this morning and said to pass it on, whoever wants to come. Dates, too."

"You bringing one?" O-kay. That came out a lot sharper than he intended.

"A date?" She said the word as if it were an alien concept.

"No, a moose." He snorted. "Yes, a date."

"You don't have to get pissy."

"I'm not pissy!" Much.

"Are, too." She paused, smirking when he glanced at her. "Maybe I'll bring Drake, if he's free."

"What, the nerdy little teacher guy? He doesn't exactly fit in with us."

"He fits in just fine, and he's *not* little," she drawled in a tone that suggested the man sported a ten-inch dick.

Against his will, his blood started to boil. "You said Drake was just a friend," he pointed out. There. See him be reasonable.

The witch blinked at him, the picture of innocence. "When did I say that?"

"I . . . I don't know. A while back, but you did say it."

"Oh. If it's been a while, I can't be held accountable for what I said. Things change, you know."

If he'd been Superman, he would've bent the steering wheel in half. The thought of Drake's skinny neck between his hands was much more satisfying. He'd squeeze until the pip-squeak's eyes bugged out—

"Yeah, I might give him a call," she said, almost to herself.

"You do that."

"I will."

"Fine."

"Fine!"

Fuck! What the hell just happened here? Women were so fucking difficult! He should stick to his horses; they couldn't talk. Still, some perverse and insanely jealous devil on his shoulder made him ask.

"Eve?"

"Hmm?"

"I'm your friend, right?"

Her voice softened, snarky tone gone. "Are you kidding? After all we've been through? We're friends. Believe that."

"Then go with me tomorrow night."

"What? Like, *with* you?" Her voice rose on the last two words, incredulous.

Yes! Finally, he'd penetrated her armor and gotten her attention.

"Sure, with me. Two friends going to hang with the others. Why not?"

"Well . . . sure. Okay, why not?" She sounded as amazed as he felt.

"Great. I'll pick you up around seven?"

She blinked at him. "Sounds good."

And that would be the end of that Drake bullshit. Eve wanted a friend to blow the evening with? She had one right here, no need for that wimpy little flake. Sue him, but he felt pretty darned smug about derailing her plan before it was put into action.

That settled, his mind drifted back to the guys not telling him about the upcoming night out. And he hated the logical conclusion.

"Eve, I'm not going to fall off the wagon, if that's what they're worried about. I've come too far to fuck myself up." If he said that a hundred more times, it would be true.

"I'd be lying if I claimed they weren't concerned, but I swear to you nobody was going to keep it a secret," she insisted. "We all know you need us to be real around you. We've discussed it."

Wasn't that special? Another top secret "Help Sean Recover" op. What a mortifying thought. But at least they cared and supported him, which was more than many recovering alcoholics had going for them. More than that, they were his family.

"I appreciate it," he said, more to ease her mind than his own.

The rest of the ride was spent in silence, and once back at the station, the guys and Eve drifted off to get dry and then tackle various chores. After changing out of his wet clothes, Sean headed to the kitchen to put on a pot of coffee, just what he needed to chase away the chill from the river.

"Oh *yeah*." He made a beeline to the pot, already filling with the aromatic brew, and stepped around Six-Pack and Clay, who were lounging against the kitchen counter. "Is this the good stuff?"

"Starbucks, man." Six-Pack crossed his arms over his massive chest, grinning. "You know I won't stock anything else."

"I always knew you were good for something besides taking up lots of space."

"And for his cooking," Clay pointed out with enthusiasm. "It's the big guy's turn tonight, too. What are we having?"

Six-Pack rolled his eyes. "You're nothin' but a giant stomach."

"There's only one thing giant on me, bud, and it *ain't* my belly," their friend drawled, eyes dancing with humor. "Just ask Cherie, Beth, Stacy—or was it Tracy? Hmm."

"Man, don't you take medication or something? Your attention span is shorter than Julian's and that's saying a lot." The lieutenant snorted and shook his head. To Sean, he joked, "It's a damned good thing he's pretty, 'cause he doesn't have a lick of sense."

"Aww, you think I'm pretty?" Clay batted his eyelashes and draped an arm over Six-Pack's shoulders. "That's so sweet!"

"Get off me before I hurt you." His laugh ruined the menacing tone.

Chuckling, Sean fished in the cupboard, grabbing his favorite mug, which declared *I AM the Boss of You*, and pulled the old switchola with the pot, deftly replacing it with his mug.

"Hey, no cuts!" Clay yelled good-naturedly.

Sean replaced the pot and held up his mug, tapping the saying on the front and taking a sip. With a groan of appreciation, he wrapped his hands around it, soaking up the warmth. "Good stuff. Funny how everything tastes better when you're sober."

The other two glanced at him in surprise and he gave them a half smile. Best to keep things out in the open and dialogue flowing rather than treat the issue like the elephant in the room. He wanted the guys to talk *to* him, not around him.

"I'll bet it does. Which reminds me," Six-Pack said, giving Sean a meaningful look. "A bunch of us are heading over to the Waterin' Hole tomorrow night. You want to come?"

"Eve mentioned it." He took another sip. "And yeah, that sounds like fun."

"Can you handle the booze being everywhere?" Leave it to his best friend to cut through the bull. But that was one of the guy's finest qualities, among many.

"I don't have a choice. It's coffee, tea, and soda for me now, just like you." Like Sean, Howard didn't drink. Except the lieutenant's choice was due to a horrible childhood at the hands of the drunken, violent stepfather who'd raised him. "Won't be a picnic, but it'll help some that I won't be the only one not drinking."

"I've got your back."

"Me, too," Clay piped up.

"Thanks, guys. I'm looking forward to going out again, with my head screwed on straight. Anyway, guess I'd better get on that report from the boating accident, huh?" He made a face. "That bitch is going to take all evening."

"Want some help?" Six-Pack asked.

"Naw, you've got dinner. I'll handle it."

He left them in the kitchen, talking in low tones, and wondered uncomfortably if he was the topic of conversation, as he'd no doubt been many times. For sure, he'd be under a microscope for a while, especially off duty, but he had no one to blame but himself. Briefly, he worried what they'd think when he showed up with Eve, then decided he didn't care. She was his friend, just like one of them.

But he'd never had the burning desire to kiss any of the others senseless.

Right. The paperwork. He forced his mind to the task, one of the drawbacks to being captain. Six-Pack had his share as well, but a lot of it fell to himself. Not that he had a right to complain these days—he was simply grateful to have a job.

Once in a while, he glanced up from the computer to his cell phone resting innocently on his desk. The disturbing call from earlier hadn't been far from his mind all day. That muffled voice, the malicious intent behind his words.

Because no matter the meaning of his statement, the intent was to upset Sean.

If it wasn't a prank call. Or a wrong number.

He didn't believe either of those was the case ... but he could be wrong. He'd been wrong before, at some extremely crucial points in his life.

And each of those times, he'd lost everything he loved.

Cats might have nine lives, but not Sean Tanner.

You fuck up this time around? Everything is gone. Your career, your life.

Everything.

3

"Why don't you believe in God, Jess?"

His friend considered this for a long time. "I believe in things that I can touch, smell, and taste. I believe that men create their own destinies. There is no before or after. What's here and now is real, and nothing else."

"That's pretty grim."

"Life is grim."

"And when you find out God is real? What then?"

"I'd ask him why he let my father beat my big brother to death, why he didn't let him grow big enough to put a bullet in the fucker's brain. That's what." With that, Jesse rolled over in his bunk and went to sleep.

Sean never broached the subject again.

Jesse Rose slid out of the Land Rover and stretched his muscles, popped the kinks out of his neck. Tucking his gun into the waistband of his jeans, he surveyed the old farm that would serve as their base until their mission was complete.

The money skimmed and funneled to them by the late Forrest Prescott was serving them well, so far. The cash had paid for weapons, explosives, this place.

The men had to be paid, too, since the sons of bitches wouldn't work for free. Sugarland's deceased and disgraced city manager had proved to be a useful tool in the ongoing fight against a government doing its best to communize. A government that didn't give a fuck about its soldiers or civilians.

Yeah, too bad Prescott, the idiot, had gotten himself killed. He could've done more good before his number came up. But such was the way of war.

Jesse ought to know.

Shoving down the bad memories before they could take hold, the rage that always came with the pain of remembered betrayal, he continued to scan the area, noting the ancient but sturdy white frame house nestled at the base of the rolling, wooded hills. Beyond the rise behind the house, about one hundred yards away, he knew there was an equally ancient tobacco barn that had been modified and shored up in advance by some of his men. From the outside, nobody would think the structure to be anything other than what it appeared—a defunct relic of Tennessee history.

Inside, underneath the weathered flooring and protected in a brand-new concrete bunker? A real big, nasty surprise for the good folks of central Tennessee, and more importantly the U.S. government.

Two men stepped onto the front porch, letting the screen door bang shut behind them, and headed toward him. His lieutenants, Grimes and Hammer. Grimes was a thin, wiry guy with long, stringy dark hair and beady eyes, like a rat. Moved like one, too, quiet and furtive. Hammer got his nickname for one obvious reason—the big SOB had a fist like one. Jesse had seen the man kill with a single blow. Both were loyal, as committed to the cause as Jesse.

Grimes clapped his shoulder in greeting, speaking up first. "Been too quiet around here without you to keep the men on their toes. They're gettin' antsy."

Jesse didn't smile or return the gesture. Any hint of humanity was a leader's fatal mistake. "They won't be sitting on their asses much longer. We've got plenty of work to do before showtime." He flicked a hand at the place. "Good setup. Plenty of land, big house with a basement for us and the weapons. Barn for storing our special surprise, nearest neighbors two miles away through the woods. It's closer to town than I wanted, but I think this will suit our needs just fine."

"Wasn't no place else around that met our requirements," Hammer put in, head back, face expressionless.

"It'll do." Jesse started for the house, leaving the men to trail in his wake. "Choose several men to help you get our cargo moved to the barn."

So much to accomplish, and he was eager to get started. He scented blood in the water, and like any good shark, he was ready to tear into his prey. Almost twenty years of slowly building his army, of gathering intel, carefully planning his vengeance, and he was so near the culmination of his dreams he could taste success. He couldn't sleep for anticipating the shock and horror on his enemies' faces—the entire nation's—when they saw what he'd done. When they experienced the horror of their own making unleashed against them.

When they learned what happens to those who betray Jesse Rose.

Climbing the porch steps, he lifted a hand, rubbed at the puckered scar on his chest just there, beneath his T-shirt. Right over his heart.

The same heart that had almost been blown away,

both figuratively and literally, by a man he'd believed to be his best friend.

Jesse learned his lessons well, and he never forgot them. Three years ago, he'd finally put the last of his plans into action. And since he was a patient man, he'd worked toward this day and the ones to come.

I've enjoyed watching your downfall, Sean. Trust me, old friend. You haven't yet begun to suffer.

And suffer he would. Jesse considered it his little side bonus for a job well-done.

Sean stepped out of the shower, grabbed a towel off the bar on the wall, and briskly dried himself from head to toe. After getting off shift at seven this morning, he'd gone straight home, stripped, and stood under the hot spray, washing away the grit from the river. Lord, it had felt good.

When finished, he hung the cloth over the bar again and padded into his bedroom. A pair of black boxer briefs lay on the bed next to his jeans and he snatched them, pulling them on. The jeans were next and he yanked them up, leaving the top button undone. He'd just started for the dresser to find a shirt when the phone rang, shattering the peace and quiet.

Reversing direction, he strode to the nightstand and grabbed the receiver from its charger. "Hello?"

"Sean, my boy! How are you?"

Sean smiled and sat on the edge of the bed. "Hey, Uncle Joe. Doing okay. How are you and Aunt Clara?" His late father's seventy-one-year-old brother and sister-in-law were just about his favorite people in the world.

Joe snorted. "Same shit, different day, kid. Can't complain too much, 'cause we're still here on this earth."

"I can relate. So, what's the news from Texas?"

"Oh, a fair bit. First, Clara wanted me to call and see if you're coming for Thanksgiving this year." His uncle paused, voice growing soft. Concerned. "You know how we hate for you to be alone, son, and your cousins would love to see you."

Sean cleared his throat. "I know. And I appreciate it. The truth is, though, I'm scheduled to work this year and I don't have another day off to spare. Wish I did." He hated for his aunt and uncle to worry. God knew they'd done enough of that on his account. "But we're having a feast at the station, so you guys don't have to be concerned about me."

"Well, that's all right, then. Your aunt's been after me to find out and I told her I would. Maybe you can come at Christmas."

"We'll see." He didn't like putting them off. For his own good, he had to stop isolating himself.

"How're the AA meetings coming, son?"

Shame washed over him, but he managed to hold his voice steady. He hated how he'd let his only family down. "Productive. Therapeutic."

"You hate the hell out of them." His uncle had a way of cutting through the bull.

"With a passion."

"Someday you won't have to go anymore, or at least not as often. I have faith in you. We all do."

"Thanks, Uncle Joe. How are Eddie and Alicia?" he asked, referring to his cousins.

The diversion worked. Joe launched into an animated discussion of his and Clara's grown children and all the grandchildren, and what wonderful accomplishments each of them made in the past few months. Sean was truly happy for them, but he couldn't help but be reminded of his official status as the family disaster. Which wasn't his sweet uncle's intention at all.

By the time they said good-bye, Sean's ears were ringing and he breathed a small sigh of relief as he hung up the phone. Forgoing the shirt after all, he headed barefoot into the kitchen and inhaled, grateful that he'd set up the timer on the coffeepot last night. Coffee was quickly becoming a replacement for the booze, but if that ended up being his worst vice, he'd consider himself a fortunate man.

He poured himself a cup and then settled in his favorite recliner with the morning paper he'd fetched from the driveway when he got home, and didn't move except to refill his mug on occasion. He read until almost noon, when a knock at the front door interrupted his solitude.

"Now what?"

More curious than annoyed, he folded the paper, set it on the table next to his chair, and went to answer the door. He didn't get many visitors. Out of habit, he looked out the peephole first, and his eyes widened—partly in surprise, and mostly because of the rush of pleasure that went due south.

Suddenly, he was nervous, and this was the last person he wanted to realize that. Opening the door, he fixed a pleasant smile on his face. "Eve, what a surprise. I thought I was picking you up at seven. We're still going, right?"

"Um . . ." Eve blinked, blue eyes drifting from his face to his chest, and lower still. Her gaze snapped up to his and she gave a shaky laugh. "Of course! But in the meantime, I figured you might need these." She thrust out a hand.

Sean was barely aware of the small items he took

from her grasp. Much more important was the electric zing that shot through him at the brush of their fingers. And the fact that she'd been checking him out. Really looking him over and not bothering to hide it.

Me. A man more than ten years her senior. Does she like what she sees?

God knew he appreciated Eve as a man does a woman, and his body was coming alive as it hadn't in years. Yawning awake like a bear ravenous from a long, cold winter in hibernation. His cock began to fill, harden painfully in his jeans, and he prayed she didn't notice. Christ, he was staring at her like a complete fool.

With an effort, he forced his attention to the items he held. "My wallet and sunglasses? Where did you find these?"

"I didn't." She shrugged. "Val found them in the men's restroom when he came in for B-shift. I offered to bring them by here, but I went home and changed, ran some errands first. Hope you haven't needed them."

"No, I haven't gone anywhere." He smiled. "Guess I forgot to pick them up after I changed out of my wet clothes earlier. Thanks for bringing them."

Her answering smile lit her beautiful face. "You're welcome."

"Jesus, where are my manners! Come in for a while?"

"Sure, I'd like that."

Moving aside, he let her in and closed the door. While Eve made a circuit of the living room, curiously examining her surroundings, he admired a much better view.

Curly dark hair fell to her shoulders over her black jacket, and he wondered if it would be as soft as it looked as he ran his fingers through the silky mass.

Her pointy little chin, pert nose, and long lashes were the icing on a pretty, sweet profile—yet the woman was anything but dainty. Her body was long and lean, not an ounce of fat on her frame. Her jeans hugged a high, round ass that flexed as she moved, and his mouth watered at the thought of digging his fingers into the supple, bronzed flesh as he pounded into her.

Oh, God, stop it!

Eve wasn't just a gorgeous package; she was mentally tough as well. The woman took no crap from anyone, even her own captain when she knew she was right. She was an excellent firefighter and paramedic, strong as any man. Had to be in order to pass the strenuous physical tests. He'd seen her in action many times over the years, and she never ceased to make him proud.

She was an intriguing mix of strength and femininity, and he was mesmerized.

"Sean?"

He shook himself. "I'm sorry. What?"

"I said you have a lovely home."

Glancing around, he tried to see the place through her eyes. "Thanks, but it hasn't been a home in a long time. I've been thinking of selling."

"Really? I can't picture you stuck in town."

"Me, either, which is why if I do sell, I'll probably move to another place with acreage so I can take the horses. It's just . . ." He sighed. "When Blair and I got married, she took one look at this house and the land, and had to have it. I couldn't afford the mortgage back then, on a firefighter's starting salary, but Blair's family is old money. And what Blair wanted . . ."

He trailed off, feeling incredibly disloyal despite the old barb that remained under his skin over the matter.

"Blair got," Eve finished.

"Yeah. It always seemed more her home than mine, even when Bobby and Mia came along. Still does." He sucked in a slow breath, aware that he'd mentioned his children without falling totally apart. That was progress, for sure.

Her gaze reflected complete understanding. "I know what it's like to need a fresh start, and if this is what it takes to make you happy, go for it."

"Do you know? Really?" He studied her, suddenly aware that for all the years they'd worked together and been friends, he knew little of her background. Her life outside the station. Oh, he knew her mother was still alive and they were close, and he'd heard Eve talk about her dates sometimes. But not much else. Eve was a private person, and he felt honored that she'd opened the door even a crack.

"Yes. Rain check on that subject?"

"Absolutely." He hesitated. "Want to meet Elvis and the gals?"

"Who're they?"

"Let me put on a shirt and some shoes, and I'll show you. Unless you have to rush off?"

"No, I'm good. I've got nothing going on this afternoon that can't wait."

"Great!" He jogged to his bedroom, feeling like a teenager trying to impress his first date.

The clearheaded, straitlaced part of his conscience demanded to know what he was doing, encouraging her to stay when he was feeling a great deal more than just friendly toward her. The side of him that was sick of being lonely beat that pesky wimp into submission.

Quickly, he yanked on a T-shirt that hung low enough

to hide his erection. He hoped. After pulling on his socks and shoes, he hurried back to Eve, taking her hand. "This way."

He led her through the kitchen and out the back door, onto the deck overlooking the back acreage. Then across the deck and down the steps, heading toward the gate in the fence that separated the lawn from the pasture.

"Wow, it's beautiful out here," she said with enthusiasm as he dragged her in his wake.

"This is the one place I feel at home—outdoors with my buddies." As he drew her to the gate, he stopped and gestured toward the field with a broad smile. "Meet Elvis, Madonna, Mariah, and J-Lo."

Four equine heads popped up on cue, dark eyes studying them with great interest. Sean gave a shrill whistle through his teeth, and a chorus of deep-throated nickers answered. The horses began to lumber in their direction, whinnying more greetings.

"Oh, Sean, they're so pretty!" Her delighted laugh warmed his weary soul. "You're lucky to have horses. I'm jealous."

"I'd always wanted some, and when we moved here, Blair wasn't able to talk me out of them. I started with two quarter horse mares, and breeding became a part-time hobby."

She glanced at him, puzzled. "Why would she want to talk you out of something you enjoy? I mean, look at them!"

"Horses were never her thing. She hated getting dirty and smelly." He frowned, uneasy with comparing his dead wife with Eve, even in his own mind. "Anyway, I won that particular battle of wills, though

I lost plenty of others. The skirmish over the chicken coop, for example? Defeated, big-time." He put on a forlorn expression that earned a laugh.

"Chickens?"

"Why not? Fresh eggs, some fuzzy chicks running around—what's not to love?"

"Oh, let me see . . . chicken poop, the smell, the rooster crowing at dawn and whenever else he feels like it? Sorry. I have to say I'd be with her on that one."

"And here I had you pegged for a girl who didn't mind a little dirt and smell when it comes to animals," he teased.

She arched a dark brow. "I don't mind and you darned well know it. Take me horseback riding sometime and I'll prove it."

"You mean that?" He studied her, excited by the idea. A lazy fall afternoon doing his favorite thing— well, second favorite—with a woman he liked and admired? Heaven.

"I do, and I'd love to take a ride with you." She checked her watch. "Another day, though. I just remembered I told Mama I'd come by and try to fix the leak under her sink. With her arthritis and bad knees, she can't crawl around like that anymore."

"I could come, too, and help you," he blurted. "I'm pretty handy with fixing stuff."

"Oh, no, I couldn't ask you to do that," she said, waving a hand. "You wouldn't want to spend the afternoon under Mama's sink and get grilled by her for your trouble."

"Why would she grill me? You and I have worked together for years."

Eve looked at him like he'd lost his good sense.

"And how many times have we hung out, just you and me, without the guys?"

"Oh." He deflated some. "I guess I'm a little out of practice dealing with mothers. She'd make something out of us being together, huh?"

"And then she'd be after me like a bloodhound on the scent, despite the fact that I have nothing to confess."

She doesn't? What does that mean? That I'm imagining the mutual attraction?

Their conversation was interrupted by the arrival of his equine friends, who were curious about Eve and hoping for a treat. Elvis stuck his sleek brown head over the fence and sniffed Eve's front jeans pockets, then moved on to inspect her jacket, completely unmoved by her squeal of surprise.

"What's he doing?" She giggled, patting the gelding's smooth neck as his velvety nose whuffed at her jacket.

"Checking for apples or carrots. He knows where I keep them, so he's saying hello and searching for a snack at the same time."

"Sorry, boy," she crooned in sympathy, scratching his big ears. "I'll bring something next time, I promise."

The two of them made a hell of a beautiful picture, together in the sunshine, Elvis eating up her attentions like an overgrown dog, eyes half-closed in bliss. Sean couldn't take his eyes off the scene, and something weird broke loose inside him, rattling around, stealing his breath. He couldn't have described the feeling if he tried, only knew that this moment would remain etched in his mind as long as he lived.

He really didn't want her to go, and he mentally scrambled for a way to make it last.

"Thanks for showing them to me," she said, stepping back from her new friend. "I really have to go, though."

Disappointment rose, but he accepted his cue gracefully, nodding. "I'll walk you to your car."

As he led her around the side of the house to the front driveway, he told himself it was for the best. He had no business selfishly pushing for more between them—an ill-advised move on many levels.

Like the almost kiss he couldn't forget.

Dammit!

Eve unlocked her car, opened the door, and paused. "Seven?"

"You bet. I've got your address."

"Good. It'll be fun."

"Can't wait."

It would be pure torture not to touch her.

He watched as she turned the car around and started down the winding drive. Didn't move until the vehicle disappeared from sight. A rueful smile curved his lips and he stood there marveling at all the good changes in his life, including this new closeness with Eve.

Common sense be damned. He felt better than he had in years.

And even if this attraction between them couldn't go any further, he wasn't going to waste a second of getting on with living.

No matter how bittersweet.

Eve was aware of Sean's gaze. Continued to feel his physical presence even after she could no longer see him in her rearview mirror.

He'd wanted her to stay, or at least spend more time with him. That much was clear by the obvious disappointment that flashed in his green eyes when she turned down his offer to help at her mother's house. She'd be willing to bet he didn't have a clue where his interest in Eve was coming from or if indeed it was simply a desire to deepen their friendship.

Which was precisely why she couldn't allow them to lose their heads. Sean was like one of those chicks he'd mentioned—reborn, blinking into the sunlight, new and fuzzy, vulnerable to predators. He didn't know what he wanted besides surviving each day, and she didn't fault him for that.

But she wasn't up for a round of him using her heart as a soccer ball during his path to healing.

Keeping him at a safe distance might be easier said than done, however. When he'd opened the door, shirtless and barefoot, jeans unbuttoned . . . Lord, she'd just about swallowed her tongue! Sure, she'd seen all of her team bare-chested at some point over the years, even if it was a brief glimpse as one of them pulled on a clean shirt, but holy crap. She'd never seen Sean like that, in such an intimate setting, with his potent male beauty staring her in the face and nothing to do but look. And appreciate the scenery.

The man might not be as ripped as he'd been before he'd gone through hell, but he was still sexy. That wide, strong chest, a light covering of dark chest hair that she'd love to feel under her palms, the springy curls narrowing into a treasure trail that disappeared behind his zipper. Narrow waist, long legs. Sean totally did it for her, without question.

Oh, this was bad.

She was looking forward to tonight in his company,

more than was wise. He occupied her thoughts all the way to her mother's small house outside Sugarland. So thoroughly that she nearly missed the driveway. Braking, she made a sharp right, drove up, and parked behind her mother's ugly green rattletrap of a car, shaken to realize she'd made the half-hour drive with no real recollection of doing so.

Great. She had to get the man off her mind or her mother would *know*, in that superhuman way all moms had, and pry the truth out of her with speed and skill that would impress the FBI.

Shutting off the ignition, Eve got out and walked through the garage as she normally did—the front door was for "company." Getting her key ready, she tested the door to find it unlocked. Again. With a sigh, she pushed it open and gave a knock.

"Mama?"

"In here!"

She walked through the mudroom into the kitchen, following the direction of her mother's voice. "How many times do I have to fuss at you to lock—what are you doing?" she cried, tossing her purse and keys onto the counter. "Get up from there right now, before you hurt yourself!"

She hurried over to where Mama lay under the sink, twisted half onto her back, only her bottom half visible.

"Hey, baby," her mom said, panting from exertion. "I was just . . . trying to fix this . . . so we can visit."

Rolling her eyes, she squatted and took the older woman's arm. "We can't visit if I'm having to take you to the doctor for screwing up your knees. Come on, up."

"Stubborn child."

"I get it honest."

Amelia Marshall got to her feet with a whole lot of huffing and even more grumbling, but Eve heard the love behind the bluster. That love was always there, as steady and true as Mama herself. Even when annoyed with her only child.

"I'm not an invalid, you know. There are still certain things I can do for myself."

"I know that, Mama," she said, brushing the dirt off the older woman's sweatshirt. "You're only fifty-three and far from decrepit. You're one hot mama, pardon the pun, and if I like taking care of you, so what?"

As she'd intended, the compliment made Mama laugh and squeeze her in a tight hug. Eve was always startled by how fragile her mother felt in her arms, and worried about her constantly. Maybe it was just the difference in their physical builds that made the older woman seem like a lovely piece of blown glass. After all, not many women could hoist a full-grown man into a fireman's carry.

"I'm far from 'hot,' but I'm working on it," she said, pulling away. "And you have better things to do with your time than babysit me. Like marry that nice young man Drake, and give me grandbabies."

Eve blinked at her mother, unsure which part of that to tackle first. She opted for avoiding the subject of Drake, if possible. "What do you mean, you're 'working on it'?"

Momentarily diverted, her mother grinned and indicated her blue warm-up suit. "When do you ever recall seeing me dressed like this?"

"Not often," she replied, eyeing the outfit. "Never, in fact." Her mother was always dressed in nice pants for work, or pressed jeans. She always looked gorgeous and polished, even on a modest budget.

"Well, you might see me like this more often. I had a little extra in the kitty, so I bought myself a membership to that new gym in town!"

Eve's mouth fell open. "Seriously? I thought sweating was against your religion or something."

"Let's just say I have a new outlook on life."

"You don't need to lose any weight."

"I'm building up muscle and toning what I've got."

Her mother glanced away and Eve narrowed her eyes. "What's really going on? Fess up."

"There's nothing to confess. Yet."

She frowned. "Mama . . ."

"Oh, all right, Miss Nosybody. Remember I told you that we got a new pastor at church three weeks ago?"

"Right. So?"

Her mother stared at her like she was dense. "Come on, child. Don't tell me you're even more out of practice at man-hunting than your mama."

"You're sweet on the pastor and want to get into shape?" That made sense.

"You're getting warmer." Her sly smile was the tip-off.

"Oh! He works out at the gym! You sneaky devil," she said, amazed at the older woman's subtle pursuit. "I can't remember the last time you showed interest in anyone. This man must be something special."

"He is." Amelia's voice softened. "You know who the Rock is, right? Dwayne Johnson?"

Eve's eyes widened and she laughed. "No way! He's that hot?"

"Mmm, and then some," her mother confirmed with a dreamy sigh. "He's a big, beautiful hunk of a man, single, close to my age, and he's sweet as a teddy bear. Now, if he'd just notice me . . ."

Wrapping an arm around her mother's shoulders, she gave her a quick hug. "He'd be a fool not to fall all over a stunning woman like you. And if he doesn't, he isn't worth the ground you walk on."

She kept her tone light, but she wanted this for Mama. Badly. If anyone deserved a healthy dose of romance, it was this incredible lady who'd worked so hard and raised her only child alone.

"Now, give me that wrench and sit down while I fix the pipe." She plucked the tool from her mother's hand. "And then you can tell me all about the pastor. . . . What's his name?"

"Tyson Sherrill."

Eve crawled under the sink, fixed the leak in less than five minutes, and was sitting at the table with Mama immediately after. Sipping iced tea and listening to her mother detail Tyson's virtues, of which there were many. In fact, God Himself might have sent the man down from on high, perfect as he sounded. But it was good to hear Mama happy and hopeful of getting a date.

And it kept Mama from returning to the topic of Drake Bowers and grandbabies. If that happened, she might ferret out her daughter's true feelings for a certain captain, who would be anything but husband material in her mother's eyes.

Husband material? Good God, where did that come from?

Because Sean would never be her man, lover, husband, whatever.

And the knowledge saddened her so much she fought to keep her tears inside, hidden from the woman who knew and loved her best.

4

"I met the prettiest girl when I was home on leave, Jesse. Her name is Tracy." Sean smiled, heart giving a little thump at the memory of his week in Chattanooga. He couldn't ever remember being this excited about dating one person, and he just knew Jesse would be happy for him.

"Yeah? That's nice." Jesse took aim with the rifle and peppered the targets with bullets, all in the kill zone.

"Nice? That's it? She's a goddess!"

"Whatever you say."

Frustrated, he lined up his own shot. "Shit, I thought you'd be happy for me."

"I am, if that's what you want."

"But?"

Jesse sighed. "In my experience, including my own mother as an example, women are only as good as their last taste of cock. Once something better comes along, they're history. Just remember that, okay? I'm only telling you this as a friend."

"Sure, whatever."

Why couldn't his best friend be happy about anything? Jesse's cynical nature grated sometimes. Except Jesse would call it practical.

That's what he told himself. But when he couldn't sleep at night, a voice whispered in his brain, asking if he wasn't certain Jesse's problem was something else altogether.

Knowing Sean couldn't be hers didn't stop her from wearing her sexiest jeans.

Eve turned around and craned her neck to see over her shoulder, critically perusing her rear in the bathroom mirror. Just because she was in prime physical shape didn't mean a man would find her appealing. There wasn't anything wrong with wanting to look her best.

Facing front again, she eyed her tight, low-cut black top, wondering if it was too blatant. So what if she could hold her own on the physical-agility course with any man? Didn't she have the right to feel feminine, desirable?

She fluffed her hair, applied a touch of gloss to her lips, and snorted at her reflection. "Yeah, like the guys won't notice you've never put this much effort into your appearance around them before."

Well, screw it. Let them think what they would.

A knock interrupted her musings and she hurried for the door. Without pausing, she flung it open and suffered a temporary loss of speech at the sight of Sean standing on her threshold. And a definite spike in her libido.

She wasn't the only one who'd taken extra pains with appearance. Sean had been to many of their get-togethers in the past, and she'd never seen him looking so . . . sharp. Pressed and crisp, sexy as hell.

His long-sleeved emerald green shirt set off his eyes and was tucked in, showing off his lean frame. Black jeans hugged his long legs and cupped his package invitingly, making her mouth water. Quickly, she lifted her gaze to his face, hoping he didn't notice she'd been checking out the goods.

"Hey! Let me get my purse and I'm set."

He smiled. "Ready when you are."

Grabbing her purse and keys off the table in the small dining area, she rejoined him, locking up behind her. Immediately, doubts assailed her. Should she have invited him inside? She hadn't thought he'd be real excited to see her dinky apartment; she'd wanted to keep things sort of casual, and now she hoped he hadn't thought her rude.

"You look very pretty," he said as they walked toward his Tahoe.

"Thanks. You clean up good yourself." God, how lame! That was the sort of reply she would've made before . . . well, just *before*, and she cursed herself for not coming up with something more clever. Witty. Jeez, should she flirt? No, absolutely not. She smiled at him to cover her discomfort.

"So I've been told, but it's been a while."

He held the door open for her and she slid inside the SUV, her pulse giving a tiny jump as he slammed it shut. She glanced around the interior of the vehicle, thinking how strange to have him pick her up, to ride together to their team's hangout. And really wonderful.

Especially when he got inside and started the engine, the rich musk of his cologne invading her senses. She loved the aroma of a man, fresh from the shower. Loved the sight of damp hair clinging to his neck, shirt open to reveal a slice of bronzed chest.

"You're staring again." His lips quirked.

She cleared her throat. "Sorry. I couldn't help but notice you're getting tan. You're looking healthy."

More like scrumptious.

"I've been working outside since I got home from rehab, every chance I get," he said, pulling out of the parking lot. "I don't tan easily, but at least my skin is losing that pasty white cast."

"Well, keep up the good work."

"Will do."

He fell silent for a couple of minutes, and the tension inside the SUV rose to a palpable level. As aware as she was of him as a man, she could swear from the almost static current flowing between them that he was aware of her, too, as more than a teammate. Pheromones were a weird thing, so perhaps those were busy tripping her internal alarms. Or maybe it was the set of his shoulders, the tilt of his head. The way he didn't do more than glance at her when he finally spoke again.

"How's your mother?"

"I'm sorry?"

"Your mom. You said her sink was leaking?"

"Oh, that. I fixed it." She shook her head. "Would you believe I caught her under the sink, half inside the cabinet trying to do it herself?"

"What's wrong with that?"

"You sound just like her. You two would get along great."

"Is that a bad thing?"

"Not at all. I love Mama to pieces. She's simply very stubborn."

"You're saying I'm stubborn, too?" The slight smile gave away his teasing.

"Yep, through and through. And anyway, she shouldn't be crawling around on the floor with her arthritis."

"That's right. I remember you mentioning her health. Is she elderly?"

"No, she's only fifty-three and she's quite lovely. I'm a bit too protective of her, I guess."

"A person can never be too protective of their loved ones. Time is all too fleeting."

Which Sean knew better than most. Dammit, she'd stuck her foot right in it.

"I apologize—"

"Don't, okay? I'd prefer you not guard your words around me," he said firmly. "Keep it real, because that's the only way I'll get better."

She relaxed some. "The wise advice of the department shrink?"

"And some good friends." He shot her a genuine smile, which she returned. "Your mom must be a special lady, the way you talk about her. Like she's a queen or something."

"She is a queen in my eyes. That woman raised me after my father took off, and did it all alone. She sacrificed everything for me in those awful early years, until things finally turned around." Eve didn't bother to keep the pride from her voice. "She's been an executive secretary in downtown Nashville for the past fifteen years, and her boss already dreads the day she decides to retire. He'd be lost without her."

Just like I would.

"I'd like to meet your mom sometime," he said casually.

Her heart gave a leap. "I'd like that, too." What her mother would think of Sean remained to be seen. And heard.

"Until now, I've never heard you mention your father. Is he still around?"

She snorted. "According to the e-mails he sends me on Christmas and my birthday? Alive and kicking, with his perfect, lily-white family."

"I touched on a sore subject. I'm sorry," he said, laying a hand over hers.

She took a deep, calming breath. But it was his touch that settled her. Made her safe. "No, it's fine. I made my peace years ago with him running off, cutting us out of his life. Or I start to think so and the bitterness comes back to bite me."

"Why did he take off? I don't understand how anyone could do that to their family."

"Isn't it obvious?"

"Not to me."

"Come on, Sean, you're not that naive." She sighed at his puzzled look. "My father was white. Attitudes were different thirty years ago. He couldn't hack the pressure of being the white country boy who'd married a young, pretty black girl. The nasty slurs and the threats. One day, he lit out like his ass was on fire and never looked back."

Sean was silent for a long moment, as though weighing his words carefully. "I believe if a man is fortunate enough to be blessed with someone to love, he should hold on to that and fight with everything he's got. To hell with everyone else. If that makes me naive, then so be it."

Warmth filled her soul and emotion clogged her throat. "No, it doesn't. Just rare."

"Not really. I can name a few guys we know who've done the same."

"They're rare, too."

The rest of the drive passed in companionable silence, her hand still enfolded in Sean's. How could such a simple, everyday pleasure like a man's big hand holding hers thrill her from head to toe? Make her feel like the most important woman in the world?

She didn't want it to end, but they arrived at the Waterin' Hole all too soon. Belatedly, she realized they'd discussed her parents, but she never got to ask about his. She knew his parents were deceased from comments he'd made over the years, but not the circumstances or whether he had aunts and uncles, cousins. She knew that he had no siblings, which wasn't much, and made a mental note to try to learn more.

"Stay there," he said, shutting off the ignition. He jogged around and opened the door for her, then took her hand again, leading her toward the entrance.

As they went inside, she was surprised and more than a little nervous about what the others would say if they saw. Part of her hoped he'd keep hold, just to get their reaction. Her worries were for nothing, however, since he let go the second he spied their group against the far left wall.

He waved and headed in their direction, leaving her to follow in his wake. She didn't know whether to be relieved or annoyed, but managed to do a decent job of keeping both to herself.

"Hey, amigo!" Julian yelled, slapping Sean on the back. "Lookin' like a million, man! Got a hot date?"

"Sure do. Eve's my date tonight," he said, glancing around to make eye contact and give her a playful wink.

Julian's mouth fell open for a minute as he studied them both. Then he decided Sean was kidding. "Oh, right. That's a good one!"

Everyone laughed except Sean, she noted. He smiled, but didn't comment as he scooted out a chair and waited for her to sit.

Of the assembled group, Six-Pack noticed the gesture and his laughter died, replaced by a thoughtful expression as his eyes met Eve's.

She avoided the weight of his stare and turned her attention to Sean, who took a seat beside her and gave his drink order to the server.

"A Coke, please."

The girl hesitated. "Just a plain Coke?"

"Yes," he answered, politeness a tad strained.

"Make that two," Eve put in.

"You usually get beer." He gave her leg a squeeze.

"But—"

"I'm the alcoholic, not you," he insisted. "If you want beer, order one. It's fine."

"If you're sure . . ."

"I am. Besides, if you order Coke like me, then think how the others will feel. I don't want anyone to feel guilty about drinking what they want around me."

He had a point. "All right." She looked up at the girl, who waited with a tight smile, clearly uncomfortable. "Miller Lite, bottled."

"Gotcha!"

The girl flounced off and Sean nodded. "Thank you."

"What for?"

"Keeping it real, remember?"

"My version of that rule excludes anything that might hurt you," she informed him. "I reserve the right to break it as needed."

He grinned. "Duly noted." Propping his elbows on the table, he addressed the group in general. "Where are the rest of the women? You guys make them stay home?"

"As if you can *make* a pregnant woman do anything," Six-Pack said, making a face. "Kat's ankles are swollen and she didn't sleep good last night. She practically shoved me out the door so she could finish grading homework and go to bed."

Being seven months pregnant and teaching first grade, on her feet all day, sounded like hell to Eve. "That sucks, my friend."

"Tell me about it."

Zack made a sympathetic noise. "Same here, except Cori's just tired. The hospital has her working too many shifts, in my opinion."

"Jeez, you guys are a real advertisement for having kids," Julian said with a laugh. "No, thanks."

Clay echoed the sentiment with enthusiasm.

The two fathers-to-be glared at Jules, and Eve couldn't stifle a chuckle. Some aspects of the man's personality would never change. "Where's Grace?" she asked him.

"Going over notes for a big trial she's working. Her client is innocent, blah, blah."

"Aren't they all?" Sean took his Coke from the serving girl and set it in front of him.

"Yeah. She's damned good at her job, though." The note of pride in his voice was something to hear. The man had worked his tail off to win Grace over, and nobody had ever seen him happier.

Eve grabbed her beer and was about to ask Jules a question when a familiar and much-welcome voice dispelled the thought.

"Is this a private party or can anyone join in?"

All eyes swung toward the newcomer—and the young, blue-eyed blond man was definitely no stranger.

"You made it! Good to see you, amigo." Jules shook his hand and then pulled him into a manly hug. The others did the same, exclaiming how glad they were he'd been able come. Even Sean, who in the past had been quite reserved about showing any sort of affection in public.

Eve waited for her turn, hugged him tight. Then she drew back and eyed the scar bisecting the right side of Tommy's handsome face, as well as the one circling his right wrist, unable to see them without recalling the horrible day they'd almost lost him.

"Figured I'd better show since I got, like, eight messages on my answering machine. Dang, it's only been two weeks since the barbecue, but you guys are acting like you haven't seen me in years," he said goodnaturedly. "Not that I'm complaining about the reception. I'm an attention slut like that."

"You've got that right." Shea Ford, Tommy's lady love, a cutie with curly brown hair and big brown eyes, stepped forward and waved at the group. Another round of hugs ensued, and when it was her turn to get one from Eve, she laughed. "Wow, a girl could do worse than getting hugged by five gorgeous studs. You are so lucky to work with these guys."

"Six," Tommy corrected, arching a dusky brow. "And hugs are *all* they're getting."

"Right, six." She gave him a kiss, which soothed her man's ruffled feathers.

Shea took a seat between Tommy and Eve. As much as she loved the guys, Eve was glad another woman had shown up at the gathering. It gave her a break from their macho bull and constant teasing, and a chance to talk with someone who didn't sport a penis.

Eve leaned close to the other woman. "So how are plans for the house coming?" Like Julian and Grace, Tommy and Shea were planning to build. The younger couple's home, however, would be built on a piece of land on the Cumberland that was owned by Shea and her police-detective brother, Shane.

"We're still looking at plans, but we know we want something with a wide covered porch overlooking the river, and plenty of bedrooms for future Skylers." The last was said softly, with a dreamy smile on her face.

"Have you set a date yet for the wedding?"

"Another work in progress. Tommy's still getting settled in his new position in Arson and has to pass the state certification, so we're not rushing things. I don't want him under too much stress all at once."

"I can understand that, after what you two have been through. I've heard getting married is one of the most stressful periods in a person's life, not that I'd know."

"Me, either. But with any luck I'll soon find out. Want to shoot some pool?"

"I'd love to."

"Great! Get us a table while I grab a beer and the pool cues."

They played three games, giggling because it was a clear contest of who sucked the least. Neither of them stood a chance of becoming a pool shark. While they played, Eve became aware of a tingling on the back of her neck. A couple of times, she caught Sean staring in her direction with undisguised heat darkening his gaze. He either didn't know or didn't give a damn that the others, not just Six-Pack, had started to notice.

The room suddenly became very warm and she turned to face Shea, leaning on her pool stick.

Shea straightened from her shot and gave her a curious look. "You okay?"

"Yeah."

"Something going on with you and Sean?"

Crap. "Why do you say that?"

"Oh, maybe because the man is ogling you like he's a lion and you're a three-legged antelope?"

"That transparent, huh?"

"Yep." The other woman skirted the table and came to stand beside Eve, who grimaced.

"Great." She sighed. "Honestly, I have no idea where this is going. Or even if it can go anywhere."

"But you want him," Shea said confidently. "And the consensus is he wants you. Everyone knows that."

"What?" she croaked, startled. "Like who?"

"The guys. Tommy says they figured it out months ago." She gave Eve's shoulders a comforting squeeze. "Oh, it was nothing either of you knowingly said or did. Mostly it was the tension between you two that gave it away. But don't worry—according to Tommy, nobody's going to say anything bad if something does develop."

"But they *would* get involved. I know those guys." Not a delightful prospect.

"Only out of love and concern for you both, nothing more. You know that."

She did. Didn't make it any easier to face them, however. Their female teammate was completely, head-over-heels in love with their captain, a sticky situation that would divide most station houses and turn the workplace into a battle zone.

She'd quit the department before she'd allow that to happen.

"Eve? I'm sorry if I've overstepped." Shea bit her lip in worry. "I thought you'd want to know."

"No, I'm glad you told me. Forewarned and all that."

"Can I ask you a personal question?"

"Sure."

"How long have you been in love with Sean?"

She took a long look at the man in question, then turned back to Shea. "He had me at 'I'm Sean Tanner and I'm your captain,'" she said with a sad smile. "From the second I stepped foot in Station Five, he was my hero. He was the firefighter I aspired to be, had the courage of ten men, and he owned my heart the instant I saw him standing in the bay."

Shea sniffed, brushed at her eye with one finger as Eve went on.

"As badly as I wanted him, it hurt me so much when his family died to see him broken and lost, no longer the man we'd all known. Tell me, Shea . . . do you believe any woman could heal his heart after all he's lost?"

Shea had no answer to such an impossible question.

Unlike Eve, who was very much afraid she did.

God, why couldn't he take his eyes off the woman?

Stupid question. He'd always been attracted to Eve, but he'd been married. Happily, in the beginning. Then in recent years, he and Blair began to have problems and he clamped down on his desire for Eve. He wasn't the sort of man who'd cheat on his wife, and he certainly wasn't going down that path with a colleague.

Even if he strongly suspected Blair hadn't remained true to their vows.

Then he'd been widowed, his children dead, and he'd disappeared inside himself.

But the forbidden yearning hadn't died along with the rest of his life. If anything, his feelings had strengthened into . . . he didn't know. Was afraid to find out.

"Um, earth to Sean?"

"What?" He blinked at Tommy.

"I said, I heard you're going to participate in the fire department's bachelor auction thing."

"Howard didn't give me much choice." He curled his lip at Six-Pack, but the big guy just snickered along with everyone else.

"Hey, you'll be the coolest guy there. For your age, anyway," Tommy drawled.

"Very funny, kid. What about you? Isn't the fire marshal's branch participating?"

"Yes, but without me. Shea made it clear that I'm off the market." The younger man looked smug about it, too.

"I'm gonna do it," Six-Pack said. "We all are, right?" The others agreed.

"But Grace informed me she'd better win the bid, or I'm toast," Julian said.

"Well, hell, maybe Shea will say yes when she hears I'm the odd man out."

Six-Pack grinned. "It *is* for charity."

Sean chucked Tommy on the shoulder. "He's good with laying the guilt trip."

"No shit." Tommy lifted his beer. "Okay, I'm in!"

They all whooped and clinked glasses, and it struck Sean that he was smiling and having a great time. And that he hadn't been this content in years. He basked in the feeling of belonging for a good while, until Eve and Shea rejoined the group.

The evening was full of laughter and banter between good friends. Others paired off to play pool or darts, then swooped in again to talk and relax. By the time he and Eve rose to leave, he was flying high—a natural one. The best kind.

"See you guys Monday morning," he called with a wave.

Their grins and curious looks as he turned to go didn't even bother him. Maybe later, but not tonight.

"Seems like you had a good time," he commented as they walked to his Tahoe.

"I did. You?"

"The best I can recall."

"You need to get out more," she teased.

"I plan to do just that." He hadn't intended for the statement to come out sounding provocative, rife with innuendo. Hell, he'd never been good with the verbal man-woman dance. *So what am I doing?*

He helped Eve into the SUV and hesitated before closing the door. Her gaze held his, full of uncertainty. And promise?

Stepping inside the open door, he leaned in close, as though drawn by some unseen force. Her lips parted slightly, and in that moment, nothing mattered more than tasting them. For real, not some airy almost kiss.

One hand reached out of its own volition, cupped her cheek. "Your skin is so soft. You're so beautiful." Her eyes were wide, breath hitching. "God, I want to kiss you."

"Then what the hell are you waiting for?" she whispered.

His tenuous control snapped and he crushed his mouth to hers, groaning in need. Reveling in the pure, sheer pleasure of his tongue invading her heat, sliding against hers. She returned his hunger eagerly, fingers curling behind his neck, tangling in his hair, pulling him close. She tasted like spice and beer, and he knew he could get drunk on her alone. That she was the only mind-altering substance he'd ever want again.

When he finally broke the kiss, they were both panting, staring at each other, desires naked and exposed. There was nowhere to hide from this, no place to run. And he wasn't sure he could, even if he still wanted to.

"I want you," he said, surprised by the words. The truth of them shook him to the core.

"Take me home and you can have me," she answered breathlessly.

Stealing another kiss, he shut her door and hurried to his side. He couldn't peel out of the parking lot fast enough, and every mile that separated them from their destination was agony. His jeans were strangling his cock, and his balls threatened to erupt at the thought of burying himself in her hot, willing flesh.

"Supplies? Do you have any? Because I don't," he rasped.

"Yes, at home. Just hurry." Scooting close, she nuzzled his throat, his ear.

Shit, he was going to drive off the damned road. Or maybe pull over and fuck her in the back of his Tahoe under the stars. Now, there was an idea that had merit.

Somehow he made it back to her place without coming or wrecking, both of which he considered minor miracles. He screeched to a halt, parked a bit crooked, and jumped out, not even caring whether he'd locked the vehicle. She met him at the front of the truck and they grabbed hands, ran to the door of her apartment. After several fumbled attempts with the keys, she managed to let them inside.

They barely got through the door, Eve slamming it shut and locking it, and he was on her. Pressing her back against the wall, devouring her mouth like a starving man. She kissed him back with equal fervor, then pushed against his chest, trying to create a bit of space. He almost growled in frustration until he saw her grab the edge of her shirt, haul it over her head, and toss it aside, leaving her in a pretty, lacy scrap of a black bra.

Their mouths came together again as she worked the buttons on his shirt. When he grabbed the material, prepared to rip it apart, she pulled back.

"No! I love that shirt," she said hoarsely. "Matches those amazing eyes."

"In that case, I'll wear it every damned day."

His shirt fluttered to the floor, unharmed. She unbuttoned her jeans next and pushed them off her hips, down her legs. And what gorgeous legs they were, long, toned with just the right amount of muscle. Strong yet alluring, like the rest of her body. He couldn't wait to see her out of the bra and matching skimpy panties, spread around his cock.

He'd just started pushing off his own jeans when she grabbed him by the hand and began dragging him in the direction of what he assumed was her bedroom. He stumbled along, hopping out of each leg, finally freeing himself and leaving the jeans abandoned somewhere between the front door and her room.

Her bedroom wasn't large, but the bed was nice, queen-sized. He preferred a king, but this would do fine. Vaguely, he was aware that her tastes were more feminine than he'd expected, with frilly whatnots draped over the various surfaces of the dark furniture. However, he didn't have time to ponder this revelation because Eve was back from digging in the nightstand, a square packet in hand.

"Undo me?" She turned her back to him.

"With pleasure." He flicked the clasp on the bra, admiring the line of her back, her bronzed skin.

She turned to face him again, letting the material fall away. Sweet Jesus, she was beautiful, breasts high and firm, tipped with dark brown nipples. He wanted to suckle them, and he would, but right now he needed something else.

Clearly impatient, she hit her knees and yanked at the waistband of his boxer briefs, pulled them down. His erection popped free, flushed deep red and leaking at the tip. He nearly came undone when she captured a bead with her tongue and licked all around the head . . . and then looked up at him with a catlike smile on her face.

"Oh, God. Put it on me," he hissed.

"I want to suck you first." She stuck her lip out in a pout.

"There will be plenty of time for that later. Dammit, I'm not going to last!" With an exaggerated sigh, she ripped open the package and placed the condom over the tip. Rolled it on slowly, driving him crazy. Grabbing her arms, he hauled her to her feet. "Do you have any idea how long I've wanted to bury myself deep in your pussy?"

Answering fire flashed in her expression, and her voice was thick with lust. "Not nearly as long as I've wanted it, Sean Tanner. I'll ask you again—what are you waiting for?"

Needing no further encouragement, he slid the black panties down her legs. He was hardly aware of her kicking them aside, fixed as he was on her flat abs and lower, where a curly thatch of neatly trimmed black hair hid a treasure.

He pressed her back against the wall, loving her gasp as he pinched one pert nipple, rolling it between his fingers. He stole several kisses, nipping at her lips and his palm skimming down over her tummy, to the triangle between her thighs. His fingers brushed through the downy softness to find the wet pearly nub awaiting his attention. Throbbing cock or no, he wasn't about to take her without making certain she was physically ready to accept him.

"Spread your legs, baby," he demanded. She trembled as she complied, but her eyes told him it wasn't from fear. The woman was as lost as he, with one shaky toehold on sanity, needing his body pressed into hers, filling spaces empty and lonely for far too long.

As she widened her stance, he played with her clit, fingering it until he got a small whimper and a shift of her hips. His signal that she wanted more. He slid his fingers back, parting her flesh, marveling at the feel of her wet heat. Imagining it around his cock. Pressing two fingers inside, he pumped, stretching her. Mimicked what he'd do in a moment, letting her anticipate.

"Now, please! Don't make me wait anymore," she pleaded.

"Wrap your legs around my waist, your arms around my neck, and hang on."

He hitched her up, holding her against the wall, using his strength and hers combined to keep her in place. She clung like a burr as he cupped her bottom and shifted, nudging the head of his cock between her folds. He lowered her, let her settle, pushed deep inside until she was impaled on his shaft.

"Oh, God," he groaned. "Yeah."

"Sean . . . feels so good. Waited so long."

This was heaven. Being seated inside Eve, her body wrapped around his. Nothing else mattered now except stroking her with his cock, making her feel as good as he did. Angling his hips, he began to thrust. Slow and deep. To the balls and out again. Her whimpers became breathy moans and he thought they'd drive him over the edge. But what she said next actually did the trick.

"Fuck me hard," she rasped. "Need it hard and fast. Dirty."

"Shit, yes!"

Holding her steady, he slammed home, reveled in her glad cry. Fucked her just the way she wanted, hammering with merciless precision, rattling the pictures on the wall. But she began to slip and he needed a better position.

"Hang on, baby."

Spinning, still inside her, he walked them the few steps to her bed and eased her backward, coming down over her. He did slip out of her then, but not for long. She scrambled to the middle of the bed and lay on her back, legs spread. He crawled between them, lifted them over his shoulders, and cupped her bottom once more. Lifted her clear off the bed, and impaled her again.

"That's it. This is what I needed." He gave her a feral smile. "Hold on tight, because I'm gonna give you that sound fucking you want so badly."

"Please!"

Hips snapping, he drove into her channel. Mindless, he focused on nothing but the grip on his cock, the wild sensations battering at his control. So long. Too damned long. He wasn't going to last. Not with his cock enveloped in heaven, his balls slapping her ass.

"I'm gonna come!" she yelled, body tightening. "Yes!"

The tingling at the base of his spine warned of the explosion. His balls drew up and the orgasm rocked him, shattered his world. He came with a shout, wracked with spasms, filling her. Couldn't remember when he'd ever come that hard.

Eventually he pulled out and sought the bathroom to dispose of the condom and clean up a bit. When he returned, Eve was curled on her side, chin resting on her hand. Sound asleep. He smiled ruefully, something very much like affection stirring in his heart. Something more frightening than structure fires or even hateful phone calls.

Pushing the unwanted thought from his mind, he pulled back the covers, settled her underneath, and spooned her against him, her sweet rear nestled against his groin.

And fell asleep thinking Eve felt extraordinarily right in his arms.

5

Sean surveyed the bustling city of Bangkok, eyes wide. "Come on, Jesse. What do you need a tattoo for when we can get laid? They don't call it Bang-cock for nothing, right?" The prospect made his dick twitch. It had been a long dry spell since he and Tracy had broken up.

Jesse laughed, but didn't bite. "Here's the place I was talking about. Inside."

Sean let himself be steered through the doors, where his friend quickly got caught up in finding the perfect design. What the hell, he might as well get one, too. Something rad, like a screaming eagle on his shoulder. Or some sort of symbol, like a Celtic knot.

After what seemed like hours, his friend showed him a picture of a single rose on a thorny stem.

"Why a rose, man? They've got all sorts of cool designs. Celtic, dragons, whatever."

"Besides my name? So my enemies will remember that if they touch me, I'll make them bleed."

Eve awoke slowly. Stretched. Winced.

She was sore, aching in places she'd forgotten she

had muscles. Then she recalled why they ached and she smiled.

Sean had fucked her through the mattress, and it was fabulous.

Braving the early-morning sunlight, she opened her eyes and rolled to her side. Blinked at the empty spot next to her. Trepidation curled through her stomach, and she was about to call his name when she smelled the coffee. A faint clink came from the kitchen and she sat up, relieved that she hadn't been abandoned. Now that her brain was becoming clear, though, morning-after jitters were plucking her nerves like wound-up fiddle strings. Which she told herself was silly.

Men don't stay and make coffee if they're planning to run for the hills. Right?

Pushing out of bed, she went in search of something to cover her nakedness. That was probably like shutting the gate after the cows got out, but the tiny bit of uncertainty over her reception was enough to curtail any attempt to seduce, at least for the moment. A search of a dresser drawer produced an oversized T-shirt and she pulled it over her head, satisfied that it shielded the essentials.

And if all went well? It could easily come right back off.

Cheered by the idea, she padded the short distance down the hall, through the small living area, and into the kitchen. Sean was leaning with his rear against the counter, fully dressed, mug in hand, raising it to his lips. He spotted her and stopped in midmotion, giving her a half smile. But it wasn't a "Good morning, sexy" or even a "Let's have a repeat of last night" sort of smile.

No, this one telegraphed "This is so awkward, I

don't know what to say to you" and was underscored by the fact that it didn't reach his eyes.

"Hey, you're up," he said, his tone neutral. "Can I pour you a cup?"

Eve's gut cramped in disappointment. That was about as flat and impersonal a greeting as a girl could get, in her experience. "No, I'm good." The brew would sour right now if she even tried. "How did you sleep?"

"Fine. You?"

Not *fabulous*, not *wonderful to be in your arms*. Just *fine*.

"I slept like a baby." Going out on a limb, she beamed at him, letting him know in no uncertain terms where her feelings stood. "Last night was fantastic . . . and so were you."

His expression closed a bit. "Yeah, um . . . about that. We have to talk."

Never a good conversation starter after your boss has screwed your brains out.

Her smile faded and she crossed her arms over her chest. She could already feel her own walls going up fast, brick by brick. "So, talk."

"Why don't we go into the living room and sit down?"

"Sure."

She left him to follow her and lowered herself to the sofa, trying for a relaxed position. Leaning back, she rested her hands in her lap, willing them not to shake as he sat beside her and placed his mug on the coffee table. Schooling her face into what she hoped appeared to be nothing but curiosity, she waited.

He cleared his throat. "You're a hell of a woman, Eve."

"You're not so bad yourself," she said, playfully patting his leg.

"We're friends, right?"

"Of course. I'd hope last night didn't change that except to make our friendship stronger."

He nodded. "I'm glad you feel that way, because I let things get out of hand. We both know what part of me I was relying on to do my thinking, and I'm sorry."

"No, don't apologize. I was more than willing and I enjoyed what we did," she said earnestly. She paused, taking a deep breath, and blurted, "I want to be with you again."

Regret shadowed his eyes as he shook his head. "There are half a dozen reasons why it was a bad idea, and those haven't gone away," he replied gently. "I made a mistake and it won't happen again, Eve. It can't."

Oh, God, it hurt. So fucking bad.

She laughed and covered her mouth with her hand, tears springing to her eyes in spite of her effort to stop them. "So I'm the rebound screw after all."

"What? No, it's not like that!" He grabbed her hands, clasped them in his rough ones. "I'm not on the rebound, not after two years of being alone. You're special to me, and because you are, I can't drag you through the pile of crap that doubles as my life while I'm still trying to work through it myself."

She stared down at their hands, saying nothing, waiting for him to continue.

"And then there's the department to worry about. I don't want to jeopardize our careers over a station house affair. And let's face it, you'd take the brunt of the fallout and most likely be the one transferred."

"You have a valid point except for one detail—

we've already crossed the line! Do you honestly think no one will notice?"

"They won't if it's a onetime thing and we keep it to ourselves." He tilted her chin up, forcing her to look at him. The anguish in his eyes was palpable. "You're my friend. I think you're terrific and I respect you a great deal. But that's all there can be."

She would not cry. Not in front of him.

"Are you all right?"

The soft question, full of genuine concern, was nearly her undoing. But she gave him a bright, fake smile to mask the pain of a shattered heart. "Why wouldn't I be? We're two adults who scratched an itch, right? No hard feelings."

He frowned and studied her face intently for a long moment. Finally, he leaned over, cupped her cheek, and kissed her on the temple. Then he stood and retrieved his mug, taking it into the kitchen. Eve heard the water running as he rinsed it out. In a minute he was back, keys in hand, obviously ready to make tracks. She rose and saw him to the door.

On the threshold he turned, and his voice was hesitant. "I'm really sorry."

"Think nothing more of it." *Please, just go!*

"Okay. I'll see you."

She hoped he might pin down a day, but he made his escape, hurried down the walk with the brisk strides of a man running from the scene of a figurative crime. Moving inside, she closed the door, not wanting to see him speed off like the devil was in hot pursuit.

Slowly, she made her way to the sofa, curled up in one corner. Just folded in on herself, one arm wrapped around her aching stomach. She was no stranger to loneliness; not one of her attempts at a serious relationship had ever worked out, and she'd been sad before.

But she'd never felt more rejected, more ugly and undesirable, than she did now.

Her shoulders began to shake and she let the tears fall. God, she needed to talk to somebody. Not just anybody, but her best friend. He'd know something was wrong anyway, first thing tomorrow morning. Reaching out to the coffee table, she grabbed her purse, dug out her cell phone, and hit speed dial.

Zack's upbeat voice rang in her ear. "What's up?"

"Can I c-come over?"

"Evie? What's wrong?" he asked, worried.

"I n-need to t-talk to you." She got out between sobs. "If I'm n-not imposing—"

"You could never impose, honey. It's not your mom, is it?"

"No, no, Mom's fine." *Thank God, it's not Mom. Calm down. It could always be worse.*

"Okay, that's good. Do you need me to come get you?"

"N-no, I can drive. I'll be there soon."

"Okay, but drive careful. Give me a clue what this is about?"

"When I get there." Breaths hitching, she wiped her face and struggled to get control. "I fucked up, big-time."

Zack Knight hung up the phone and turned to his beautiful, very pregnant wife. "Eve's coming over. Jesus, she's crying."

Cori's hand stilled, a forkful of eggs suspended halfway to her mouth. "What's wrong?"

"I don't know, but I have a damned good idea." He

paused, then said meaningfully, "She showed up at the Waterin' Hole last night with Sean. And left with him, too."

The fork clattered to her plate. "With Sean? *With*, as in . . ." Her eyes widened for emphasis.

"Sure looked like it to me, the way he kept her in his sights the whole night. I'd hoped I was wrong, but this"—he waved a hand at the phone—"does not bode well."

"Shit."

"Yeah. And I'll tell you something. . . . If he's hurt her, I'll kill the asshole myself and put him out of everyone's misery."

Coward. Stupid, dumbass motherfucker.

Sean took the curves on the road too fast, half blind to much of anything except the memory of Eve's sweet face laughing, of her having a good time at the bar last night. Later, blue eyes heavy with desire, smoldering with ecstasy as he drove into her.

And this morning, anguish quickly masked when he'd pulled the rug out from under her. Proved himself to be a selfish bastard.

Every reason he'd given her this morning of why there could be no repeat performance of their tryst was the truth. Technically. Still, those reasons sounded like lame excuses.

Like a man running scared.

Didn't he have a right to be afraid? The answer was yes—as long as he didn't hurt anyone in the process. And he had.

Cursing himself, he pulled into his drive and almost missed the brown-wrapped package sitting on the ground next to his mailbox. The postman usually brought oversized packages to the door, but it wasn't a big deal. He braked, put the truck in park, and went to the box. He hadn't checked his mail yesterday, focused as he'd been on Eve. There were a few bills and the typical junk. He bent, gathered the package from the ground, and carried all the mail to his truck, placing it on the seat.

As he let himself into the house through the garage, he glanced down at the package. No return address. That wasn't what caught his attention, though. He set it on the kitchen counter, laid the regular envelopes to the side.

No postmark. Curious, he lifted the box, inspected the plain wrapping from every angle. Sort of heavy, but not too much. Maybe whoever sent it was planning to mail it, and found himself out this way, dropped it off instead. Perfectly reasonable. Leaving it, he started a pot of coffee, using the Starbucks blend Howard had gotten him hooked on. He watched the brown liquid stream into the pot, inhaling the aroma like a hit of weed.

Coffee first. The mess of his life later.

After pulling the pot-mug switcheroo, he returned to the package, trying to recall if he'd ordered anything online. Even if he had, wouldn't it have some sort of label from the company? Perhaps his aunt and uncle had sent something.

Setting down the mug, he angled one end of the box toward him and started to work on the tape. The paper ripped easily and he got it off, letting the wrap flutter to the floor. It was just a regular cardboard box, taped closed at the top. Picking off one end, he stripped off the tape, balled it up, and let it join the paper. Then he opened the flaps and peered inside.

Bubble Wrap. Lots of it protecting the object within, and a shard stabbed his lungs as he recalled how Mia used to squeal, "Let me pop it!" She'd loved the crinkly stuff. And he recalled how he'd finally snap at her to stop, and take it away because the noise was getting on his last nerve.

Breathe, right through the agony. You can do it, even with that gaping hole in your chest.

It was the memories of the everyday things that hit the hardest. Always would.

Reaching inside, he lifted out the object and began to unwrap it. Before he even got the stuff all the way off, he realized what he held, and his stomach clenched in dread. He banged it heavily onto the counter and stood staring, shock warring with anger.

"Fucking Jack Daniel's?"

A big-assed bottle of Tennessee's finest whiskey. Enough to drown his sorrows all the way to next weekend. Who would've sent this? None of his friends, for sure. They all knew he was recovering, and that he planned to stay that way. Christ, he had to get rid of it. Give it to Clay or Jules, today. He'd call one of them.

First, he peered into the box again, looking for a note or some sort of clue as to who'd sent the damned thing. Carefully, he moved around some of the Bubble Wrap left in the box . . . and saw an envelope in the bottom. Fishing it out, he held it up and turned it over, inspecting both sides. Just a plain, yellow greeting card envelope. Strange. No name on the outside. Didn't most people automatically write a person's name on one, even when it wasn't necessary?

Wary, he tore into the paper, lifted the flap. At a glance, he could tell the sole contents consisted of a single photograph, and he removed it. An amateur night-time shot of a fire? Yeah, with people in the perimeter of the picture, a couple of firefighters with hoses. Taken on a hill or rise, from quite a distance, so far you almost couldn't tell—wait.

From out of the inferno, on the right-hand side, the nose of a vehicle could be seen. And part of a cab. They belonged to an eighteen-wheeler. Hands suddenly clammy, he scanned to the left. In the flames, the faint outline of a car. Bred to the back end.

He knew the scene all too well. He saw it in his nightmares, both sleeping and awake.

"Oh, God," he moaned, knees almost buckling. He staggered to a chair in the breakfast nook, fell into it. His hands were empty—he'd dropped the photo onto the pile of wrapping paper.

"Why? Why would anyone do this to me?"

And who?

A wisp of an idea seeped into his mind like black smoke, stifling. Deadly. But no, it had been too many years. A lifetime.

Did you ever ask yourself . . . what if it wasn't an accident?

The call. The photo.

Someone had known about his family's wreck. Had somehow known enough to stand on a hill in the darkness, undetected, and snap a tangible memory of hell. The hell that had begun his slide into the depths of alcoholism.

The booze. They knew about that, too.

The room spun, and he buried his face in his hands. He needed to do something, but he didn't know what. Couldn't think.

So he just sat, frozen.

Blown apart, all over again.

* * *

Eve sat on Zack and Cori's sofa between the couple, elbows on her knees, hands clasped to hide their trembling. Cori's palm was rubbing comforting circles on her back, and Zack was patting her knee, gazing at her in real concern.

"I'm so sorry to barge in on you guys like this."

"Stop that," Zack admonished gently. "Tell us what's wrong and maybe we can help."

Eve gave a bitter laugh. "That's just it—you can't help. I feel so stupid. I mean, I'm tougher than this, right? I should be able to handle it on my own."

"Eve," Cori said softly, "the beauty of having good friends is that you don't have to be tough. You can fall apart and know you're safe to do it here."

That got her. The tears she'd been suppressing on the drive over filled her eyes, overflowed, ran down her cheeks. "I messed up so bad. I might have to transfer to another station, or put in for the Nashville Fire Department. Or Clarksville, or the fucking West Coast. Anywhere but here."

"You slept with Sean, didn't you?" Zack asked quietly, no hint of accusation in his tone.

"I'm such a moron." Eve buried her face in her hands. "I love him."

She broke down then. Cried as she hadn't since she was twelve and a boy at school had called her Oreo— black on the outside, white in the middle. She'd been shocked to the core because her skin wasn't much darker than his, her eyes blue. But that hadn't stopped the hateful slurs the scum and his posse had thrown her way for the next couple of years until high school, when she'd outgrown her awkwardness and blossomed. And gained her confidence to boot.

This hurt so much more, her insides being ripped apart.

Cori's voice broke through her misery as she handed Eve a tissue. "Sweetie, what did he say to you? Was he mean?"

Eve took it and wiped her face. "Would've been easier if he were. I can fight against mean, you know? But no, he was nice. He can't drag me into the cesspool of his life, blah, blah. I'm an incredible woman, and, drumroll, 'we're still friends.'"

"That bastard," Zack hissed. "I'm gonna kill him."

"No!" Panic seized her. "You can't let on that you know! If you do, the others will find out and things will get out of hand. Promise me you won't say anything to him."

Her handsome, dark-haired friend visibly struggled with her request for several long moments before pinning her with laser blue eyes and giving her knee a squeeze. "All right. For you, I'll keep it to myself—unless he asks for it by hurting you again."

"Thank you." She gave him a hug, which he returned, hard.

"I'm so sorry this happened," he whispered into her hair.

"It's partly my fault. I knew what I was facing and I bit the apple anyway."

"How long have you loved him?"

"Always." Her voice shook. "Even when I had no right. And *surprise*, I still don't."

"Are you really thinking of putting in for a transfer?"

"Yeah. I think it's for the best." She straightened, letting go of him. "I can't carry these feelings around with me anymore and face him every shift. It's too hard, especially now."

His expression fell, became immeasurably sad. "I wish it didn't have to come to that, but I understand."

"Thanks."

"When will you make the move?"

"As soon as I tell him. Despite everything, or maybe because of it, he deserves to hear it from me, beforehand." The very thought of leaving Station Five, her home these past several years, caused a hollow ache inside. But as she'd told Zack, it was partially her fault.

"Stay and have some breakfast," Cori offered. "We have bacon and eggs."

Eve's stomach lurched. "There's no way I could eat, but thank you, both of you."

"Coffee, then?" Zack's jaw tightened in stubbornness. "You're not going anywhere until we're one hundred percent sure you're all right."

In that case, she could be here for eternity.

She mustered a wobbly smile. "Coffee sounds fine."

And so went the morning of turnabout, Eve doing her best to reassure her friends she was fine when nothing could be further from the truth. She was dying inside. Her love for Sean wasn't just a festering secret anymore; it was an open, bleeding wound.

And she was the one responsible for handing him the power to deliver it.

Just look him straight in the eye and tell him. What can he do? Nothing.

Eve parked behind Sean's Tahoe, and got out, tough outer shell in place. For the most part. She'd been shredded, but the visit with Zack and Cori had gone a long way toward patching up the ragged seams to where they were almost invisible to the naked eye. Sort of like putting wall plaster over a crack in the Hoover Dam.

She left her purse in the car and locked up. This wasn't going to take long.

At the front door, she rang the bell and waited. After a few moments she tried again, and still no sign of Sean. Of course he wouldn't come to the door and let her get this over with, especially when her nerves were shot. Always the hard way with Sean.

A nicker from around back caught her ear and she tensed. If he was outside, even better. Might make this go quicker and make for a faster exit. Leaving the porch, she walked around the side of the house. As soon as she rounded the corner, she saw his long, lean form sprawled in a lounger, the backrest propped upright. His head was back, and as she got closer, she saw his eyes were open, staring at the pasture and the horses, who were observing her approach curiously.

Her running shoes were making plenty of noise crunching through the grass, so she couldn't imagine why he hadn't turned his head to see who was approaching. Reaching the deck, she ascended the three steps, skirted his chair to face him . . . and a cry of dismay escaped her lips when she spied the small table beside him.

"No! Jack Daniel's? What are you thinking?" A highball glass sat beside the bottle, half-full of amber liquid.

He raised his eyes and blinked slowly, as though noticing her for the first time. "Why are you here?"

She flinched. "That can wait. Why do you have a

gallon of whiskey? Tell me you didn't go out and buy this."

"Sunday. Liquor stores are closed."

"Then where did you get the bottle, Sean?"

"It was a gift. From someone who hates me." His laugh was harsh, his eyes bleak. "And no, I haven't taken a drink."

"There's whiskey in the glass," she pointed out.

"Didn't say I didn't *want* to."

She took a cautious step forward, scrambling to make sense of this. "Back up. How exactly did you come into possession of the bottle?"

"You sound like a detective," he said dully. "Maybe that's what I need."

His attitude scared her. "Answer the damned question."

"I never picked up my mail yesterday. When I got home this morning, there was a package wrapped in brown paper sitting beside the mailbox. I brought it in, opened it, and found the bottle inside."

"That's it? Why would you say someone hates you? Could be from an old friend who doesn't know you're on the wagon." She didn't really believe that, though, and from his expression neither did he. Something else was going on.

Without a word, he reached behind the bottle and picked up something from the table. A photograph. Since it had been lying facedown, she hadn't seen it before. He simply handed it over, and waited.

Flipping it over, she peered at the pic, frowning. A big fire, obviously. Involving a truck? What . . . ?

The instant she realized what she was looking at, the blood drained from her face. "Oh my God." Cold horror gripped her and her knees grew weak. She sat heavily in the lounger beside his, staring at the hideous photo.

"Someone watched my family die. Took a fucking picture and sent it to me two years later." He looked at her with wrecked eyes, voice cracking. "Why?"

"I don't know," she said, reaching out to grab his hand. "But considering this and the phone call that upset you the other day, I think we need to call the police."

"What can some beat cop do? I haven't actually been threatened and there's no real proof this is anything but meanness."

"First, we're not going to call a uniform. We're going to use our tie to the police department and go straight to the guys who can really help." Her tone brooked no argument. "I'll make the call. Can I use your phone? I left my cell phone in my purse, in the car."

He nodded, looking lost. No way could she address the real reason she'd come. Not now.

"I'll be right back. In the meantime, don't touch the bottle or that glass anymore. If someone hates you that much, the whiskey could be tainted. Did you think of that?"

His eyes widened. "No, I didn't. But the bottle was sealed. . . ."

"That doesn't mean squat. Just sit tight until I get back."

Slipping inside the house through the sliding glass door, she went straight to the phone sitting on the far end of the kitchen counter. Picked it up and scrolled through the numbers on his speed dial. She found the one she was looking for with no trouble. As captain, Sean kept all of his team's numbers handy, and as she'd guessed, this one was still included.

Tommy Skyler answered on the third ring. "Hey, Cap! What's up?"

She smiled at the way he still called Sean "Cap" even though Skyler was now working in Arson. "Wrong person. It's me, Eve."

A pause. "Eve? Oh! What's going on?" His voice was cheerful, but clearly puzzled about why she was calling from Sean's number.

"I have sort of a situation here and I need your help, old friend."

"Sure—shit, he's not drinking, is he?" he asked in alarm.

"No, but there's some stuff going on that needs to go on record with the cops. Preferably a detective."

She proceeded to tell her former teammate about Sean's phone call, the awful "gift" in the box, and the implications. When she was finished, Tommy cursed softly and got right on board, just as she'd known he would.

"I'll call Shane right now," he said, referring to Detective Shane Ford. His future brother-in-law, and a good man who'd helped out the guys at Station Five more than once. "He's in Homicide, but I know he'll send someone out to talk with Sean. Someone good, whom he trusts."

"You don't know how much that means, buddy. Thank you."

"How's he doing?"

"Not great, but hanging in there."

"Let me know if there's anything else I can do. I'll stop by and see him in the next day or so."

"I know he'd like that. He needs his friends around him."

"Is that what you still are, Eve? Just a friend?"

Crap. "What makes you ask that question?"

"My eyes worked just fine when I was at Station Five," he said, a trace of wry humor in his voice. "And you're there, protecting him from the boogeyman. Gonna spill?"

"That's a story I'll have to tell you another day."

"Aha! So there is a story."

"Bye, Tommy," she said softly. "And thanks again."

"Anytime."

She hung up, thinking she missed the kid, missed his constant teasing and flirting. But for all his acting like a big, goofy puppy, Tommy was a very perceptive, intelligent man. Much too perceptive.

And she was a fool for letting Sean Tanner rule her heart.

6

"Have you ever noticed how a gun feels better in a man's hands than any woman?"

Sean, lying on his back on his bunk, hands behind his head, craned his neck to laugh at his friend. "Man, you have some seriously fucked-up priorities."

"I'm not joking." Those dark eyes held his. "A piece of ass can be had anywhere, but the respect a leader commands from his men, the power he holds? Better than any orgasm."

Sean stared at his friend, not liking the implication of those words. "And you think a weapon will get you respect and power? You don't get those things by using force, Jess. They're earned, not commanded."

"Semantics. How you get them isn't the point."

"Then what is?"

Jesse stared at him so long, he began to feel weird. Like what his friend said next might change everything.

"The point is what you do with them once you have them. Let me ask you something. . . . Do you believe every person has the right to eat, to have clothing and shelter, to defend themselves? No matter what country they're from?"

"Of course I do. Why do you think I'm here, serving our country?"

"And if you found out the country you so proudly serve gives with one hand and takes with the other, same as it's done since it beat the shit out of the Native Americans? If you found out that not a fucking thing has changed and that soldiers like you and me are feeding into a warped system designed to kill the ones we're supposedly trying to help? What then?"

"I have no idea what you're talking about." Jesus.

"Oh, come on. Rip off those goddamned rose-colored glasses, my friend, and answer my question."

He knew damned well there was more than a grain of truth to what Jesse claimed. History spoke for itself. "Sure, our government does some stuff I don't agree with. But we're just the peons, and I don't know what either of us could do to change that."

"But if you could right those wrongs, would you?"

"Christ, I don't know," he muttered irritably. "I suppose. Can we drop this?"

A smile played about Jesse's lips. "For now. I've got big plans for us, though."

"Whatever."

Much later, as he mulled over the conversation, he worried about what Jesse was up to. And whether the man took his answer to heart.

Eve was here. Thank God.

That was all he could think over the numb shock that had stormed his brain. She was taking action like a trouper, keeping her head on straight and handling his nightmare.

My nightmare, not hers.

He should do something. Take this out of her hands, because she didn't deserve any of this. His past, his present shit. None of it. Yet he was paralyzed. The horrible photo brought back that night like it was yesterday.

The flames.

The stench of gasoline and burned flesh.

His wife's license plate curling, blackening.

He lurched out of the chair, gasping, clutching his chest. The memory was a razor blade to his throat, slicing deep the way he wished he could slice his wrists.

Parents expected they'd die before their children. Not *with* them.

Why my son, my baby girl? Why?

"Sean! Honey, look at me." Strong fingers dug into his shoulders. "Look at me, now!"

Her voice penetrated his self-inflicted hell and he stared into her face, the fog lifting. Until then, he hadn't realized he was standing by the deck railing, hands fisted in his hair as though ready to pull it out by the roots. Gradually, he relaxed, dropping his hands to his sides . . . when what he really wanted to do was to take her in his arms and never let go.

"You're going to get through this, you hear me?" Her worried face hovered close to his. Beautiful.

"Do you see now why I don't want to drag you into my shit?" he rasped. "Do you get it?"

"Come inside and sit down."

"But I—"

"Hush."

She pulled him inside, through the kitchen and into the living room. Pushed him down onto the sofa and he didn't resist. His legs just sort of surrendered and he sank, defeated. Her footsteps moved off in the direction of the kitchen and he heard her rustle in the fridge, remove a glass from the cupboard. In a few seconds she returned, holding out a glass of juice, which he took with a question in his eyes.

"Apple," she said. "It'll go easier on your stomach than coffee."

That wasn't the main question on his mind. "Why are you taking such good care of me, especially after I ran off this morning?"

"I'm into pain."

His lips curved into a half smile at the joke. "Inflicting or receiving?"

"Well, I'd thought receiving, but I might've changed my mind. Might want to inspect that apple juice carefully, and keep me away from sharp objects."

"I'm amazed you can joke with me after what I pulled."

"What else am I supposed to do? My hair shirt is at the cleaner's." The sadness in her eyes was quickly covered, her expression neutralizing.

"I'm sorry," he said softly.

"Let's get the detective up to speed on your situation before we worry about anything else, okay?"

He sighed, staring into his unwanted juice. If he pretended it was a few shades darker and tasted like Jack, it might go down better. Fat chance.

He hated what he'd done to her this morning. Hated *himself*. But God, he was scared. No, terrified. To let any woman in, to let her matter.

Because he'd never survive another loss.

The doorbell saved him from another round of self-flagellation, and he rose, setting down his glass. "I'll get it." Now that the shock was subsiding a bit, he wasn't willing to act like a helpless victim in his own home, and in front of a stranger.

He opened the door to find a man with dark blond

hair and brown eyes, not as tall as himself, but close. More muscular, too, built like he could put a man on the ground without much effort, if necessary. And the guarded expression in his eyes, the tense stance that appeared natural to him, suggested he'd done just that a time or three.

"Captain Sean Tanner, Sugarland Fire Department," he said, offering his hand with a smile. Or what he hoped passed for one.

The man's tension bled out some, and he shook the offered hand with a return smile that made him appear much more approachable. Even friendly. "Detective Taylor Kayne. I understand you've got a slight problem, some harassment going on."

Sean nodded. "I hope that's all it amounts to, but that's what I'd like you to tell me, given your expertise. Come on in."

The detective stepped inside, his gaze going straight to Eve and settling on her. Sean moved around him to stand next to Eve, bristling inwardly at the man's rather frank appreciation of the woman in front of him. As Kayne introduced himself and shook her hand, Sean edged closer to her and draped an arm over her shoulders. He felt her stiffen in surprise and sensed her glance at him, but his attention was on the cop.

Let Detective Muscles admire the view all he wanted—from afar. Real fucking far.

And yeah, that gasping noise was his resolve to remain *just friends* dying a swift death.

Shit.

"Can I get you some coffee?" Eve asked the man.

Sean tried not to frown and barely managed to keep to himself that the detective wouldn't be there long enough to enjoy it.

"That would be great. Thanks." The cop beamed at her, and she disappeared into the kitchen.

"Have a seat, Detective." Sean gestured to the easy chair at one end of the coffee table and took up a seat on the sofa.

To his credit, the cop wasted no time getting to business, removing a small notepad and a pen from the pocket of his long-sleeved shirt.

"I'm surprised you guys aren't using electronic devices of some sort to take your notes on by now," he commented.

Kayne looked up from scribbling something at the top of a page. "To me, nothing beats good old pen and paper, at least in the field. Then I transfer my notes on each case to computer, expand on clues, interviews, my own observations, and such while the details are fresh. It's a system that works for most of us."

"Do you ever run into any trouble?" he asked, curious. The cop didn't look like a man who got his build from a gym membership.

"You kidding?" He laughed. "Nine times out of ten *nobody* is happy to see me coming, unlike your job. Got scars from a knife and two bullets to prove it."

"I'll remember that next time I think I've had a bad day."

Eve returned with the man's coffee, and he thanked her politely. After handing over the mug, she took a seat on the other side of Sean, with him planted firmly between her and the detective. Not that he'd left her enough room to sit anywhere else, and a secret part of him smirked.

It vanished quickly, however, as Kayne began the interview.

"Captain Tanner, give me a rundown of what's been going on. I got only a brief version from my colleague Shane Ford." All his attention was now focused solely on Sean. When it came to his job, the man obviously didn't allow any distractions of the female variety. A major point in his favor.

Sean steeled himself against reliving the story, and knew keeping it factual was the only way he'd get through the telling. "Almost two years ago, my wife, son, and daughter were killed in a traffic accident. At least I thought it was an accident until I received a call on my cell phone at work on Friday."

"Who was driving the car?"

He swallowed hard. "My son. He drove into the back of an eighteen-wheeler that was parked on the shoulder of the highway." *It should've been me.*

"I'm very sorry." The detective sounded sincere, and gave Sean a few moments before he continued. "What did the caller say?"

"He said, 'Did you ever ask yourself, what if it wasn't an accident?' It took me a few seconds to make the connection as to what he could possibly be talking about."

"He? You're sure?"

"Yes. But his voice was low and there was a lot of background noise. I couldn't identify him."

The detective's pen paused over the paper. "What sort of background noise? People talking, car horns, dishes clanking? Anything that stands out would be a help, especially if it indicates a specific place."

He thought back, concentrated hard. Put himself in the moment and . . .

"Road noise," he said. "Like when someone has a

window open and you can hear the whine of the wheels on pavement, cars rushing past going the other way? And a radio with music playing. Heavy metal."

"You're certain?"

"As sure as I can be without having been there, yes."

"Okay, so we think he was on the move, possibly traveling. This is good." He paused, pen tapping the paper. "You didn't delete the incoming number, did you?"

"No. I started to, but something told me to keep it."

"Excellent. Get your phone and let me get the number off there. I'm playing a hunch."

"Which is?" Sean rose.

"The phone was one of those disposable jobs, or it was stolen. If it was stolen, we'll have his last known location, that being the city or town he stole it from. Perhaps even the exact location of the theft."

"That won't tell us who we're dealing with."

"Not directly, no. But it would give us a map of where he's been as well as a time line, particularly if he made other calls. One more piece of the big picture."

Quickly, he retrieved his phone from the kitchen counter and scrolled through the received calls. There weren't many, and he found the one in question with no problem.

"This one," he said, walking over and handing the phone to the detective. The man took the phone, jotted the number down, and gave it back to Sean. "Thanks. I'll follow up on this number, see what turns up." He pinned Sean with his brown gaze. "Detective Ford tells me you were a witness to the accident that took your family."

Oh, Jesus. Help me. "Yes. I was on shift and we got the call."

"I'm going to ask you to tell me about that night. Believe me, it's necessary or I wouldn't ask," he said quietly. "Just take your time."

Sean wavered, emotion threatening to silence his voice. But Eve's hand gripped his and he found the courage to recount the evening, in horrid detail, every event beginning with Blair being pissed that he missed Bobby's important game, to passing out cold when he realized the burning car belonged to his wife. When he finished, he was certain there was no blood left in the hand that was clinging to Eve's, and he struggled not to give in to the black spots dancing in front of his vision.

"I know how hard that must've been," Kayne said, his gaze sympathetic. "Just a couple more questions along this line, I promise. Okay?"

Sean nodded, and the man continued.

"You said your wife was really angry that you elected to work overtime instead of attending your son's game, and that she made a heated remark along the lines of, 'If you can't appreciate what you have, someone else will.' Do you have any idea what she meant by that?"

God. Here was one wound he hadn't bared before. Absolutely no one knew what he'd suspected and hoped would never have to see the light of day. What if he was wrong?

What if you're not?

In the end, Blair was gone and couldn't be hurt by speculation. She would've bared the truth herself if it meant justice for her children.

"At the time, I thought . . . I believed my wife might be having an affair."

Eve sucked in a breath, but the detective showed no reaction at all. Sean figured the man had heard much worse.

"Were there any other indicators you considered red flags?"

"Yeah. There were small things that added up, stuff I didn't want to acknowledge at first. I'd spent a lot of time thinking about her leaving for work early, staying late. She came from family money, but she had built a lucrative career as an advertising exec. Suddenly her cell phone was off-limits to me. Sometimes she'd get a text message and claim it was a client. Those sorts of things. But no actual smoking gun, and after she was gone, there wasn't any point in finding out."

"I don't suppose you still have her phone, computer, things that might yield clues?"

Sean stared at him. "Her computer is still in her office. I haven't touched it since before the funeral. We think her BlackBerry burned in the wreck, but the rest of her stuff is probably in a box somewhere in the basement with her clothes and other belongings. I don't know because I didn't pack them—my team at the station did."

"All right. I don't need to see them right now, but don't get rid of those items just yet, if you don't mind."

"I . . . sure."

"Back to the harassment." The cop flipped a sheet of paper on his pad. "Tell me about the items you received here."

"This morning I found a package sitting on the ground beside the mailbox. That's a little unusual because the mail carrier will normally bring oversized packages to the house and leave them on the porch by the front door. When I brought it inside, I noticed it didn't have a postmark on it, that whoever it was from had brought it by instead of mailing it."

The detective's brows lifted and his expression clearly communicated what he thought of that move. "And you opened it anyway? Brilliant. You could've been blown to pieces."

Sean glanced at Eve and winced at the fear on her face before looking back to Kayne. "I'm not used to thinking like a cop, Detective. I've probably alienated some people in the department because of the mistakes I've made, but I never considered getting threats. And I sure as hell wasn't expecting to find a bottle of whiskey and a photo of the accident scene."

"What's the significance of the bottle?"

"After my family died, I used alcohol to numb the pain, more and more frequently until I had a real problem. I came to work hungover a few months ago and made a grave mistake, and one of my former firefighters was almost killed. I went into rehab and just recently got out, returned to work."

The cop nodded. "You're recovering. Good for you." No judgment. "Let me take a look at the bottle and the photo."

They rose and Sean led him through the kitchen, Eve following. On the way out to the deck, he said, "There's the box they came in."

Outside, Kayne squatted next to the small table to look at the photo, but didn't touch it. He studied it for several long moments before he spoke. "Did both of you handle this?"

"Yes," he said, feeling stupid. "I guess we shouldn't have."

"I doubt we would've gotten much off of it even if you hadn't. It's rarely like on TV where the print is all perfect and the culprit is rounded up neat as can be. But we'll check, 'cause you never know. I'll need you both to come in and get printed so we can rule yours out." Kayne stood, gestured to the bottle and glass. "You didn't drink any of that, I hope? Could be doctored."

"No, my stupidity level is about maxed for one day," he muttered.

"Good. I'm gonna go and get some evidence bags out of my car and I'll be right back."

As soon as the detective disappeared through the sliding glass door, Eve spoke up. "I like him. It seems like he's taking this seriously, and not because we called in a favor."

"Is that the only reason you like golden boy?" Dammit, he hadn't meant to say that out loud.

She squinted at him. "Golden boy?" A slow smile spread across her face. "You're jealous."

"I'm not."

"Ha! You are." The smile turned mischievous. "I could probably have a date with him before he leaves. Want to place a bet?"

"No, I damned well do not," he said, low and dangerous. "There's no need because you're not going anywhere with him."

She feigned an innocent look. "I'm not?"

"No, you're fucking not, so drop the subject." Jesus, he was growling like a rabid wolf.

"Wrong tactic," she said sweetly. "Rewind and try that again."

The idea of her following through, going out with the cop, eventually allowing him into her bed? Letting him do the things Sean had done to her last night?

He pulled Eve into his arms and brought his mouth down on hers. Kissed her like he meant business, and he did. Because no matter how bad an idea it was to get involved with her, allowing another man to take his place trumped that one as king of the bullshit ideas. His tongue slipped past her lips and she melted against him. Warm and soft, just the way he liked. He was really getting into it when a throat cleared behind them.

Sean broke the kiss, but took her hand before facing the detective. "Sorry about that." But he wasn't and they both knew it. From the cop's rueful smile, Sean had effectively burst his bubble. Good.

"I bagged the box and wrapping paper in the kitchen so the lab guys can test those, too. What, if anything, they'll tell us, who knows? The most innocuous-looking objects can talk and sometimes tell a hell of a story." He proceeded to bag the bottle of Jack and the photo, and prepared to leave. "You'll be around if I have more questions?"

"Absolutely. You can reach me here or at Station Five. Let me give you a card." Reaching into his back pocket, he extracted his wallet and fished out a business card while Kayne did the same. They exchanged cards and pocketed their wallets.

"Given what you've told me, I'm treating this as a threat," the detective said. "It's unofficial at the moment because an *actual* threat hasn't been made, but the implication is there. I've seen mean pranks, but frankly, the tone of this strikes me as sinister. Until we find out different, that's how I'm approaching it. I'll let you know something soon."

"I really appreciate this," Sean said. He meant it, too. "If this asshole had anything to do with my family's death, he's going to pay."

"I'd feel the same way. Let me ask you one more question." He pinned Sean with a narrow-eyed look. "Do you have any idea who's behind this?"

He considered the answer, lead settling in his gut. "Almost everyone in the fire department knows what happened to my family, and me as a result. My mistake got a good man hurt. One of them might hate me enough to try and push me out." The past niggled at his brain, like a worm pushing through soil. "There was someone else, once. We parted on bad terms, but that was over twenty years ago and I haven't heard from him since."

"Twenty years? Most people aren't that patient. You piss them off, they react. The first scenario seems far more likely," Kayne agreed.

Sean walked him to the front door. Items in hand, the detective reminded him about getting fingerprinted, said his good-byes, and left. Sean's prints were on file with the military, but he figured going in would save the cops some time digging them up, so he didn't argue.

For his part, Sean was glad to be rid of both the "gift" and the cop, for very different reasons. Both posed a subtle threat to the inner peace he was trying so hard to establish.

He turned to find Eve standing in the middle of the living room, arms crossed over her chest. He knew that look, the one of a woman in self-protection mode. She might have melted into his kiss before, but she wasn't going to be distracted now. He went to stand in front of her, unsure what to say.

"What was all of the breast-beating about? You don't want me, but the second someone else shows an interest, you go caveman. What is that?"

He pushed a hand through his hair. "I wish I knew."

"That makes two of us."

"All I know is whenever I see another man sniffing around, touching you or making eyes at you, like that fool Blake—"

"Drake."

"—whatever, or the detective . . . Christ, it drives me crazy!"

"You can't have it both ways. You're going to have to deal with me dating other men, or come up with some rules we can live with, because I can't do this ping-pong thing. Not with you. I can handle anything but being yanked around—that I won't tolerate, and I don't give a shit how much you snarl. What's it going to be?"

"You're asking me to—what?—make a decision about us when this thing between us, whatever it is, is a whole day old? In the middle of trying to keep sober, reestablish the respect of my men, and figuring out who wants to ruin it all?"

She looked away, jaw clenched. "Of course not. I'm flying as blind as you are, and I just need to figure out what we're doing. Besides fucking."

"Look at me." When she did, he cupped her face. Her gaze was wary, shadowed, and he hated that he'd put that look there. "Last night was more than sex. Why the hell do you think I'm so scared? It doesn't help that I still don't think I'm the greatest thing that could ever happen to you."

"So where do we go from here?" she asked miserably. "What do you want from me, Sean?"

Everything. I want it all, and I'm terrified to get it only to have it taken away. Again.

"To take things one day at a time. Can we do that?"

"I can't settle for being friends with benefits. I can

have that with Drake or anyone else, without risking my job or my heart," she said softly.

"Are you risking your heart by taking a chance on me?" He stroked her cheek, and fell into her ocean blue eyes.

"Do you even have to ask?"

"I guess not. But the risk isn't one-sided." He took a deep breath, and took the first step out on a very thin limb. "You're much more than a friend to me, baby. I've been in denial about it for the past several months. Then we acted on our feelings and I panicked because I've lost it all before and can again. I'm starting my life over, and it's terrifying. It doesn't excuse what I did this morning, but those are my reasons."

"You're not going to fail, or lose the people you love a second time. I refuse to believe that fate, or whatever is responsible, could play out that way again."

"The odds are with you being right, but my messed-up head still needs screwing on straight. I don't know why you'd want to put up with me, but . . . are you willing to take things slow? See what happens?"

Her expression lit with excitement, but was tempered with caution. "Only if we're exclusive while we're 'taking things slow.' I don't share well with others."

"Neither do I, baby," he murmured into her hair. "You've got a deal."

"We're going to have to keep this on the down-low at work."

"An understatement. And it won't be easy, because those guys will be worried about you and pissed at me if they find out. I don't care for my sake, but I don't want any of our personal issues affecting their concentration on a call."

If the guys thought he might hurt Eve, the fragile

new trust he'd begun to rebuild with them could degenerate into a hellish situation, fast. He couldn't put them through that. But he couldn't walk away from her. He'd already tried, and failed spectacularly.

"There's one exception." She looked him straight in the eye. "Zack knows."

"What? Already?" Damn, this was going to be awkward.

"I was upset and I had to talk to somebody," she defended. "Besides, he's my best friend and knows me well enough that he would've put two and two together in a heartbeat."

"I know, it's just . . . jeez, who are we kidding? They're *all* going to figure it out."

She deflated some. "Yeah. And Six-Pack will be the first one because he's *your* best friend and he doesn't miss a beat. The way he was staring at us last night, he suspects."

"You're right. I'm surprised he hasn't called or dropped by to ask me flat out."

"If you're thinking that, he probably will. Look, there was a reason I came over. After I saw how upset you were about the package, I was going to postpone bringing this up, but it seems I don't have a choice." Releasing him, she dropped onto the sofa. He'd never seen her so conflicted.

He sat beside her, trying to catch her eye. Someone as direct as Eve, not looking at him? Not a good sign. "I can tell I'm not going to like this."

"I'm putting in for a transfer," she said, her voice painfully sad.

He'd have been less stunned if she'd shot him. "Forget it. I won't send in the form, so get that idea out of your head."

At that, she snapped her gaze to his face. "It's for the best and we both have to accept that."

"I don't have to accept shit. It's not gonna happen."

"You're impossible!" she cried, throwing her hands in the air in frustration. "An arrogant, stubborn jackass!"

"That's what you like about me," he said with a confident grin. "Otherwise, you wouldn't be here."

"I came to tell you I was leaving for another station!"

"But you wouldn't have gone through with it, paperwork or not." Reaching over, he hauled her into his lap.

"Infuriating," she whispered into his lips.

"Yep, that's me."

God, claiming her mouth was fast becoming his favorite activity. Well, second favorite, next to claiming the rest of her. Swooping in, he captured her lips, deepened the kiss. Drank in her essence. Nothing like the taste of Eve, the feel of her nestled in his arms, and he wanted more.

She pressed against him, fingers twined in his hair. Heat ignited between them, rising in a tide of desire, sweeping him away in the current. Why swim against it? Holding her tight, he stood, erection swelling, hot and aching. His need for this woman was incredibly strong when it had been muted to near silence before, and he could only guess that the alcohol—or more accurately his inability to kick it—had been to blame.

"Let me take you to my room? Please." He'd beg if he had to.

"Yes."

Her upturned face, the fire that reached out to touch him, was all the extra reassurance he needed.

And he planned to ride that fire all afternoon.

* * *

No man had ever carried her before. Not as in swept away to be ravished.

And there could be no doubt that was exactly what Sean had in mind as he hurried toward his bedroom. She must be an idiot at best. Insane at worst. But she needed him over and around her, pressing into her, owning every inch of her body, as he'd done last night. Despite the fact that it was stupid as hell, might alienate many of their friends, put their jobs in jeopardy. All of it.

Didn't matter. Her need for this man was as simple, and complicated, as that.

At the end of the hallway, he made a right and carried her into a big bedroom filled with tasteful, dark masculine furniture. As he crossed the room and laid her on the king-sized bed, she admired how the large window let in plenty of light, bathing the gorgeous space in golden tones. There was nothing feminine about the space with its clean lines and no frills.

"When I got out of rehab, I bought new furniture and redid the room," he said, answering her unspoken question. "No one has slept in this bed but me."

Relief nearly overwhelmed her. Until that moment, she hadn't realized the prospect of making love on the same bed he'd occupied with his wife would be so abhorrent. But she should've known Sean would not be so thoughtless a lover.

"I'm glad. And the pieces are beautiful."

"I needed a new start, and for me, the bedroom was the most important place to begin. I wanted to turn a place of misery into one of peace and sanctuary." His green eyes shone. "I never dreamed it could become more."

She didn't ask what he meant by *more*. For now, being here with him would feed her starving soul, fuel her fantasies. The future seemed an elusive thing, a dream without a promise, and the present might have to hold her when the dream vanished into mist.

Sean walked into his bathroom and she could see his rear as he bent over, rummaging in a drawer. In a few moments, he returned and flashed her a smile. "How old do condoms have to get before they disintegrate into dust?"

A giggle escaped, sounding strange to her ears. "I have no clue. But I have some in my purse if—"

"That's quite all right. These will do." He tossed a couple onto the nightstand, leering. "Strip for me, honey."

She arched a brow. "We're really going to work on your delivery. When we're in the bedroom, you are *not* my boss."

His feral grin was all the warning she got before he bounded onto the bed, pushed her onto her back, and straddled her hips. His hard-on rubbed low on her abdomen, right above the pubic area, as he crouched, placing his palms on either side of her head. "I beg to differ, baby," he murmured.

He kissed her senseless to back up his claim, an activity that was fast proving to be one of his favorites. Hers, too. The spike of arousal plucking her nipples, heating between her thighs, attested to the fact that not all of her objected to his taking charge—in the bedroom or anywhere he wanted.

She might as well face that the man was the perfect match for her strong personality. In every way. Whatever she gave, he gave back in spades. No other man had ever turned her on like Sean, and no other ever would.

He finally broke away and sat up, giving her a bit of room to maneuver. "You're too clothed."

"So are you."

"Ladies first."

"Lady, singular."

"Figure of speech. You're stalling."

"I'm not."

Pushing up, she pulled off her shirt and tossed it. When she went for the bra, he forestalled her, flicking the clasp himself. He peeled the cups apart, baring her breasts to his hungry gaze, and pushed her down again. Despite his demand for her to undress, he continued to do the task himself, taking off her shoes and socks, then unzipping her jeans.

After working them off her hips and down her legs, he shoved them off the bed along with her underwear. His own clothes went next, and she could only stare in appreciation at the sight of his hard, muscled body. His wasn't the form of a man in the bloom of his youth, but that of a mature man who'd seen plenty of battles and lived to tell. No question about it, Sean was in amazing shape and could hold his own with any guy.

Ogling him, her attention focused on the tattoo she'd noticed last night but hadn't asked about. With her finger, she traced the eagle on his upper right arm. The bird had an American flag in its talons, and its wings were spread to wrap around his bicep. "The artwork is beautiful," she said, admiring it. "Where did you have this done?"

"Bangkok, when I was in the service." A fleeting

shadow crossed his face. "During one of the many stupid moments of my youth."

"I think it's gorgeous."

"No, gorgeous is you." Crouching over her again, he nipped and suckled each breast, sending little shocks through the brown nubs. "What do you want, baby? You need my mouth?"

"Please," she said, voice thick.

He tongued the peaks, lavishing each one with equal attention before venturing south, to her tummy. She was ticklish there, which he quickly discovered and ruthlessly used to his advantage, making her squeal as he nibbled and blew raspberries, licked her insy. But when he moved lower still, she gasped in delight as his mouth found her sex, laved the folds with a sound of pure male satisfaction.

He wasn't shy about seeing to her pleasure, and indeed made it his mission to be certain she was writhing mindlessly, legs splayed, surrendering to his mouth. Gripping his hair, she bucked her hips as he suckled the bud of her clit, sending off little sparks that danced behind her eyelids.

"Sean, please . . ."

He lifted his head. "Yes?"

A whimper escaped, and she would've been embarrassed if she weren't so far gone. Hell, she never made noises like that—much less begged—for any man. "Please! I need you inside me."

Moving to the side, he retrieved a condom from the nightstand and ripped open the package, sheathing himself quickly. "Roll over on your stomach."

Stomach? Apparently Sean wasn't much for missionary, if their encounters so far were any indication.

The idea excited her, and she knew there was definitely something to be recommended for having a *man* for a lover instead of a boy. She complied, wondering what he'd do next.

"On your knees."

His tone, and maybe a bit of intuition, told her that he might have something in mind besides simple doggy-style. Eager to find out, she presented herself on all fours, feeling completely slutty. Free. Always before she'd held a part of herself back, but with this man, there was no reason. He'd take care of her.

One hand gripped her hips while the other brought the head of his cock to her folds. He nudged with care and she opened for him with a moan, loving how he filled her inch by inch, his thick length sliding deep. At last he was seated to the hilt, stretching her more than she'd thought possible, their position adding to the delicious friction.

"God, yes." His fingers dug into her hips as he began to move.

His thrusts were strong, steady. A long slide in, then all the way out. In again, not too fast, just enough force and control to let her feel the unleashed power, thrill her to every nerve ending. A few more thrusts and he had her writhing on his cock, owning her, small sounds of pleasure escaping her lips.

Before she realized his intention, he rose up and sat back, wrapping an arm around her middle and taking her with him. Now she was sitting in his lap, back to front, impaled. So decadent, erotic. Connected in a way she'd never been to another man, and the sheer sensuality made her fly.

He began to move his hips, and her head fell back

onto his shoulder. If she'd been free before, she was soaring now, dancing with this man making love to her like a dark angel.

"God, Eve," he rasped. "I've wanted . . . for so damned long . . ."

Me, too. Oh, yes!

But she wasn't sure if she said the words aloud or only in her head. Wasn't sure of anything but the stroke of his cock, fingers splayed on her throat, lips nuzzling her neck. Unintelligible rumbles of encouragement, satisfaction. Arousal built to a fever pitch, a white-hot ball gathering, growing heavy. . . .

The explosion swept her into space and she cried out, pulsing around his length. Another thrust, two, and he stiffened, arms tightening around her with a hoarse shout. He held her through the storm, rode it gently back to earth with a sigh. Soothed her with lips and hands, made her feel like the most wanted woman alive.

All too soon reality intruded. Eve disengaged and rolled to her back, a smile lighting her face. One that was short-lived when she saw him staring wide-eyed at his condom-clad cock.

The condom that was split and leaking cum onto his new comforter.

"I . . . shit, Eve! I'm sorry," he said, stunned.

Oh, God. Elation morphed to a sick sinking in her stomach. Still, she tried for a bit of levity. "Guess that answers your question about when condoms will disintegrate."

"Jesus, I'm such an idiot." He raised stricken green eyes to hers.

She shrugged, feigning calm. "Hey, we're both clean. We know that because we have regular tests through work, and on top of that, I've never had unprotected sex until now. Plus, I'm on the pill. We'll be okay."

Some of the panic drained from his expression. "You're on the pill?"

"Yep, no worries." The knot of dread grew cold, especially given the relief evident in the slump of his shoulders and relaxing of his body.

"All right, that's good. Not that I wouldn't do right by you, but—"

"Sean, breathe. We're fine."

He nodded, pushed a hand through his hair. "Okay. You're right. Why don't I get us a washcloth to clean up?"

Without waiting for an answer, he jumped from the bed and ducked into the bathroom. She blew out a breath and tried not to imagine his reaction if her reassurances proved wrong.

Fortunately, the chances of that were slim.

Thank goodness.

7

1991

"Line up, losers! Operation Desert Storm, here we come!"

"Hey, Rose," one of them called. "Think we'll get to kill anybody?"

"Does a camel shit in the desert?" He said it like a joke, and that's how everyone took it.

Everyone but Sean. A cheer sounded among their buddies, but Sean managed only a hint of a smile as they lined up in front of the helicopter for a picture. God, he missed Blair and his son. What the fuck was he doing here?

"Get me a copy of that pic, will ya, Wilson?" Jesse said, slapping the man on the back. It was more of an order than a question.

"Sure thing, Jess."

Sean never did get around to asking Wilson for the same favor.

Amelia Marshall pulled an apple pie out of the oven, just about the time another one of those big blasted trucks came barreling down the road in front of the house. All hours of the day and night, rumbling past, not constant, but frequent enough to annoy. And raise her curiosity.

The activity certainly was an unwelcome change from when the previous couple had owned the place down the road. The Byrds had been quiet, friendly. They raised some livestock, dropped in to visit from time to time. But they'd been getting on in years and wanted to sell, take their money, and move to a condo in the city. Less upkeep and more amenities for two older folks who couldn't run a farm anymore, a farm their kids and grandkids hadn't wanted.

Lester Byrd had been deliriously happy the day he'd dropped by a few weeks ago to tell Amelia the news that not only did he have a buyer willing to pay the asking price, but he'd paid in cash. And Amelia had been happy for Lester and Beatrice, but who in the world had that sort of cash handy in this economy? When she'd posed the question to Lester, his eyes had clouded.

I don't know, Amelia, but Bea and I ain't gettin' any younger. Best not to look that gift horse too close in the mouth.

Well, after days of listening to that racket, Amelia had no such compunction. Curiosity might not kill the cat if the cat showed up bearing apple pie and a neighborly smile. Humming, she covered the pie with foil, then grabbed her purse and keys. Using pot holders, she carried the pie to the car, placed it in the passenger's seat, and headed in the direction of the Byrds' old place.

On the way, her mind drifted toward her only child. Something had been going on with Eve for a while now, not that her daughter would let on. Eve had always been the light of her life, and she couldn't fool her mother. A mother knows when something is wrong in her child's world, and Eve's had been about two inches off its axis for months. Longer, maybe.

Before she could think on it more, she reached the Byrds' driveway and turned. Until she had a new name to put with the place, she'd always think of it as belonging to Lester and Bea. Perhaps she always would even after being introduced to the new owner.

As she parked, the first thing she noticed was . . . stillness. Almost as if the land itself held its breath, waiting for the other shoe to drop. How odd, after all the noise of the trucks traversing up and down the road. When the Byrds had lived here, the property had bustled with life. Chickens, cows bellowing, a couple of hired hands always around doing some chore. She opened the car door and there was simply nothing in the way of life. Not even a dog came out to bark and greet her.

Around the side of the house was a squat, square vehicle she thought was a Range Rover. About fifty yards out, next to the barn, something heavier. One of those half-ton pickups? A Dually? She didn't know a lot about trucks.

Gathering the pie, she made her way to the house, up the porch steps, and knocked on the door. Movement could be heard inside, a shuffling of footsteps on creaky boards. Then the door swung open and she found herself face-to-face with a good-looking man with long, dark blond hair pulled back into a ponytail. She normally didn't care for long hair and tattoos on a man, but on this one, the look fit him.

Not to say she approved, because she didn't. There was a difference.

The long hair and tattoo suited the man's deceptively loose stance, like a cougar preparing to pounce. An air of nonconformity, rebelliousness, settled about his shoulders like a black cloak he wore well and never removed. Perhaps that image was perpetuated by the tilt of his chin, the way his smile of greeting came nowhere close to those cold, dead eyes.

"Ma'am?"

Remembering the purpose of her visit, she shook off the impressions and hefted the pie. "I'm Amelia Marshall, your neighbor. I thought I'd welcome you to the area, and what better way to do that than with homemade apple pie?"

"Homemade?" The man whistled through his teeth. "Yes ma'am, that'll do it. Why don't you come in?"

Said the spider to the fly.

Her smile faltered, but she shoved aside her misgivings. The man didn't look like any of her friends and neighbors, but one could hardly hold that against him. Her Eve knew better than most how it hurt to be judged on appearance.

He stepped aside to let her in, and she studied the interior of the Byrds' former home, noting the changes. Before, the house had looked like a home, complete with well-loved furniture, pillows, doilies, and photos of family parked on every surface. Now the inside was . . . barren. Desolate. Only a minimal amount of furnishings graced the living room, and what she could see was cheap, functional. There were no personal touches, no photos.

Save one.

"Can I take that, put it in the kitchen?"

"What? Oh, yes! Here you go. Enjoy." She handed over the pie and her host disappeared into the kitchen to put the dessert away. Immediately, her gaze homed in on the one concession to any sort of nostalgia. She walked over to the scarred coffee table and picked up the framed picture, a close-up snapshot of a group of soldiers in combat fatigues, smiling for the camera.

She easily identified one man by the tattoo on his neck—her host, who'd answered the door. Former military. Much, much younger, his hair buzzed in a high-and-tight, but there was no mistaking him. Well, that would certainly explain the utilitarian feel of the Byrds' old home, him being military and all.

What arrested her was her host's open, carefree expression. In the picture, his arm was around the shoulders of another young man, one with a rugged but handsome face, brown hair and brilliant green eyes shining in the sun. The closeness between the two was unmistakable, and so at odds with the man who'd answered the door.

"Desert Storm, 1991."

Startled, she jumped, clutching the frame guiltily. Wasn't like she was snooping, exactly, since the picture was in plain sight, but those cool eyes left her trembling. "I'm sorry. It's just that this photo caught my eye. Such handsome young men you were, and you looked so close."

"That we were."

No emotion. Strange.

"Anyway, where are my manners?" He offered his hand. "I'm George Sparks. I bought this place from the Byrds, but I guess you already know that. I'm not much for keeping animals like they did, but I prefer my space."

Was there a warning in that statement? If so, she couldn't detect it as she shook his hand.

"What do you do, Mr. Sparks?"

"George, please. I dabble in electronics, computers,

video games, and such. I'm developing a game now called *Total Annihilation*." He smiled.

"Oh! How . . . interesting."

"I enjoy what I do, though it's hard to break into gaming. Very competitive. How about you, Amelia?" On his lips, her name sounded like an intimate caress, one she didn't care for.

"I work in downtown Nashville as an executive assistant. Really that just means I'm a glorified gofer, but it will pay the bills until I retire."

"Retirement," he mused. "What a concept. I don't think I'll ever see that day, but it's a nice idea."

She laughed. "You're awful young to be talking like that! You'll need time to relax one day, spend lazy days with your family."

An odd look entered his eyes, quickly masked. "Family. Sure. One day, maybe, when I have the time."

What on earth did that mean? It seemed to her then that this man didn't have the foggiest concept of family, or warmth of any sort. "Oh. So you live alone?"

"I have a few buddies in and out, helping me with a couple of projects on the place, but it's just me for the most part."

"That must be some project, what with the trucks going in and out." She was only prodding him out of curiosity, hoping he'd reveal more. But she earned a hard stare instead.

"Yes, it is. Sorry about the noise, ma'am." But he didn't sound sorry in the least. His jaw tightened, and if she didn't know better, she'd believe he was considering putting his hands around her throat. Silly, but . . .

Some sixth sense urged her to find a graceful way to bid good-bye to George Sparks.

"No problem. Well, I won't intrude on your day any

longer," she said with false brightness. "I just wanted to introduce myself and let you know if you need anything, don't hesitate to call on me. Let me leave my number."

The same inner voice warned her not to let this man know exactly which house was hers, though he could learn the information without too much trouble. Instead, she wrote her cell phone number on a Post-it he retrieved from the kitchen, and made as graceful an exit as she could muster.

"Enjoy the pie, George."

"Oh, I surely will, Amelia." His lips curved upward, cold eyes glittering. "Apple is the fruit of temptation, after all. Have a good day, now."

He closed the door after her and she stared at it a moment, heart thudding in her chest.

Apple. The fruit Eve gave to Adam, leading him astray to fall from grace.

The man couldn't have meant anything by the remark.

Amelia hurried off the porch and to her car. Fired it up and drove away as sedately as possible. One thing was certain—she wasn't coming back here.

Ever.

Grimes stepped from the hallway, smirking. "You're losing your touch, Jesse. She made you like a bloodhound on the scent."

Jesse whirled, grabbing the man's shirt and slamming him against the wall. "The bitch made what I let her, nothing more. I already knew who she was, smartass, and I expected her to do the 'welcome the neighbor' thing days ago. So don't go getting all superior with me or I might forget how useful you are and do something rash, and messy. You feel me?"

Fear flashed in the other man's eyes, quickly masked. "I feel ya. We're good."

Jesse gave the man an "affectionate" pat on the cheek, hard, and released him. "I've got a job for you."

"Shoot."

When he finished, Grimes was shaking his head. "This deviates from the master plan, Jesse. Never a good thing and you know it."

"I know I'm in charge and you'll do what I tell you," he stated coldly. "I've waited a lifetime to pay back that fucker for what he did to me, and I'm going to love every single second of pain he suffers."

"You're the boss."

"Don't forget it."

Grimes walked out, and Jesse picked up the framed photo, peering into the face of the man who'd been his friend, protector, brother.

His downfall.

The man he was going to rip apart. Piece by agonizing piece.

Zack was biding his time, Sean could tell. Only a load of calls and the fact that Sean hung around the others all day kept the FAO from cornering him and ripping him a new one, from the glares he shot Sean's way.

As hard a time as he'd given Zack in the past, he probably deserved it. But he knew Zack's anger wasn't for himself, but for Eve. He was a good man who thought of others first, a quality that would serve him well when he finally made lieutenant, and then captain.

He was in for a surprise, however, when he found himself alone with Zack that afternoon and the man remained silent as they watched some mindless talk show on TV. About twenty minutes in, he couldn't take the suspense anymore.

"Aren't you going to give me the third degree?"

Zack, feet propped on a table, scratched his stomach and looked at Sean. "Believe me, I'd love nothing more. But Eve made me promise to lay off."

He didn't know whether to be irritated or grateful. "I can fight my own battles."

"Which is why you've been avoiding me like I have the flu."

"Hey, I don't *want* to argue with you, but I'm fully capable of taking whatever you need to dish out. Just prefer it's done in private."

"Not a courtesy you gave me, not so long ago."

The words shamed him deeply. "You don't know how much I regret that," he said sincerely. "I know it's not an excuse, but I wasn't myself. The man I really am would never have unloaded on you in front of the team."

"Yeah, I know." He sighed. "Look, the truth is I saw this thing with you and Eve coming a mile off, even if you didn't. The attraction has been there, building for months, and anyone with eyes can see the explosion was inevitable. I don't have to like it, but that's reality."

Sean didn't know how to respond. He'd become the guy his own friends would warn women away from, and it stung. Damned bad, though it was his own fault.

"I don't want Eve to end up with her heart pulverized," Zack went on. "She deserves better than to be your booty call on the road to self-betterment."

Anger churned in his gut. And a bit of guilt. "Eve is nobody's *booty call*, especially mine. You aren't giving her enough credit. She's a strong person who values herself more than that."

"In every respect except when it comes to you." Zack paused, lowered his voice. "You didn't hold her while she sobbed her heart out over that lame-assed 'Great fuck but we're still friends' bullshit you pulled, but Cori and I did. I know you don't want my advice, but tough shit, you're going to get it—if you're not playing for keeps, keep your dick away from Eve."

"His what? I think somebody better rewind and fill me in."

Sean turned his head toward the doorway to their television room, and groaned. "Now I'm gonna get double-teamed. Fan-fucking-tastic. Somebody shoot me now."

Six-Pack strode in and lowered himself into a chair, concerned brown eyes bouncing between him and Zack before setting on Sean. "This have anything to do with Saturday night?"

"Yeah."

"Tell me it didn't get as far as it sounded when I walked in."

Sean didn't have to say a word—his pained expression said enough. Howard pinched the bridge of his nose and laid his head against the back of the chair.

"Christ, man. You had to finally go there? You couldn't give yourself a few more weeks to get back on even ground before getting involved?"

"Wow, guys. Really, don't worry about my self-esteem or anything. It's not like I have any illusions that I'm a great catch." He was going for angry sarcasm. Instead, he just sounded hurt.

"Cut the crap," Six-Pack grumbled, sitting up straight. "We're just worried about both of you. Your sobriety is like five minutes old—and you're doing great—but I hate to see either of you rush into something that's gonna put too much stress on you and end up being too much to handle."

"I appreciate your concern, but it's my problem, and Eve's," he said firmly.

Zack cut in. "If word gets out, it's going to be *everybody's* problem. Our guys will be worried, like us, but they'll do their best to keep it in the family. However, people have eyes, and once the news spreads, there are those in the department who'll be less than thrilled about two firefighters on the same team developing a romantic relationship, or whatever it is, especially between a ranking officer and a subordinate. Tell me I'm wrong."

He couldn't. And that pissed him off. But even more so that Zack's assessment made it sound so dirty. He wasn't sure what he and Eve had going yet, but while it wasn't advisable to throw their newfound relationship in everyone's faces—and yes, he could be reprimanded for crossing the line—he wasn't in any way ashamed of it. "What would you have me do? Give up what could be a very good thing for both of us to make everyone else more comfortable? Fuck that."

"Nobody's suggesting anything of the kind," Six-Pack said, shaking his head. "Just be sure what you have is worth fighting for, and if so? Don't let any fool stand in your way."

"I wouldn't."

"Don't mess with her head. If you're simply scratching an itch, go find another post, because Eve deserves more. Things would be strained for a while, but she'd get over it."

His best friend's lecture echoed Zack's, but he was wrong about one point—he didn't know Eve was so upset she'd been planning to transfer. Zack probably knew, but it wasn't something Sean wanted to get into, especially since he'd never let it happen.

He'd leave the department first. It wasn't as if he needed the money.

But he did need a reason to get up every morning, stay sober one more day. A reason not to reach for the sleeping pills and succeed where he'd failed once before.

"I get it." Sean pushed to his feet. "Well, if we're done with this little heart-to-heart, I've got work to do in the office."

They were probably talking about him after he left the room, but he didn't care. The office he shared with Six-Pack as captain and lieutenant was the one place he could remain relatively undisturbed, unless one of his team had a problem to discuss, or dispatch relayed a call.

As if he'd conjured the loud tones on the intercom, they sounded three times the second he entered the office. With a soft curse, he strode back the way he'd come, toward the bay. So much for an hour of peace and quiet. The others were quickly bunking out in their gear, moving like a well-oiled machine while listening to the computerized female voice.

A three-alarm structure fire. An explosion in a restaurant at the strip mall east of downtown Sugarland, the flames rapidly spreading from the original site to the connecting businesses. Multiple injuries.

This was going to be a bad one. His gut never lied.

"Gas leak?" he speculated as he and Zack jumped into the cab of the quint. Clay and Julian climbed in back, the lieutenant and Eve in the ambulance.

"Could be, since it's a restaurant." Zack fired up his baby and led them out of the bay, hitting the lights and sirens.

Despite his previous hopes for some quiet office time, Sean would be lying if he said that sound, the roar of the engine, didn't shoot a rush of pure adrenaline through his veins. Ever since he was a boy, the wail of sirens had made him equal parts sad and excited: sad for whoever was in trouble, excited that maybe he'd be grown-up enough one day to jump into the action, help people.

He wasn't sure whom they'd be able to help today; the scene looked even worse than described. People were running around, some still spilling out of the businesses from the mall into the parking lot. A few were lying on the pavement a fair distance from the inferno, being treated by firefighter-paramedics. As Zack pulled into the parking lot, Clay voiced everyone's thoughts.

"Holy shee-it, boys, we've got a raging bitch on our hands! Hope y'all are ready to rumble."

Ready as they'd ever be. They'd practiced this drill, performed the real deal more times than he could count. No two fires were alike, however, and they had to stay sharp. The last time they'd worked a fire this involved, he had a meltdown, fucked up, and Tommy had almost been killed.

The memory had him breaking into a cold sweat as they jumped out. *Focus.*

Captain Lance Holliday from Station Two jogged over to give him the rundown. Sean hadn't seen the man since the day of the boat accident, but there was no time for pleasantries.

"Tanner," Holliday said loudly, to be heard over the crackle and roar of the blaze. "We've got four businesses involved. Started with an explosion in China Fang." He pointed to the restaurant, which was belching flame and smoke.

"Point of origin?"

"Witnesses swear it came from the restrooms."

"Say *what*?"

"Yeah," the captain said grimly. "We've already called the police and the bomb experts are on the way, along with Arson. In the meantime, we've got two known missing persons from the restaurant. A woman and an eleven-year-old boy. My guys have made one sweep so far and found some others with a variety of injuries, but haven't found the woman or the boy."

"We're on it. What else?"

"Fire spread to the video store on the end to the right, and then to the shoe and computer stores on the left. Our guys and Captain Reynolds from Station Three are trying to get it contained and search for victims inside. Video place is clear."

"That leaves a lot of area to cover. I'll fan out my team and we'll keep looking for the woman and the boy." Sean frowned at the blaze. "We'll still be spread too thin. I think we need to call in another engine company."

"I agree. I'll call the battalion chief and we'll get it rolling." Holliday loped over to Reynolds to confer with the older captain.

Sean turned to find Zack already finished with the preconnected hoses and climbing on top of the quint to man the high-powered gun. He'd use it to hose down the roofs of the buildings that had the all clear—because of the water pressure, it was too dangerous for firefighters or anyone else to be inside during this procedure.

The rest of the team was quickly shrugging on their Air-Pak tanks over their heavy coats and donning the black face masks of their SCBAs, or self-contained breathing apparatuses. These tanks were supposed to be good for thirty minutes of air, but they varied depending on the individual. A low-air alarm would sound when it was time for a firefighter to get the hell out to safety. He spared a glance at Eve and forced himself to tamp down the fear and let her do her job. She'd been pulling her weight for years and she deserved a better shake than he'd given her lately.

He stepped up to his four firefighters and gave his orders. "Eve, you and Clay help scour the restaurant. We've got a missing woman and an eleven-year-old boy in there and time is wasting."

"Yes, sir." Given the situation, Clay's natural exuberance was dampened. He and Eve fastened their masks and jogged for the building. The urge to call her back was almost unbearable.

She'll be fine. Get a grip and let the woman do her job.

"You two man the hose and let's see if we can slay the dragon," he said to Julian and Six-Pack.

After signaling Zack the go-ahead to hose down the roof of the video store, Sean eyed the inferno and considered whether to don his own Air-Pak and SCBA. As captain, he rarely had to leave his post—he could count on one hand the number of times that had ever been necessary—but every man must be prepared.

He decided to wait. His equipment was close at hand, on the quint, and more firefighters would arrive soon.

Every muscle tense, he practically vibrated in place as he watched the firefighters work in almost choreographed precision. Two in, two out. Repeat procedure.

Trust your superiors to bring you out if the situation turns. More than that, trust *yourself*. Know where every comrade is at all times; leave no one behind. Find the victims, bring them out.

Stay alive.

The men were having a tough time subduing the blaze at the left end of the row of stores. Two firefighters from Station Three, Jones and Blackwell, stumbled from the shoe store, Blackwell's arm around Jones' shoulders. Captain Reynolds met the men halfway, assisted Jones in getting Blackwell to an ambulance, where he collapsed onto the ground. Sean wanted nothing more than to go over and check on the man, but that would have to wait.

Where the fuck was the fourth engine company?

They were taking too damned long. The teams were battling the blaze with everything they had, but the tide was turning too slowly. Black smoke belched and flame shot from every broken window, cutting precious minutes short for whoever was still inside. The familiar, terrible helplessness crept through his veins like poison, whispered into his ear that he was as ineffectual as he'd been twice before. Damned to do nothing while the world burned to ash and fell around him, dragging his soul to hell.

He paced, rising panic at war with logic and respect for proper procedure. Every instinct screamed at him to get in there, find the woman and boy, help his team. Something. Anything but stand here and watch them burn. Watch them—

His thoughts ground to a halt as his gaze passed over the crowd of displaced shoppers and diners. His attention was caught by a tall man striding away, long dirty blond hair flowing down his back, and his heart skipped a beat. Blood froze. Then the man was gone, swallowed in the chaos.

"No. It couldn't have been."

That man was probably rotting in prison somewhere. Or dead.

A shout pulled him back to the situation at hand and he spun to see Eve emerge from the restaurant, a person in jeans slung over her shoulder in a fireman's carry. Clay followed on her heels, limping badly and holding a rip in his coat sleeve, blood streaming between his fingers.

Sean jogged to meet them and supported Clay, the man's good arm around his shoulders. "What happened?" he asked, steering the other man toward the ambulance.

"Got the woman," Eve called, voice muffled by her face mask. "Part of the roof fell on Clay while he was searching for the boy."

"Shit!" Now he had an injured firefighter, a still-missing child, and not enough men to treat the victims, fight the fire, *and* look for the kid. As they reached the ambulance, he helped Clay lean against the side of the vehicle, then jerked open the back doors and pulled out the gurney. He assisted Eve in laying the unconscious woman gently on it and then keyed the microphone on his coat. "Howard! I need you and Julian back here, now!"

"Copy that. Be right there."

They slid the gurney into the back of the ambulance and Eve climbed in, jerked off her SCBA, and began to take the woman's vitals. Sean stepped around the side to find Clay sitting on the ground leaning against the vehicle, SCBA removed, gritting his teeth and holding his bare, bloodied arm, lines of pain around his mouth.

Squatting, Sean lifted the man's chin to peer into his eyes. Pupils looked normal. Good.

"You all right?"

"I'll live, Cap. Nothing a few stitches won't fix." A wan smile punctuated the claim.

"All right. Hang tight and we'll get another unit to take you in. We've got to transport the woman first."

"I'll keep."

"Good man." Sean squeezed his shoulder and stood. Before he even thought about what he was doing, he sprinted to the quint, retrieved his own tank and SCBA. Yanked them on, fixed the mask over his face, started the air flowing.

Julian and Six-Pack came at a run, Jules stopping to see about Clay. Six-Pack, however, bore down on Sean, eyes wide. "What the hell are you doing?"

"We've still got a kid inside. You're in charge," he said, his tone making his orders clear. "Get on the radio and find out where that fourth fucking crew is and tell whoever isn't asleep over there that we need them fucking *now*! Tell Julian to transport the woman with Eve, and then find one of the other teams to take care of Clay."

"Wait a damned sec—"

"Just do it!"

He ran, and the wail of more sirens was a welcome sound. But the relief was temporary. They still had a kid inside and time had about run out, a fact that filled him with fear. He wasn't going to lose this one. *Jesus, let me be in time. Please. I can't fail again.*

Just as he reached the entrance to the restaurant, a shout from behind him made him turn. Eve was closing the distance fast, shrugging on her equipment once more. He paused, allowing her to catch up.

"What the fuck are you doing? You're supposed to take care of the woman!"

"Saving your ass from getting written up," she snapped back, fixing her mask. "Help is here, so Zack and Jules will transport her. Let's go!"

They headed inside and were immediately plunged into a murky black soup. The missing boy's only saving grace would be if he was lying on the floor where the smoke was thinner. Even so, the outcome wasn't likely to be good.

They swept the dining area with their flashlights, attempting to stay close together. As they worked their way deeper into the restaurant, he studied the amount of damage caused by the blast. Tables and chairs were upended, food and other debris littering the floor. All appeared to have been blown toward the front of the place, indicating that the blast had come from the back. If there were no fatalities resulting from the various injuries, it would be a miracle.

Who could have done this? Why?

At that moment, a shrill tone emitted from his equipment and he paused, stunned to realize it was the alarm indicating low air in his tank. Fuck! All the tanks were supposed to be ready to go, and his team was meticulous about equipment maintenance. This call had clusterfuck written all over it from the second they'd arrived, and he wondered whether any call went according to the textbook and the drills. *Hell, no. That would be too simple.*

Eve grabbed his arm. "We've got to get you out of here!"

"I'm not leaving without that kid."

"I'll stay and keep looking—you send someone in to help me."

"And risk you? Forget it."

With that, he continued his search, aware of her anger despite their limited communication. He'd have a lot to answer for and smooth over, not only with Eve and the rest of the team, but with the battalion chief as well.

Right now, none of that mattered. All that did was the boy. Nothing else.

Mia's sweet cherub face swam in his mind. Five minutes had been all that separated him and his baby girl for eternity. Five minutes made all the difference. The vast canyon that could never be spanned.

But he could make a difference to the boy. To the mother outside, going out of her mind.

He could not—would not—fail again.

As he peered around a fallen table, he drew in a breath . . . only to discover it wasn't there. His lungs strained to take in the last drop of air, and then he had no choice but to rip off his mask, letting it dangle around his neck. Immediately the foul smoke filled his lungs, burning like acid. Trying to breathe a vat of tar might be similar, and about as successful.

Still, he pushed on, grateful that either Eve was too caught up in their search or visibility was too bad for her to notice his predicament.

He tossed aside chairs, trash. Poked into every corner. His breath grew short quickly, exerting himself as he was, and his vision began to grow hazy. Or was that the smoke? Defeat became a distinct possibility, yet he couldn't bring himself to turn away. To write off an innocent life without knowing for sure whether the boy was alive. He didn't have it in him to leave.

He stumbled over a board, lost his balance. Went down, hit the ground on his hands and knees. Was about to push up when he saw a shoe. An athletic shoe, inches from his face. Reaching out, he grabbed the shoe and found a foot. Then a leg.

"Got him!" he shouted, though it came out as a hoarse croak. "Eve!"

Carefully he crawled forward, pushed aside a chair and some plaster to find the boy curled in a fetal position, arms over his face. *God, please let this kid be alive.*

At his side, Sean nudged the boy's shoulder, gently rolled him onto his back. Gut clenching in dread, he felt the slender, grimy neck for a pulse. Found nothing, and tried again.

"Oh, no. Come on, son. Please . . ."

A faint throb answered his plea, barely discernible. But present. The kid had a chance, and that was more than he had a minute earlier. Sean scooped the skinny body into his arms and stood, scanning for Eve and the entrance.

His partner was at his side in moments, guiding them toward light. Toward fresh air and life. She might've said something, but he wasn't sure what; he knew only that she kept tugging him forward, urging him on, moving fast.

And then they were out, bursting into bright sunlight, so abruptly he was blinded. Through the fog in his brain he heard shouts. Blinking away grit, he saw Six-Pack and another firefighter rushing forward, one from another station. The firefighter took the boy and it was as if Sean's body knew it was okay to let go. To simply fall like a puppet with cut strings, weightless. The pavement rushed up to meet him and the breath might've been knocked from him, had there been any left.

This prompted more shouts as hands relieved him

of the SCBA and tank, rolled him onto his back. Six-Pack hovered over him, one big hand slapping his cheek, the other on his chest. His best friend's expression was stricken as he spoke, some of what he said filtering to Sean's consciousness like a bad radio signal, fading in and out.

"... on, buddy. Don't ... okay? Hang ... help ... Sean?"

His lips moved and he tried to answer, but no sound emerged. He blinked and Eve was there, too, tears running off her chin. He tried to lift his arm, wanted to wipe them away. But he couldn't move.

"Breathe," she whispered.

Sorry, baby.

A dark veil descended over his eyes and he began to drift. How ironic that finally, for the first time in two years, he didn't want to leave this world behind and now he might not have a choice.

"Goddammit, I need help over here, right fucking now!"

Six-Pack. His steady friend who never drank and rarely cursed. That order had certainly been loud and clear. Sean might have smiled at the image of a bunch of firefighters leaping to do the big man's bidding, but he couldn't hang on.

Darkness sucked him under, and he knew nothing more.

8

Sean recalled the note from Jesse, given to him earlier by one of the men in the group that was clustered outside in the darkness of the barracks. A missive stating simply that he was to be at the "meeting" taking place tonight, far enough from the sleeping quarters to not be overheard, no excuses. Like he knew what it was about. Hell, he just wanted to go to bed, but as he approached, their conversation filled him with dread.

"Twenty million, man. That's the bottom line," Jesse said coldly.

"Come on, Rose. That's too much for our buyers and you know it. Their country is too poor to front the cash."

Jesse waved him into the circle, gestured for him to have a seat. And like an idiot, he did, listening as they kept on without a bit of concern as to his presence.

"If they want the rifles, they'll pay. If not, I'll find another buyer. That's the deal. And if he doesn't take it, kill him. That'll set an example for the future."

"What?" Sean sputtered. "Kill who?" No one paid him any attention.

"Whatever you say, Rose."

The men made noises of agreement and left, and Sean

rounded on Jesse. "What the fuck was that? You're dealing in stolen weapons?"

"No, we're dealing. You and me."

The blood drained from Sean's face. "No. Leave me out of this, Jess. I'm not involved."

Jesse grinned. "Sure you are. I sent you a note to attend our first meeting, and you came running. You're in this same as me."

"I didn't know!" God, what a nightmare.

"But you do now. And you're still sitting here, aren't you?" his friend had the audacity to explain patiently, as though talking to a child. "Look, I know you're not going to side against me. We're like brothers and that means you're with me all the way. You needed a little push is all, and I gave you one. Now get your shit together because we have business to handle. Got it?"

Without waiting for an answer, Jesse left him there, staring into space, his heart in tatters. His best friend was dealing in illegal arms, and now he was guilty by association if not in deed.

What the fuck was he going to do?

Sean didn't sleep that night. Or the next.

Sean's beautiful green eyes drifted closed, and Eve fisted his coat, shook him hard. "Sean? Sean! Oh, my God," she said, voice cracking. "Howard, he's not breathing!"

The lieutenant placed two fingers on his friend's neck. Eve knew she'd never seen Six-Pack so scared. "He's got a pulse. We've got to clear his lungs."

Two of Captain Holliday's team pushed into the circle, carrying their equipment and gently ordering Six-Pack and Eve aside. "Scoot back and let us help him, okay?"

Eve stood on rubbery legs, hand over her mouth, as

the men began efforts to resuscitate her boss. Friend. Lover. She was hardly aware of a similar drama being played out over the boy Sean had rescued, possibly at the cost of his own life.

She'd known that he wanted to die. But that was before he'd gotten sober, started counseling. Was it all just a cover while he waited for the opportunity to check out?

No, she couldn't believe that. No way was he faking his determination to turn himself around. But something told her that their superiors wouldn't be as easy to convince.

If he survived.

"All right, let's get him moving," one of the firefighters barked, slipping an oxygen mask over Sean's nose and mouth.

Eve nearly fell over in relief, but she knew better than to celebrate just yet. Victims succumbed to smoke inhalation all the time, even after they'd been revived. The results were always unpredictable; he could recover quickly after treatment and go home, or they could all be in for a long, agonizing wait.

The hardest thing she ever did was watch, helpless, as the other team lifted Sean onto the gurney and whisked him away to Sterling, Sugarland's newest hospital, a few miles away. Not to know what was happening to him was torture, but it was a burden every single one of them shared, no matter which station they called home. A pall was cast over the group even as they doubled their efforts to get this bitch under control.

The boy was taken away as well, the mask strapped over his face and the men talking to him in soothing tones.

Six-Pack helped the other three captains coordinate the fire-control and rescue efforts. Eve was crouched over a woman, tending her superficial burns, when Zack and Julian returned with their ambulance. After making sure the lady didn't want to be transported to Sterling, she walked over to meet the guys.

"How's the woman from the restaurant?" she asked. She crossed her arms over her chest to ward off the growing chill that had little to do with the fall weather.

"Didn't make it," Julian said, shaking his head.

They shared a look. The ones they couldn't save always hurt more than anyone could understand, except the victims' families.

"Where is everyone?" Zack asked, frowning. His gaze surveyed the smoldering rubble of the mall, fire-fighters dousing it, poking, making certain the blaze was out.

She knew he meant Sean and Clay, and her stomach dropped. "Clay's over there assisting Jones, since Blackwell had to be transported." She hitched a thumb toward the shoe store. "Idiot refused to be taken in until everyone was out of danger. Had one of the other guys wrap his arm."

Julian snorted. "Dipstick. Say, where's Cap?"

"He's . . ." Eve's voice failed. Suddenly, a big hand landed on her shoulder and Six-Pack was at her side, lending his support. Not only to her, but to all of them.

"Sean's been transported to Sterling. Smoke inhalation."

The lieutenant's quiet words, effective as much for what they didn't say as for what they did, fell into the space between them like a boulder, with crushing weight.

"What the fuck?" Zack sputtered. "How? He's not supposed to go inside!"

"We were seriously shorthanded at the time," Six-Pack said grimly. "He ordered me to stay and he went inside with Eve."

That was fudging. She and Howard both knew it. Sean was going in with or without her, but that would remain unspoken.

"But he should have sent you," Julian countered. Suddenly, his confusion cleared. "Shit, it was the kid, wasn't it? He went in after that kid. God, the brass is gonna roast him for this."

"Shut up, asshole," Zack growled. Rarely did he give his temper reign over his normally gentle personality. When he did, others listened. He addressed the lieutenant. "How is he?"

"Wasn't breathing when he collapsed, but he was when they left with him. Soon as we get out of here, we'll go straight to Sterling and find out something."

"*Madre de Dios.*" Julian fished his gold cross from under his shirt, held it tight.

"The quicker we get this mess dealt with, the quicker we can go to him. Let's move it."

The lieutenant's voice was tired, worried. Eve joined the others in poking through the shell of the stores, checking for hot spots to avoid a flare-up. Forcing her mind to the task wasn't easy, but it had to be done. No way would any of them put another team at risk by not concentrating on their job.

Only when they were finished and Six-Pack got the go-ahead from Holliday to leave did she allow herself to think of Sean. Worry over how he was doing. They loaded their gear and dragged themselves into the vehicles, the lieutenant riding shotgun in Sean's seat in the quint. He'd sat there many times over the weeks Sean was in rehab, but it had never hit her harder than now.

Julian drove the ambulance and made a protesting Clay ride in the back. Not liking his pallor, Eve rode in the back with him, taking his vitals and peeling up the bandage to examine the cut high on his arm. The wound was deep but only about four inches long and wasn't in too bad a spot, considering. Still, it bled profusely and had to hurt like a bastard. His ankle was another matter. It appeared to be just a sprain, but would need to be X-rayed.

She cleaned the gash and left the rest to the doc in the ER. No one spoke for the remainder of the drive, especially to utter false reassurances about Sean. Seemed too much like inviting fate to step in and render a blow from which they'd never recover.

Tired, bedraggled, they shuffled into the ER, every one of their faces a mirror of trepidation. Eve turned to Zack. "Is Cori working tonight?" If so, Zack's wife might be able to slip them some inside info if the doctor was still busy.

"No, she's at home," he said regretfully. "Maybe Shea is working?"

"Good thought. I'll ask."

She approached the nurses' station and saw a woman she recognized. The charge nurse, a worn-down blonde named Dora. "Hello. We're here—"

"About the captain. I know, hon," she said in sympathy. "Dr. Brown and some others have him back there, treating him for smoke inhalation. I can't tell you anything about his condition, but the doctor should be out before too long."

"Thank you for telling us that much." She peered past Dora's shoulder. "Is Shea Ford working tonight?"

"No, she's off. But she wouldn't be able to say much, either, even if she was here."

*Not with me guarding the desk like it's a matter of na-
tional security* was what Dora meant. Damn. They had
no option but to wait.

Clay was taken back to get patched and the rest of
them settled into the unforgiving vinyl chairs, flipping
through boring magazines that nobody actually read.
Six-Pack kept his radio on low, but at least they didn't
get any more calls, being shorthanded. Unless absolutely necessary, dispatch wouldn't send them out again
until they left the hospital.

About thirty minutes later, Clay emerged, stitched
and bandaged, with the okay to return to the job as
long as he was careful. His ankle was merely sprained,
and he wasn't limping as much anymore.

More than two hours crept by before the doors
swished open and an older doctor in scrubs approached,
expression unreadable. They leaped to their feet as a
unit, Eve's heart pounding as he stopped in front of
them.

"Captain Tanner is going to be fine." He smiled,
happy to be the bearer of good news.

"Thank God," she breathed. The rest echoed her relief, slapping one another on the back and grinning
broadly. When they'd quieted, the doctor continued.

"His lungs sustained no permanent damage and
he's breathing well enough now, but I'm keeping him
overnight for observation. He gave us quite a scare at
first, so I'd feel better not letting him go home just yet."

"Sounds good, Doc," Six-Pack said. "How soon can
he come back to work?"

"Oh, I'd say after a couple of days' rest, if he feels
up to it. As soon as he's moved to a room, Dora will let
you know. You can all see him—just don't wear him
out."

"What about the eleven-year-old boy who was brought in earlier?" Zack asked.

Dr. Brown nodded. "He made it. A near thing, but I believe he'll recover, in time."

More good news. They understood the doc couldn't give any other details, but their relief was palpable. Sean hadn't risked his life for nothing, and the boy's family would be extremely grateful. A fact that would help soothe their superiors a lot if push came to shove.

Nothing like good PR to save the day.

Another forty-five minutes later, Dora gave them Sean's room number and they took the elevator to the third floor. After some debate, they decided that all five of them converging on him would be too exhausting and too many crowded into the room. Eve and Zack agreed to go first, and stay no more than ten or fifteen minutes.

When they walked in, Sean appeared to be sleeping. She and Zack quietly took up seats on opposite sides of the bed, simply watching him for a few moments. His brown hair was mussed, dark lashes fanned on his cheeks. The silver at his temples had never been as noticeable as it was now, but she wouldn't change one hair on his head. She loved him so.

And she'd nearly lost him.

She knew Zack was watching her in concern as she took Sean's hand, rested her free one on top of the covers, on his leg. She couldn't care less. Her best friend knew the score and the tears burned, some escaping to scald her face and drip onto the sheets.

"Hey, none of that." Sean's throat sounded like he'd gargled with gravel.

She looked into brilliant green eyes that she hadn't been certain she'd see again. "It's your fault, you idiot." The words held none of the sting she'd intended, instead coming out on a sob and sounding like, "Thank God you're okay. I was frantic."

He heard what she didn't say, and gave her a wan smile. "I'm sorry."

"But you'd do it again."

"To save a child? Yes." His eyes, shadowed with old horror, begged her to understand as he squeezed her hand back. And she did.

Breaking the silence, Zack asked softly, "How do you feel?"

"Sorta rough. Headache, and my throat hurts." He paused as though afraid to know. "Was I in time? Did the kid . . . ?"

"Dr. Brown said he's most likely going to recover. You did good, Cap."

He coughed a couple of times and seemed to sink into the pillows. "Thank Christ."

"Sean, what happened in there, with your SCBA?" Now that the danger was past, this was a serious question that demanded an answer.

"Ran out of air."

"That's impossible!" Zack exclaimed. "I filled them myself and Clay checked all the equipment this morning."

"You're sure he checked the tanks specifically?" she asked.

"I'm sure."

"Well, it would seem he missed one. Or you did, and he didn't catch it." She hated to accuse anyone, but the source of this near-fatal problem had to be hunted down.

"I'm telling you, every one of those tanks was full. I *know* it."

He was so adamant, she had to believe him. But that left them with no solution. "All right. Let's inspect the tank when we get back to the station, see if there's anything wrong. Maybe it had some sort of defect that caused a slow leak."

She'd never heard of that happening, but she supposed anything was possible.

"Thanks, you two. You'll figure it out. I'm in good hands and everything will be fine."

Zack's brows lifted. "Except for the part where you'll probably get your ass chewed out and your visits to your shrink extended."

"Can't wait."

Eve wiped her face and chuckled in spite of herself and the harrowing afternoon. The man definitely sported a big, steely pair of balls. Once he'd made up his mind to do something, nobody was going to get in his way. That was either good or bad, depending on your viewpoint.

Good if you were a child in desperate need of rescuing.

"We've got your back," Zack said. "You know that."

"Yeah, I do. You guys have many times, even when I didn't deserve it."

"That's what family does, or should do, and I consider you mine."

Sean looked away for a moment, appearing overcome by that declaration. "Coming from you, that means a lot to me. I feel the same about each of you."

Zack smiled. "Group hug?"

"Not gonna happen."

They all laughed, and Sean's humor ended in an unfortunate bout of coughing. She and Zack looked on in concern as he struggled to regain control of his irritated lungs. Once he was settled again, she smoothed the covers over his chest.

"I know you'd rather go home, but I'm glad they're keeping you overnight," she said.

"I'd rest better at home. They're going to poke and prod me around the clock."

"Tough. You can sleep tomorrow, at home."

"Mean woman." He yawned.

"You know it." She stood. "You're tired. We'd better let the others have their turn before you pass out."

"See you tomorrow, Sean."

He lifted a hand and tried to smile, but she saw the smudges under his eyes. The exhaustion. She wanted to stay, take him in her arms, and feel his heart beating against hers. Give him a lingering kiss, reassure herself that he was real. Alive. Not being able to do either of those things was almost physically painful. She thought she saw regret in his expression, too, and somehow that made her feel better.

She waved back and followed Zack out before she was tempted to make a scene the guys would be talking about for years.

The way things were going, that day might come sooner than she thought.

As soon as they pulled into the bay and parked the vehicles, Six-Pack jumped down, calling out, "Line up all the tanks and SCBAs. Show me which ones you wore and which ones were left on the quint."

Any problems they should be able to trace from there. When Eve finally had a chance to tell the lieutenant what happened inside the restaurant, he'd been as floored as she and Zack. He immediately agreed an inspection was in order. If the fault lay with any of them, fur was going to fly.

When they each had their own equipment at their feet, Six-Pack continued. "Check over every crevice of your Air-Pak, hose, and mask. Every piece. Leave nothing unaccounted for." He paused while they took a few minutes to do as instructed. "Any problems?"

One by one, they all replied in the negative. Nothing wrong with any of the tanks and masks they'd been wearing.

"Okay, on to the spares. These were on the quint, side compartment, which was unlocked for easy access given the situation we were dealing with." He pointed to one that sat slightly apart from the others. "That's the one Sean grabbed from the quint and wore inside. He said it ran out of air, but he should've had the full thirty minutes. I damned well want to know why he didn't. Everybody grab one and do a check."

They got busy. Eve had just started on the one she'd picked when Clay spoke up.

"Uh, Lieutenant . . . the hose on this one has been cut."

Everyone froze, stared at him.

"What the hell did you say?" Howard strode over and squatted, peering at the part in question. His brows drew together and his mouth flattened. "It's been sliced, vertically, right between the grooves. Cut almost in two."

"This one, also," Zack said, voice rising.

"And this one." Julian slammed his tank on the ground, all sorts of pissed. "What the fuck is going on here?"

"Mine, too," Eve put in, staring at the cut in the hose.

"They all checked out fine this morning, I swear!" Clay cried, glancing around the group. "I know for a fact they were good."

The lieutenant checked Sean's unit last, just to confirm their suspicions. "This one is cut, too. All the extras on the quint were tampered with," he said, seething with a white-hot rage Eve had never seen. "Which means someone had to have done it while we were all busy and the scene was in chaos. A knife or a pair of cutters, and he only needed seconds to do the job. I'd like to get my hands around his neck."

His sentiments were echoed with enthusiasm.

"What do we do now?" Eve's question had them all looking to Six-Pack for guidance.

"I'll call the chief. He'll know what to do, who else to notify." Howard's father, Fire Chief Bentley Mitchell, was a legend in Sugarland. He was supposed to retire at the end of July, but had postponed the event, much to everyone's relief. "I have to say, though, I'm flying blind on this. Who the fuck would tamper with a firefighter's equipment, knowing he could get someone hurt? This is so out of the blue, so vicious. I don't get it."

That statement hit Eve like a fist. Until this second, she hadn't even considered the events could be connected. Sean might get upset, but the guys had a right to know, under the circumstances.

"Maybe not so out of the blue."

Six-Pack pinned her with his angry gaze. "Explain."

She swallowed. "The day Sean returned to work after rehab, he got a nasty phone call. Came in on his cell phone, in his office. The caller asked whether he'd ever thought maybe 'it wasn't an accident,' and when he figured out it might mean the wreck that killed his family, I thought he was going to pass out."

The others stood there, watching and silent. Howard appeared more livid every second. She hoped he didn't stroke out.

"Has he received any more calls?"

"No, but he got an equally nasty package at home. Inside was a big bottle of whiskey and a snapshot of the actual wreck as it was burning. Thank God I got there in time to help. . . ." She trailed off, realizing she'd just revealed more about their relationship than she'd intended to do in front of Julian and Clay. From the looks thrown her way, she'd get grilled later. For now, they let it go.

"Did he notify the police?"

"Yes. Tommy called Shane, who sent out a detective. After talking with Sean, he decided to take these things collectively as a threat. He took the package and its contents, and he's going to try and trace the origin of the phone call. It's a place to start. I'd hoped the guy, or whoever, would just go away, but now I have to wonder if he's behind the tampering."

"Christ Almighty." The lieutenant scrubbed a hand through his spiky brown hair and blew out a breath. "Okay, I'll call Dad and this detective—what's his name?"

"Taylor Kayne."

"Kayne. Right." He headed for the door leading inside the station from the bay. "Leave all this stuff out and don't touch it anymore."

A strained silence followed his departure.

Julian spoke up first. "I find out who's doing this to Sean? I'll kill him with my bare hands, first chance I get."

"You'll have to stand in line," Zack told him.

* * *

Sean twisted in the sheets, fevered dreams refusing to give him peace. He'd longed to die, once. To join his family in the beyond, if he believed such a thing was possible. Trouble was, he wasn't sure he believed in much of anything. Until Eve.

The feelings he had for her weren't wrong. Not after the years spent alone, grieving, mired in the bottom of a bottle. He'd done his time, deserved something pure and good.

So why did he feel so guilty?

The door opened quietly and a figure stalked to his bed. Like a panther singling out his prey. The man's face remained in shadow, hidden just there. He felt the weight of the man's stare, of accusation, before he even spoke.

"I trusted you," the man whispered. "Traitor."

Sean's heart pounded in terror. "Do I know you?"

"As well as you know yourself." His nemesis gave a bitter laugh. "That's how you destroyed me, after all."

"I don't know what you're talking about!"

"Don't you? Don't you recognize the Reaper when he comes to call?"

"Get away from me!"

Another laugh, sinister, as the man opened his shirt to reveal the scar over his heart. "Blew me away, just like I'll return the favor. Told you I'd make you pay, Sergeant Sean Tanner."

"No! Get away from me!" Sean bolted upright in bed, gasping. He clutched the bedcovers, and blinked, trying to get his bearings in the dimly lit room.

Hospital. He was alone.

Nightmare. There was no one here with him.

Just a nightmare.

Then he wasn't alone anymore as a nurse hurried inside. "Mr. Tanner? I heard you shouting," she said, reaching out to grab his wrist and take his pulse. "Way too fast. Are you all right?"

"Had a nightmare," he said. As the terror abated, he started to feel stupid. "It was nothing, really."

"Must've been a doozy. How about I give you something to help you sleep?"

The whole bottle ought to do it.

"No, thank you. I'll be fine now."

She didn't look convinced, but left him alone once more after extracting a promise to buzz her if he changed his mind.

He wouldn't. He didn't want to close his eyes and dream of shattered friendships and betrayals. About vows of vengeance.

He didn't want to close his eyes and imagine he'd seen Jesse Rose anywhere. Not in his worst nightmares.

And not in reality, ever again.

At some point he must've slept whether he wanted to or not. Sean opened bleary eyes to find the fire chief sitting quietly at his bedside, expression worried.

"About time you joined the living. I'll ask the stupid question—how do you feel?"

"Shot at and missed, shit at and hit," he croaked.

"I'll bet. Quite the day you've had. Quite the week, in fact."

Uh-oh. "Meaning?"

"Come on, son. Don't yank my pecker. I know all about the phone call and the so-called gift you got in the mail. When were you planning to say something?"

"Who told you? Eve?" He stared at Bentley Mitchell, incredulous. "She had no right."

"Wait a damned minute before you get pissed. She only told your team and me because of the air tanks being sabotaged. Or, rather, the hoses."

"What?" The full import hit, and he sat up, fumbling to push the button and raise the bed some. "The hoses were tampered with?"

"Yep. Some sumbitch cut all the spares while everyone was busy. You got hold of one, and damned near got killed as a result."

His mind reeled. "And Eve thinks this is the next step of his campaign? That he wrecked the tanks on the off chance of hurting me? The bastard couldn't have known I'd go inside the restaurant, so that doesn't work as a theory."

"True, but he knew *someone* might need a new tank. I think his goal was to hurt you indirectly, through your team, and that you were an unexpected bonus."

Terrific. "I don't know if the detective will agree—"

"He does. He said he'd catch up with you later, though."

A horrible thought occurred to him. "The explosion at the restaurant . . . Bentley, you don't think . . ."

"It was deliberate? We'll know soon enough." The man shifted, his serious demeanor telling Sean that he was about to get to the main reason for his visit. "Sean, we've known each other for, what? Eighteen years?"

"Almost. At least as long as I've known Howard."

He crossed his arms over his massive chest. "And in all those years, I've never known you to be impulsive. You've always thought out every move, taken command like a born leader. Part of that military background, I suppose."

"I guess." Christ, he felt like a kid in the principal's office. He knew where this was going.

"So what in the goddamned hell possessed you to leave your post and put yourself in danger when you have a team waiting for your direction?" He waved a hand, agitated. "No, don't answer that. I know the reason was the boy, and we could get all into the psychological implications of that shit if we had a few weeks or months to discuss it. Let me rephrase—allowing your team to see you slightly unhinged and going off half-cocked is unprofessional. Worse, it's dangerous."

Lead sat in his gut. "I'm sorry. But all I could think of was the kid, trapped in there. Believe me, it would've been more dangerous had I sent someone else and the rescue had failed. Because *I* would've failed by not acting."

Bentley sighed, suddenly looking every inch the back side of sixty. "That's a mindfuck, son. You can't put that sort of pressure on yourself and hope to make retirement."

Sean rubbed the grit out of his eyes and then looked at his mentor. His friend. "Are you here to tell me I'm done? Is that what this is about?"

"Hell no. Do you *want* to be done?" Sharp eyes pierced his.

"No, I don't. I love my job and I can't imagine not having the station, the guys. They're my home," he said truthfully.

"You could quit tomorrow, play with your money and live it up."

"I'd be dead within the year." That was no exaggeration.

"Now you know why I put off retiring," the older man said, lips quirking. "Though in my case, that feeling isn't so dire anymore. Which brings me to my point."

"You *are* done," he said softly.

"Yeah. End of the year."

"Damn." He swallowed the lump in his throat that had nothing to do with soreness from the smoke.

"Time to pack my bags and go play in the sand with Georgie. That Alaskan cruise Howard sent us on in July only whetted her appetite for me to be a free man." He sounded excited, yet his smile was wistful. "It'll be good to do all the stuff we've always wanted, go to the places we haven't seen. Anyway, as you could guess, I've been asked who might make great candidates to fill the vacant positions created by my leaving."

Sean sat up, a strange thrill going through him. He couldn't allow himself to hope this visit meant what he thought. "A domino effect of promotions all the way to the top. I hadn't given a ton of thought about how it would affect anyone but the man replacing you." Which would probably be Assistant Chief Lawrence Patrick, though Bentley would never say until the official announcement.

"Exactly. A list of names is already under consideration for the vacancies, and several captains in particular are being looked at to fill one battalion chief's position."

The statement hovered between them, and Sean sucked in a harsh breath. He couldn't believe what Bentley was telling him in so many words. Never dreamed his name would make it onto the list, even with Bentley's support.

"Every hope and doubt in your brain is etched on your face." The older man leaned forward, elbows on his knees, hands clasped. "Let me tell you something. You want your name to stay on that list? Shit like yesterday cannot happen again. You saved the kid, and that saved you in regard to the promotion. A mistake can be overlooked when there's a child involved, one who's alive because of your actions. I spun the story a tad so my successor won't think you went off your rocker. *This* time. The rest is up to you."

"Thank you," he said, meaning it.

"Don't thank me. Just get your goddamned act together once and for all, because in nine weeks, I'm gone. I won't be able to cover your ass anymore, son."

"I *am* getting it together, I swear. I'll never be perfect, but I'm coming out the other side and I know I'm going to make it."

"That's all I want for you, to be settled and find some peace."

He stared at the man who was his friend, and as close to a father as he'd known since his dad passed away. He cleared his throat. "That day, when I hit rock bottom and Tommy was hurt . . . you saved my life. Forced me to get help. You and Howard. I don't know how I'll ever repay—"

A big hand shot out, gripped his shoulder. "By moving on, being happy. By forgiving yourself for a tragic outcome you couldn't change."

Barely able to speak, he clasped the older man's arm. "I'm doing my best."

After the chief was gone, he spent more than an hour staring at the wall, waiting to be released. And contemplating everything the man had said.

Sean had never been great at handling change, and

it seemed everything that touched his life was doing just that, at an alarming rate.

Everyone was growing, changing, moving on.

He just hoped he had the courage to do the same.

Right after he tapped that elusive well of self-forgiveness.

9

Sean just wanted to go to bed, but a knot of men were clus-
tered around a bunk, speaking quietly. As he neared, their
conversation stopped him dead. He hovered out of sight,
catching enough.

"What's Rose into, man?"

"Word is, he's dealing. And maybe not just drugs. Stealing
and selling arms," Wilson claimed.

"Shit," one breathed. "How's he doing it?"

"Don't know. I hear Tanner's thrown in with him."

"No fucking way," another hissed.

God, did they know about the meeting? Spurred by fear,
Sean made himself known as the group jumped apart. Glar-
ing at Wilson, he pushed the man hard in the center of his
chest. "I don't have shit to do with anything illegal. And as
far as Jesse goes, do you have any proof? Any of you?"

Wilson raised his hands in a self-protective gesture. "No,
man. It's just what I've heard."

"Right. No proof. Which is why you're all standing
around gossiping like old women!"

"Sean, we know he's your friend, but Rose is a bad seed.
Open your eyes, man."

"My eyes are open, and I don't like what I'm seeing right

now. Don't destroy a man's reputation without proof, especially his, or you'll answer to me."

Spinning on his heel, he stalked around the corner . . . and walked right into Jesse.

"Good man," his friend said with pride. "I knew I could count on you."

Eve walked into Sean's hospital room, saw him sitting on the edge of the bed . . . and giggled. "Rainbow scrubs? Aww, aren't you precious?" It morphed to a laugh when he scowled and grumped like a little boy.

"My uniform is dirty and they didn't have anything else clean for me to wear."

"Sure they didn't," she drawled, teasing. But it seemed he didn't appreciate the humor of being caught in powder blue nurse's scrubs adorned with colorful rainbows and fluffy white clouds. Much less being reminded that he'd have to leave in them. She decided to give him a break. "Ready to go?"

"I was ready hours ago. Just waiting on the doctor to sign my release papers and I'm out of here. I was going to call a cab, but . . . take me home?"

She hoped she wasn't reading too much into the unspoken question in his eyes. As though he was talking about more than a simple lift to his place. "Anywhere you want to go."

Real subtle. She might as well stamp her feelings across her forehead. He'd said he was willing to see where things went between them, but she had no doubt he wasn't ready to make a commitment. What it would take to bridge that gap between them, or whether it was possible, she didn't know.

A half hour later a nurse wheeled him through the corridors and downstairs, per hospital policy, while his cheerful outfit earned giggles and a few comments from the nurses. She'd expected him to be grouchy, so his taking the ribbing with good humor was a pleasant surprise.

While the nurse waited with him at the curb, she jogged to fetch the car. After pulling it to the front, under the awning, she tossed his clothing bag and release papers in the backseat and he climbed into the passenger's side without assistance.

At last they were under way, and she threw him a glance. "Are you hungry? We could do a drive-through on the way."

"I could eat. I slept through dinner last night, and the rubber eggs and dry toast they brought this morning looked less than appetizing."

"I can imagine. Burger?"

"God, that sounds good." His stomach rumbled in agreement.

"You've got it."

On the way through town, she picked up a couple of burgers, fries, and shakes at Stratton's. He dove into the bag and had his burger and half his fries eaten by the time she pulled into the drive near his front porch.

"Here you are." When she made no move to get out, he frowned.

"Don't you want to come in?"

"I didn't want to presume."

"I might have a relapse. In that event, I'd need a paramedic to give me mouth-to-mouth." He grinned.

"I just happen to know one of those!" Putting the car in park, she shut off the ignition. "What kind of medic would I be to leave you in mortal danger?"

"My point exactly."

Despite their banter, she couldn't help but remember that he might very well be in jeopardy. Whoever was tormenting him had greatly upped the stakes by tampering with their equipment. What if next time he decided to take a more direct approach? That seemed to be the way this was headed, and the idea chilled her.

"Coming?"

"Sure."

Bringing her food, she trailed him into the house and to the kitchen. He discarded his trash and she sat at the breakfast table, noting the tired slump of his shoulders.

"You look like you could use a nap."

"Told you I wouldn't be able to sleep in that place." He glanced away, a shadow crossing his expression, quickly covered. But not quick enough.

"What's wrong?"

"Nothing."

"Uh-huh." Sticking her legs out, she leaned back in her chair and crossed her ankles.

"Had a nightmare. Nothing big."

Liar. At her arch stare, he relented some.

"Ever had one of those weird dreams inside of a dream? Where you're lying there and you think you're awake when something bad happens, and then you wake up for real and your heart's about to explode?"

"I have, and they're damned creepy. What was yours about?"

"I dreamed this guy showed up in my hospital room. I couldn't see his face, but I knew him. I think— I *know* he was planning to kill me." Sean lowered himself into a chair across from her. His face was a bit pale, and he seemed shaken by the recollection.

"Do you really know him? Or was he someone you just thought you knew in the dream?"

"He was someone I knew, a long time ago. My best friend from high school. We went into the marines together, fought side by side. Jesse always had a wild streak a mile wide, but for years I ignored the meanness lurking behind that magnetic personality. Jesse was brilliant, fun, a god among men. The guys followed him like the Pied Piper . . . but I discovered some were loyal to him for all the wrong reasons, and by then it was too late. When my blinders got ripped away, everything went to hell."

The sadness and regret in his tone were tempered by a distance of many years, as they should be.

"What was he doing?"

"He started by dabbling in the drug trade and quickly graduated to stealing American military weapons and supplies, selling them to the highest bidder. Allies, enemies. Didn't matter to Jesse. Finding out was bad enough, but the real kick in the gut was when I learned he was also stockpiling weapons for himself."

"Building a private army," she guessed.

"Bingo. All our lives he'd burned to leave his mark on the world, and he'd finally found a way to accomplish that."

She could picture the type; they haunted the news on the anniversary of every tragic act of violence. America had been dealt plenty of scars left by bastards like that.

"And when you found out . . ."

His voice was bitter. "I did nothing."

That gave her pause. "But surely you went to a superior, somebody who could help?"

"Not at first, and that was my mistake." He stared past her head, remembering. "Looking back, there were signs all along that Jesse had the potential to turn bad.

Shit I ignored or made excuses for, like when he started spouting antigovernment views. But it wasn't until he lured me to a meeting for his first big arms deal that I knew for sure I was in deep trouble."

"Because you were at the meeting, and didn't act right away."

"Yeah. Jesse was convinced I would support him and would never betray him, that I was merely misguided and would come to share his vision. When I got scared and failed to go to our superiors right away, I only reinforced his faith in me. He wanted to bring me into the fold as his second-in-command, for us to work side by side for a better America or some such crap. What he was really spewing were plans to commit acts of homeland terrorism. He shattered every illusion I'd had about him and our friendship."

"He broke your heart."

"Yeah."

"And *then* you reported him?"

He shook himself and waved a hand at her forgotten food. "Listen to me, rambling on about ancient history. Eat while I take a shower. This grit and stink from the fire is getting to me."

She knew her cue to drop a subject when she heard it, but she was still curious about his nightmare. "Wait. Going back to this dream, do you think it's significant at all? Is there any chance he'd come for you now?"

The question visibly upset him, but he recovered fast. "The man I discovered he really was under the riveting facade was capable of anything. But after all these years? Why? I'm sure he has more important things to do than screw with me. Be back in a bit."

After he left the room, she chewed slowly on her burger, thinking. That last part bothered her—*someone* was trying to get to Sean. She wished he had finished the rest of the story, but figured he would at some point.

Finishing her lunch, she disposed of her trash and wandered out to the living room, crossing it to hover near the hallway. She didn't hear the shower running and thought he must be done. But he had just been released from the hospital after a life-threatening ordeal, and worry got the better of her. She tiptoed down the hallway, feeling like an intruder entering his personal domain, though she'd been here a few days before. Worry was stronger.

In the master bedroom, she paused at the sight before her. Sean lay curled on his side on the bed, dressed in nothing except a fresh pair of sweatpants. His hair was damp from the shower, the towel on the floor by the bed. His chest rose and fell in easy rhythm, a comforting and dear sight after yesterday.

The man was sound asleep.

Smiling, she toed off her shoes and crawled in beside him. Snuggled in, spooning him from behind. His contented sigh and the way his pushed his rear into her lap told her he had no objections.

Holding him close, she drifted off. Content, but not counting her chickens.

Yet.

Sean stirred slowly, sat up, and stretched. Disoriented, he took a few seconds to get his bearings. Home. His bedroom. Eve?

Beside him, her place was empty. A sharp stab of disappointment caught him off guard and he quickly shook it off. They'd had a nice, lazy day yesterday napping like spoons in a drawer. She'd refused to let him do anything too strenuous despite his insistence that he was fine.

Okay, so he hadn't protested too much. When was the last time he'd been fussed over, even a little? No sane guy he knew would turn down some lovin' from a pretty lady.

And where was his?

His. Now, there was a scary thought. A possessive one that came more and more frequently, as though he and Eve were a given. Were they?

He told her personal stuff he'd never shared with another living soul, not even Howard. They connected on the most intimate level two people could. Even now, he looked forward to how her smile and sass would brighten his last day off and how they'd enjoy the hours together. He was ready to leap from the bed and go hunting for her, sneak up behind her. Pounce and kiss her breathless.

The world was new, filled with promise and—

"My God."

I think I love her.

More terrifying than any blaze, more daunting than some wacko out to drive him to drink. Because embracing what he could have with her meant moving on, leaving the memories of his family behind as just that. Beloved treasures to tuck away in a box, slide onto a shelf.

Six months ago, the guilt would've killed him, and now . . .

Am I ready? Can I follow everyone's advice and let go?

He didn't have to know today, right this minute. A classic avoidance trick he was going to employ for his sanity, for the time being.

Sliding out of bed, naked, he headed for the bathroom, a spring in his step. He hadn't had this much sex in a single week in, well, never. His marriage to Blair in later years had consisted of a lot of cuddling and kissing; her sex drive had never been as overcharged as his, and she'd hated getting messy.

And now the amazing encounters with Eve made him feel like Rip van Winkle waking up after a twenty-year slumber. All had changed.

After a quick shower, he toweled off and dressed in worn jeans and a dark blue T-shirt. He wasn't nearly as tired as yesterday, his throat not as sore. But he still had a nagging cough and a weight on his chest he supposed might linger for a few days. Nothing serious.

The house was quiet and empty as he walked through on his way to the kitchen, and again he squelched a shard of disappointment. Eve didn't answer to him and certainly wasn't his keeper, but he'd hoped to find her here. Maybe curled up on the sofa or making breakfast.

In the kitchen, he spied a slip of paper by the coffee-maker and made a beeline for it. Read it and grinned. *Went home to change clothes—can't go naked ALL the time. LOL. Coffee is set up. Be back soon. Love, Eve.*

Just . . . damn. A bubble of happiness expanded his chest so much it hurt. Over a stupid little note. *Love.* A simple thing, yet when was the last time anyone had cared enough to write it down? Switching on the coffee, he realized he was humming. Another weird symptom of whatever bug had bitten him.

On impulse, he grabbed his jacket and stuffed a pocket with baby carrots from the fridge. Next he made three ham sandwiches on hoagies and placed those in a lunch cooler along with some chips and bottled water. Last, he filled a travel mug with coffee and, slapping on a lid, grabbed the lunch container, and left the house through the sliding glass door, crossing the deck and striking out for the barn. The fall day was gorgeous, leaves bursting in every tint of red, orange, and gold, and he planned to make the most of it. A certain blue-eyed woman with creamy latte skin and dark wavy hair was going to play a key role in those plans, too.

In the breezeway of the barn, he parked his mug and lunch box on a crate and strode into the tack room, fishing out two halters with lead ropes attached. He hadn't been on a ride in far too long, and today the freedom of the lush, rolling hills was calling. Throwing one halter and rope over his shoulder, he held the other halter by the earpiece and looped the rope around his hand. As he exited the barn and headed for the gate, two of the four heads popped up and watched him curiously.

When he whistled through his teeth, Elvis and Mariah started toward him despite the halter, which could only mean being caught and saddled. They hadn't been caught in so long, left to laze about every day, he hadn't been completely sure they wouldn't bolt. But Elvis was a good boy, standing still as he slid the halter over his nose and behind his ears, fastening it at his jaw.

"That's it, big fella," he said softly, scratching the furry ears. "Want to get out for a while, huh?" He continued heaping the praise, laughing when the mare nudged his shoulder, determined not to be left out.

Letting Elvis' rope drop, he stepped on it and repeated the process on Mariah, who shied only a bit as the halter went on. The other two mares, who had moved away from them to graze, whinnied as he led their companions out the gate and closed it behind him. Horses were social creatures and reacted when any of their number left, greeted them when they returned. Sean had always thought it was kind of funny, but now he wondered if horses became truly distressed. He took comfort in knowing that in a couple of minutes they'd forget and go back to grazing.

Back in the barn, he fastened the horses' lead ropes to rings on the wall, leaving a few feet between them to maneuver. Next he fetched two brushes and combs, then set all but a brush on the crate and went to work on Elvis. The big gelding practically sighed in bliss, leaning into the hard strokes as Sean cleaned away weeks of dirt and mud from his sides and belly.

"Feels good? Wouldn't mind getting the same treatment myself."

"I'll tie you up and see what I can do."

Eve's sultry voice—not to mention that image—set his groin on fire and had him grinning as he straightened and met her amused gaze over the gelding's back. "If anyone's going to be tied up, it's you, honey."

"Think so?"

"I know so."

She strolled toward him, her mood playful. "Will I like it?"

"Guaranteed or your money back."

"Oh, I don't think I'll require a refund."

Sweet Jesus, she looked edible in snug jeans, her hair loose around the shoulders of her rust-colored cotton shirt. A little defiant, too, and he liked that. A lot.

"Come here and grab a brush."

"I just got here and already you're putting me to work." But she appeared eager as she approached.

"Slow," he cautioned. "Never approach a horse too fast or make any sudden moves, no matter how tame they are. And if you walk around their back end, don't get too close in case one kicks."

Taking his advice, she slowed her steps and gave both horses' rear ends a respectful distance. "Is it their day at the salon?" she teased, coming around to where he stood brushing Elvis.

"More like a quick brushing, a workout, and then a grooming. Up for a ride?"

Her animated expression betrayed excitement. "I'd love to. I haven't ridden since Girl Scout camp, though."

"It's not hard. I'll be with you every step of the way." He handed her the extra brush. "Why don't you spoil Mariah? She loves to be brushed and she'll be your best buddy from now on."

"Sure." Tool in hand, she turned to the mare and applied the bristly side to her smooth neck. Like most novices, she barely put any muscle into the strokes.

"Harder, like this." He demonstrated, putting his elbow into it, chuckling as Elvis practically lay over on him in pleasure.

"Okay." She copied his example, and soon both horses were ready for saddling.

"All right, that should do it. Let me get the tack and we'll saddle them."

He made a couple of trips fetching thick blankets, saddles, and bridles, then motioned her to watch while he readied the gelding. The blanket went on first, and then he tossed the saddle onto the gelding's back. He reached under the horse's belly to grab the cinch and tighten it through the ring on his side—and laughed.

"What?" Eve looked on in curiosity.

"See his stomach? An old equine trick. He's holding his breath."

"Why would he—oh! He doesn't want the strap thingie to be tight."

"Exactly. And in the middle of our ride, he'll let out his breath and the cinch will loosen, which can dump a rider on his or her ass when the saddle slips sideways."

"So how do you prevent that from happening?" She seemed truly interested.

"Watch."

Reaching under the gelding's belly, he tickled the big guy's stomach just like one would tickle a baby. The horse released a breath and he tightened the cinch, tying it off before the stomach bloated again.

"See? Easy."

She laughed. "Neat tactic."

"It works almost every time. Want to saddle your ride?"

"Sure. How difficult can it be?"

"Quite, if your mount is in a surly mood. Most days, though, these guys are very cooperative."

In short order, she had Mariah saddled. He helped show her how tight the cinch should be to prevent a fall, and then all that was left was the bridles. Removing the halter, he slipped the bit between the gelding's teeth and fastened the bridle, holding the reins securely.

"Good boy," he praised, fishing a baby carrot from his pocket. He held out his hand, palm flat, and Elvis snatched the treat with his lips and began to chew. Giving his attention to Eve, he said, "Your turn."

After a brief hesitation, she mirrored his procedure. She might be a rookie, but she wasn't afraid, he gave her that. It made him beyond happy to see her sharing one of his passions. Even if Mariah clamped her teeth together and refused to take the bit.

"Uh, what now? She won't open up."

Reaching into his pocket, he handed her a carrot. "Give her this. Put it in your palm and hold your hand out flat. When she takes the treat, slip in the bit."

"Sneaky." It worked like a charm, and she squealed in delight. "I did it! Why do they fall for that? I wonder."

"I don't think they fall for anything so much as they simply choose to tolerate us. If a horse truly doesn't want to do something, no man can make him."

"Hmm, makes sense. Are we going now?"

"Let me strap the blanket and our lunch on the back and we're ready."

"Lunch?" She eyed the container, apparently noticing it for the first time. "A picnic?"

"Nothing fancy, just ham sandwiches and chips. Is that all right with you?"

"Sounds great!"

Her enthusiasm was catching and he realized he was looking forward to this immensely. "Come around on her left side, grab the saddle horn with your left hand, and place your left foot in the stirrup. I'll be right here beside you and she's not going anywhere."

As Eve got into place, he looped the reins over the mare's head and tucked them into Eve's left hand. "Hold the reins and the saddle horn—this way when you mount, she'll be in your control. Now bounce a couple of times, haul yourself up, and swing your right leg over."

The first attempt was aborted as the mare sensed that Eve didn't know what she was doing and danced a bit. Sean calmed the horse and urged Eve to try again. This time was successful, and she grinned from ear to ear.

"Oh, wow. This is like sitting on top of a building!"

"Always feels that way the first few times." He took her hands and showed her how to hold the reins. "Not too tight or she'll back up. Just a bit loose, like this. When you want to go left or right, just move your arm in that direction, lay the reins on her neck gently, and she'll follow directions. When you want to stop, pull back gently and say, 'Whoa.' Don't ever jerk back hard because their mouths are very sensitive. Got all that?"

"I think so." She didn't look sure.

"Don't worry." He patted her knee. "I'll take the lead and she'll follow Elvis. She's a sweet-tempered soul, so I don't think you'll have to worry."

After securing the blanket and lunch container, he swung onto Elvis' back, urging him out of the barn. He guided them alongside his fenced-in pasture to where it finally ended, taking them into the hills and to freedom. Her giggles did nothing to ease the stranglehold his jeans had on his cock, or loosen the vise around his heart. God, he was a goner.

Once they'd gone half a mile or so, the trail widened some. He waited for her to bring the mare alongside him, and they rode in companionable silence until she gave in to the questions he could see churning in her head.

"Sean?"

"Hmm?"

"You don't really talk much about your life growing up. Did you go to school here?"

"Chattanooga. My parents lived there until right before I married Blair, when I was still in the service. My dad was a pilot and was killed in a single-engine plane crash, and my mother died of cancer the next year. We were all close."

"Oh, Sean. I'm so sorry."

"It was a long time ago." But the pain of loss never completely went away. "I have family in Texas, my uncle Joe, aunt Clara, and my cousins and their kids. I'm pretty close to them, too, though I don't get to visit often. So, when do I get to meet your mother?"

"Soon, maybe."

Her hesitance grated. "Are you ashamed of me?"

"Because you're white?" She stared at him, incredulous.

"Because I'm an alcoholic."

"No. I'm absolutely not ashamed of you for any reason, and don't think otherwise," she said firmly.

"You're the one who assumed I meant because I'm white," he pointed out. "Will I already have that strike against me because of your father running out on you both?"

Her lips thinned and her eyes flashed. "Listen to me good. My mother is a wonderful, gentle soul who was badly hurt by that man. And yes, she might worry because she doesn't want me to repeat her mistakes, but she's going to love you once she gets to know you. Just be yourself and let's put the color issue to rest, okay?"

"All right," he promised. "You won't hear another word about that from me."

"Good."

He couldn't help but worry about the issue rising later, but he'd heed her wishes. The tension dissipated as they rode on, soaking up the sunshine. They talked about the upcoming charity auction and Sean grimaced at her suggestion.

"I think you should do a striptease."

"What! Oh, sure, that'll go over well with the general population of Sugarland." He snorted, imagining himself shucking his fireman's coat, doing the bump and grind.

"You couldn't get naked or anything, but you guys can work the room, get the ladies excited."

"I'll leave it to the young guys to get them 'excited,' thanks." Might be funny to see their reactions, though. "What about you? Are you going to strip? That idea has merit."

"We'll see."

Her secretive smile raised his suspicions, but he let it go. He suddenly didn't want to know how she planned to get the men all wound up to bid on her, or *who* would do the bidding. Eve should be stripping only for him, dammit.

When they reached a small clearing near a stream, he brought them to a halt and dismounted. "Lunch?"

"It's a little early, isn't it?"

"I can think of something to pass the time, make sure we get good and hungry."

"In that case . . ."

After helping her dismount, he led the horses to a nearby fallen log and tied them off with just enough slack to allow them to graze. Then he brought the blanket over, spread it, and seized her hand, falling onto it and pulling her down on top of him.

"This I can get used to," he said, gazing up at her.

"Me, too."

She kissed him, sweetly at first. Then with more hunger, straddling his hips. Pushing at his T-shirt, she smoothed her palm over his stomach, his chest. It felt so good, he'd never get enough.

"Don't ever stop touching me, Eve. Please."

She scooted down, kissed his belly. Began to work on his jeans. "You sound starved."

"I am. Blair never—" He stopped, afraid he'd ruined the moment. But she looked at him in sympathy and understanding.

"Never touched you like this?" She unzipped his jeans, parted the material. Exposed his eager cock, gave it a long lick. "Never loved you like this?"

"Rarely," he said hoarsely. "She didn't care much for sex. Too messy and inconvenient."

"I'm sorry. But you don't have to be alone anymore— it's your choice."

"Then I choose you."

He kicked off his shoes and she pulled down his jeans, retrieving a condom from his pocket before setting them aside. His shirt went next, flung away into the grass. Mesmerized, he watched as she did a slow striptease for him, baring her bronzed skin an inch at a time. She was a goddess standing naked in the sunshine, and he was sure he didn't deserve her.

But he would have her anyway.

She knelt between his thighs and cupped his balls, squeezing with slight pressure. He groaned, spread wider. Her fingers were warm around his shaft, holding him steady as her mouth took him in. Hot, delicious wet heat. Sucking him between those pretty lips, tasting the salty drops. But he wanted her, too.

"Spin around and straddle me, baby."

Pulling herself off his cock, she did, placing her knees on both sides of his head. He adjusted himself, lining up with the pouty folds, and wrapped his fingers around her thighs. Tongued her slit, loving how she melted into him. Let him have his way.

They feasted, laving every inch of flesh in tandem, Eve bobbing on his erection with wonderful suction. Him tonguing her clit until she writhed against his face. When he could take no more, he pushed, urging her off.

"Ride me, baby. I want to watch."

The lust in her eyes matched his as she grabbed the condom from the blanket, sheathed his erection, repositioned herself. Slid down onto his cock, seating him fully. Hands splayed on his chest, she began to move. Impaled herself on his cock again and again. The sun shining on her beautiful body, the expression on her face that was so much more than desire—an emotion he didn't want to name—was a sight he wouldn't forget until he left the world for good.

She took him higher, his breaths short, body strung tight. His balls drew up and he did his best to stave off the impending orgasm, but it was no use.

He shot with a moan, filled her, wishing it could go on forever. That he never had to leave her heat. Especially when her walls tightened around him and she cried out her own climax, wringing the last drops from him.

"God. It was over too soon."

Leaning over, she gave him a soft kiss. "That just means you get to recover so we can do it again, in an hour or so."

"An hour!" He made a face. "Honey, I'm forty-three, not twenty-three."

"Oh." She made a show of pretending to consider this. "Well, I guess I'll have to find a virile young stud to make mad love—"

With a mock growl, he rolled her, pinning her underneath him. "One hour it is."

Her answering smile was all the incentive he needed.

10

1991

Sean's guts twisted as Jesse approached. The man knew something was wrong, no matter how he'd tried to hide it.

"What's eating you, old friend?"

"You know what," he said, voice low. "I won't do this!"

Jesse was unconcerned. "You already are. Have you forgotten that you're in this, same as me?"

"No, never the same as you. I don't want to live the life of a criminal, and I won't. I never asked for this."

"Come on, Sean. Back in the Colonial days, the American patriots were considered criminals when they told King George to shove it, remember? How's this any different?" He clapped Sean on the shoulder. "I'm going to make you my lieutenant. My right-hand man. You've always had my back and I've had yours, right? You and me against the world. What do you say?"

"You're insane! I'm not going to run guns or help you do it!"

"You're turning me down?" His expression was incredulous.

"Of course I am! Christ, what am I going to do?"

"Nothing, that's what," Jesse said coldly. "I'm your best friend and you owe me. Don't forget that."

It wasn't until Jesse spun that they both saw Connors there, standing in the shadows, listening.

"We need to talk, Rose."

"Are you sure you want to go with me?"

Eve straightened the collar of Sean's blue button-up shirt, then cupped his anxious face. "That's at least the fifth time you've asked. Are you sure you want me to go?"

"Of course I do! If you want. But I don't want you to think—I mean it's not exactly a great date and—"

"Sean! Chill, please. Deep breath."

He managed one, then nodded. "Christ, I'm sorry. I don't remember when I've been so nervous about an AA meeting. It's not like this is my first one."

But she was coming, and he was desperate to make a good impression. The knowledge puddled her heart at his feet.

"You'll be fine, and I want to go. This is what friends do, remember? Show their support."

He gave her an odd look, and then a tremulous smile. "Right. I guess I'm ready."

"And then don't forget my mother is expecting us for dessert."

"That should be interesting. She'll probably grind my bones to make her bread."

Eve snorted. "Would you stop! Let's get out of here before you work yourself into a state of psychosis or something."

Sean drove the Tahoe, which gave him other things to focus on besides tonight. She got the chance to observe him, and recall their lovely ride and interlude by the stream. This had been one of the best afternoons she could remember, even if her rear was a little saddlesore. They'd ridden for at least three hours, but she'd had fun.

Now his confidence had taken a backseat to nerves, and she felt for him. Enabling him to hide, however, wouldn't help him at all. She'd do everything in her power to restore the man she loved to his former self, or even better.

A few minutes later, he parked in front of the spacious community building where all sorts of civic meetings were held, and where the firemen's charity auction would be held in just a couple of weeks. Shutting off the SUV, he sat for a minute, gathering courage.

"It's not easy, standing in front of a room of strangers and admitting you're a fuckup," he said quietly.

"First of all, you're *not* a fuckup, and second, they're all there to kick the same problem." She took his hand. "I know what you mean, but remember what I said."

"I will. Thanks."

They got out and she slipped her hand into his, showing her support, as they walked inside. The crowd was bigger than she'd expected, perhaps fifty or so people. Some of those were sponsors, folks who had been sober for years and were here to lend their strength to those like Sean, just beginning the journey.

Sean introduced her to a few people he'd met, and they mingled a while before taking their seats. The meeting began and Eve found herself caught up in the various stories of each individual's path to self-destruction, and the often messy climb back to the light. A few started as social drinkers; some had more painful reasons. But none were as horribly tragic as Sean's.

When it came to be his turn, her lover stood tall and

faced the group. "Hi. My name is Sean and I'm an alcoholic."

"Hi, Sean!"

He took a steadying breath. "I started drinking to numb the unending pain of losing my wife and children in a car accident. I'm a captain at my fire station, and we got the call. I saw them burn."

No one moved, or spoke.

"My six-year-old daughter . . ." His voice broke and he cleared his throat. "She could've been saved. Five more minutes. That's all I needed, but I was too late. I crawled into the bottle and stayed there for almost two years. I wanted to die, or thought I did. Then my mistake at work almost got one of my men killed, and I knew I'd hit rock bottom."

A couple of sniffles sounded loud in the stillness.

"I'd come to the crossroads—either live or die. Ultimately, I wanted to be a man my daughter and son would've been proud to call their dad. It won't be easy, but knowing I'd disappoint them by giving up would be even harder. So here I am, and I believe I'll make it, thanks to friends and some very special people."

Glancing down at her, Sean held out his hand. Eve stared at him for a couple of heartbeats before she realized he'd publicly declared her to be one of those "very special people." She beamed at him and he returned the smile.

"Thank you," he said to the group. Taking his seat, he planted a sweet kiss on her lips.

She drew back, touched his face. "You did great. I'm so proud of you."

"I have the best incentive in the world."

The confident words, the heated look, sustained her

for the rest of the evening. She hardly knew what the remaining speakers said, or paid attention to the small talk they made with members of the group on their way out after the meeting. All she knew was that she and Sean had something real. Despite his fears, and other obstacles.

They could make it. Had a good shot.

He followed her directions to her mother's house and a short while later pulled into the drive. Before they got out, he grinned at her.

"I have a feeling those meetings will seem like a piece of cake compared to this. Facing a firing squad might be easier."

She rolled her eyes. "Come on, you. Into the lion's den."

No way was she going to admit she was a little unsure of his reception as well.

He was right—this should be interesting.

Sean wasn't sure what he'd expected when Amelia Marshall opened the door. All he could do was stand there like an idiot, trying to find his tongue.

The woman wasn't just lovely, as Eve had claimed—she was a knockout.

Amelia was shorter than her daughter, more petite. Her face was delicate with large brown eyes, her smile wide. She had a curvy figure made for a man's hands to go roaming. Not *his* hands, those were taken.

But, holy God. It was damned easy to see where Eve got her beauty.

"Hello, Captain Tanner," she said, voice smooth as whiskey. "Won't you come in?"

"Sean, please."

"Sean, I'm Amelia." She nodded in acknowledgment and moved past him to hug her daughter as he stepped inside. "Hey, baby."

"Mama. You're looking good." Eve waggled her brows. "Any luck with your preacher?"

"Maybe. A woman never tells *all* her secrets." She waved them in, leading them to the cozy living room. "Pie with ice cream, and coffee? I've got apple and peach."

"Peach sounds good to me, Mama. I'll come help you. Sean?"

"Um, that's fine with me, too."

"Coming up."

The ladies disappeared into the kitchen and he glanced around, taking in Amelia's home. Every space was filled with fat pillows, knickknacks, and framed photos, most of Eve. The place was lived-in, love oozing from the very walls.

He'd had a home like this, once.

The women made a couple of trips bringing the coffee and pie, finally settling in with Eve next to him on the sofa, Amelia in a stuffed chair across from them.

"Eve told me about your accident at work. Are you feeling better?"

"Much, thank you." He didn't mention the persistent irritation in his lungs. Maybe he was trying to fend off a cold now, but he didn't want to worry Eve. Shoveling a spoonful of pie and ice cream into his mouth, he groaned. "God, this is fantastic. You should open a bakery."

She preened a bit under the praise, but waved him off with a laugh. "Except that I don't know a thing about running one and I have an aversion to getting up hours before dawn to cook."

"Good point."

"But I do enjoy baking, taking treats to friends and neighbors." She looked at her daughter. "Which reminds me, I took a pie to my new neighbor, the man who bought the Byrds' old place, as a welcoming gesture. His name is George Sparks."

"Really? That was nice of you. What's he like?"

"He's in his forties or so. Odd. As my mama would've said, he 'ain't our kind of folk.'"

"How so?"

Sean watched and listened to the exchange with interest.

Amelia took a sip of her coffee, and considered the question thoughtfully. "He's friendly enough, but . . . cold. Like he's wearing a mask, but it can't hide the hollowness in his eyes. And he's strange, too. No, that's not quite right. There are things about the place that are strange. All those vehicles running up and down the road, but when I visit, there wasn't a soul to be seen except Mr. Sparks. No people, no animals. Quiet as church on a Monday."

"Weird."

"Yes. And inside the house, it's as bare as can be except the minimum of furniture. There was only one framed photograph of the man and some buddies a long time ago, when they were in the military. Desert Storm, he said."

Sean's neck prickled. But George Sparks? That wasn't anyone he knew.

"Anyway, I was so uncomfortable when I left, I won't be going back," she concluded.

Eve looked relieved. "Good. Your instincts are always right."

"Not always, baby girl. But this time, I think they are." The older woman turned her attention to Sean. "How long have you and Eve been seeing each other?"

The fact that Eve could've satisfied her questions, and at some other time, was irrelevant. Amelia was feeling him out, and not bothering to hide it.

"Not long. This is new for us."

"You two have worked together for years."

"Yes, ma'am. I was married for most of them." He pushed aside the ache in his mind and heart.

Some of the sharpness left her tone. "I was saddened to learn of your loss. No one should have to endure what you did."

"Thank you."

She paused, studying him as though trying to dissect him. "May I be blunt?"

"Mama—"

"No, it's okay," he said, taking Eve's hand. "Please do, Amelia."

"I truly applaud you for working so hard to get your life in order," she said sincerely. "But surely you can understand my concern when it comes to Eve. No mother wants to see her child unhappy, and most of the time in the past few years when I've seen her that way, it has to do with you."

"I'd never hurt Eve," he protested, shaking his head.

"You won't mean to. But you have a long way to go and I don't want to see my daughter dragged down if you fall." She glanced between Sean and Eve. "Having said that, I'll give the two of you my full blessing and support—provided you're not yanking her around," she advised, addressing Sean.

"I'm not, I swear."

"Good. Because if I find out you are? I'll cut off your balls and use them as Christmas ornaments. We're clear?"

"Mama!"

He nearly choked on a bite of pie. "Crystal."

Amelia graced him with the full force of her angelic smile. "Fantastic. More pie?"

The next two weeks passed swiftly, Eve savoring every moment of her days off with Sean. He'd survived her mother's grilling—the recollection of Mama's threat still amazed and embarrassed her—and they were none the worse for wear.

Things at work had been somewhat awkward between her and the other guys, but she thought perhaps it was all on her part. Nobody actually came out and addressed her and Sean sleeping together, though she was sure that Julian and Clay were now aware of the not-so-secret affair.

Eve weeping over Sean's prone body at the fire might have been a tiny clue.

Peering into the bathroom mirror, she put the finishing touches on her makeup and hair, turned, and checked her ass in the mirror. Her best jeans accented her rear as well as any could. Not a perfect rear, but the only one she had. That it pleased Sean was all that mattered.

Sean. He was in for a big surprise at the charity auction tonight. Just imagining his reaction brought a grin to her face. In fact, all the "attached" men on her team had better be ready—their women weren't going to allow any barely legal sweet thing to make off with their guys.

Finished getting ready, she scooped up her purse

and keys. Time to meet the ladies for some fun hooting for the beefcake on parade.

She arrived at the community center about forty minutes before the start of the auction to get a good table. Not that she minded standing, but with Kat and Cori being in their third trimesters of pregnancy, those two needed to sit. Being early had its advantages; she found a good spot close to the front and sat down to wait for the others.

What were the men doing right now? She'd bet they were in the back getting ready, discussing the order they'd go onstage. Where to stand, how to drive the crowd wild. Stuff like that. She knew there hadn't been a formal rehearsal because it wasn't that fancy of an event. Just a bunch of people from the city of Sugarland and surrounding areas coming to support the cause of giving to the families of fallen firefighters. She'd heard that quite a few were expected to attend.

That prediction turned out to be correct, and then some. By the time Cori and Shea walked in together, the place was jumping, upbeat pop music blaring through the speakers.

"Thank goodness," she said, hugging both women. "I've fended off half a dozen people who wanted our chairs. How are you guys?"

"Running late," Cori said. "One of the doctors gave us a ride over so we could go home with our guys and not have an extra car, but he got called to an emergency first. But he got done, so here we are!"

"Where's Kat?" Shea asked.

"Here!" The bubbly blonde pulled out a chair and sat heavily. "Damn, I hate being fat. Can't move faster than a turtle."

Cori nodded with a grimace. "Same here."

Eve couldn't help the tiny spark of envy. Even if she and Sean made it as a couple, the likelihood that he'd ever want more children . . . the probability was next to nil.

"Pregnant women glow," Eve countered. "And neither of you is fat—you have baby bumps. That's different."

Shea leaned forward, expression conspiratorial. "Okay, I've been dying to know something. Does your being pregnant turn on your man?"

Both women laughed and rolled their eyes, but it was Kat who answered first.

"Oh, my God, are you kidding? Howard's a machine!" A round of giggles met this announcement. "Seriously! You'd think no other man in the history of the universe has ever managed to impregnate a woman before, and he's either strutting around bragging about it, or horny as hell. He wants it *all* the time."

More giggles.

"So does Zack, but he's afraid he'll hurt me," Cori put in. "If he doesn't stop being so damned careful, I'm going to scream."

The others cooed over how sweet that was of Zack, despite Cori's annoyance. Shea wasn't finished with the inquisition.

"What's the first thing you're dying to have, once you're able?"

"Caffeine," Cori answered. "Zack won't even let me have half-caff."

"A twenty-ounce margarita," Kat said dreamily. "With an extra shot of tequila." The others chimed in their sympathy.

Before Eve thought the better of it, she asked, "How does that work out, since Howard doesn't drink?"

"Oh, he never has and isn't tempted, so it's not an issue. Why . . . ?"

The reason for Eve's question connected and all three woman gazed at her knowingly. Eve sighed. "Never mind. I'm sorry I brought it up."

Shea patted her hand. "Listen, we know you and Sean have something going. All I want to say is, if he means the world to you, if you love him, do whatever is necessary to keep him safe and happy. Whatever it takes."

Including keeping their home—should they ever make one together—booze free. She'd never have peace of mind knowing temptation was only one cabinet away from the man she loved.

Grace, Julian's fiancée, showed up late and took a seat just as the lights dimmed and the crowd cheered. The interim city manager, who'd taken over the rest of the term from the late slimeball Forrest Prescott, acted as the MC, smiling and greeting everyone, thanking them for coming out to support a good cause.

The event would kick off with each "bachelor" strutting across the stage, though some of the men were very much taken, dancing a bit to the music so the ladies could get an eyeful of the goods and decide whom to bid on. Then each man would come out one by one and be auctioned for a date with the highest bidder. All in good fun.

The event kicked off with some of the guys from Stations Two and Three, to much whistling and catcalls. Personally, Eve thought her team far surpassed the others in the hotness department, but they were okay. Things were just getting warmed up.

When their men began to parade out to the throbbing tempo, shucking coats and baring buff chests and torsos, the heat level skyrocketed. Tommy went first, looking so much like Brad Pitt it was eerie, despite the long scar on his face from the warehouse collapse. Julian was next, a smooth, dark-haired Latin lover who had Grace nearly panting, along with everyone else. Then sweet, sexy Zack, who looked like he'd rather be anywhere else, but took it with good-natured humor.

Clay was a hit with his good-looking cowboy charm, and Eve had no doubt he'd score a gorgeous date. Six-Pack proved he still lived up to his nickname when his coat came off, revealing a ripped body that was simply stunning. Kat could do much worse than having this man wanting it *all the time*, as she'd said. Lucky girl. But when Sean came out . . .

Eve forgot anyone else existed. Forgot to breathe. As far as she was concerned, no man in the room could light a candle next to him, not even with a flamethrower. He might be the oldest man on the stage, but he was so incredibly handsome. Tall and lean with those green eyes sparkling under the lights, his smile wide as he hammed it up for the audience, flexing his rather nice biceps. And it could have been her imagination, but it seemed the audience cheered louder for him than for any of the others.

God, he'd come so far. Tears pricked her eyes as she yelled the loudest of all.

Except for a stacked blond chick nearby who was really going nuts, jumping up and down, boobs bouncing like basketballs. Eve set her jaw. Breast-Enhancement Barbie could bid as high as she wanted.

No way in hell was she going to win.

* * *

Sean stood under the hot lights, thankful he couldn't see much of the wild audience of screeching women. Sweat trickled down the side of his face as he flexed his muscles.

I can't believe I'm fucking doing this. Jesus, I hope no one's laughing at me.

What difference did it make? He was here, and it was for charity. He repeated that mantra a few times, but the thirty seconds or so still seemed like an hour. When at last he was given the signal to exit, he beat a path to hide back behind the curtain.

His team was waiting to pound his back and give him a ribbing, but he didn't mind that part. These guys he knew. They calmed and grounded him more than they realized.

"Good job, man," Six-Pack said, and the rest agreed.

"God, do we have to go out there again? Can't they just bid without us?"

"Nope, they gotta see us. Too many guys to remember our names."

"Can't I put on my shirt?"

Tommy snorted. "You're forty-three, not eighty. Chill."

"Wonderful."

Clay put an arm around him. "It ain't so bad, Cap. Women eat up this shit, huh? Guaranteed nooky if you play your cards right."

It was on the tip of his tongue to retort that he had all the nooky he wanted, thank you very much, and then he thought the better of it. Considering.

Five minutes later, they were all called back to the stage for the lineup. Sean pasted on a smile and took his place in front of the crowd again, wondering how in the hell rock stars and other performers dealt with screaming people wanting a piece of them. He figured he was lucky that this would be the closest he'd ever get to finding out.

The city manager had each of them step forward when he called their name once again, quickly going down the line. Sean's turn came and he stepped out of line, scanning the sea of blurry faces, looking for Eve. Still hard to see much, even though the dance lights had quit flashing. He resumed his spot in line and kept looking—and froze.

There. To one side of the room, next to the wall. A tall, lean man standing in the shadows. Long blond hair. The man's gaze seemed to be locked on Sean, though it was impossible to actually tell. He was too far away, the crowd separating them, and there were other guys standing near Sean. The man could be staring at any of them.

But a chill chased over his skin as the man ducked his head. Turned and disappeared into the mass of bodies, heading toward the exit.

Sean's heart pounded and his legs felt like lead. The man couldn't be Jesse. What business would he have in Sugarland?

A honed sense of self-preservation whispered that he didn't want to know.

The bidding began and took his mind off the stranger. Each of the firefighters fetched a respectable sum, though his guys did better than most. Some of the local single girls were determined to get a piece of them, hitched or not, and their women were equally determined to send their competition home lonely.

When it was his turn, Sean cringed inwardly as the bidding began at a pathetic hundred bucks. They all started at that price, but his worry that nobody would bid on him made him feel like an awkward thirteen-year-old all over again. His team had each fetched over five grand, for God's sake.

Then the bidding started in earnest, and he soon discovered he needn't have been nervous.

A woman's voice called out clearly, "Five hundred!"

Okay, not shabby.

"One thousand!" came a counterbid. Eve's voice.

She was bidding on him. In public, no matter who among their colleagues was watching. Hell, in front of the entire damned town. He warmed inside, his smile genuine. It also didn't kill his ego when the two opponents upped the stakes, each prepared to outdo the other.

"Fifteen hundred!"

"Two thousand," Eve shouted.

"Three thousand!"

"Five!"

The crowd murmured excitedly.

"Seven!" the woman countered.

"Ten thousand dollars!"

No counterbid came from the woman this time, and the audience shrieked. The city manager beamed into the microphone.

"Ten thousand going once . . . going twice . . . one eligible bachelor sold to the pretty lady for ten thousand dollars!"

Sean felt light-headed and ridiculously happy. Jeez, did she have that kind of money? He guessed so or she wouldn't have done it.

Six-Pack poked him in the ribs. "Damn, my friend! Two women duking it out over you? Can I be you when I grow up?"

"Shut up." But he couldn't stop smiling.

The rest of the auction passed in a haze and was over before he knew it. He and the others trooped backstage to put their civilian clothes back on and join the audience for an after-party. In the makeshift dressing area, he dressed in his jeans and a nice gray sweater, and gathered his fireman's coat, pants, and suspenders. He hadn't worn the hat.

"Hey, I'm gonna go put this stuff in my truck before I find Eve," he called to Six-Pack. "If you see her, tell her I'll be there in a few minutes."

His friend waved as he exited through a side door and out into the fall night. The air was clear and cold with that first bite of winter, one of his favorite times of year. It had been Bobby's, too. Football season. The memory made him sad, but it wasn't crippling this time. Didn't send him to his knees, begging God to take him, too.

Reaching his Tahoe, he clicked the lock on his key ring and opened the back window to throw his gear inside. Just then a faint shuffle sounded from somewhere behind him, and he spun, staring into the darkness beyond the parking lot. He could've sworn it sounded like boots crunching on gravel, a tentative step.

The stranger came to mind, the one he thought he'd seen twice. His skin prickled again and he was absolutely certain he was being watched. Stalked? By the man who'd tormented him with the call and the shit in the box? Maybe the same one who'd destroyed the Chinese restaurant?

"What do you want, asshole?" he snapped. "I've seen you twice and I know you're there. Why don't you quit hiding like a pussy and come deal with me face-to-face?"

Now he wasn't imagining the footsteps, coming closer.

"Who the hell are you yelling at?"

Pulse leaping, Sean whirled to see Julian striding toward him, carrying his own gear. "What? Nobody. I mean, I thought somebody was out there." He waved a hand toward the gloom beyond the lights. "Obviously, I'm hearing things. Going back inside?"

"Yep." Frowning, Jules glanced from Sean to the area where he'd been staring. "Let me put away my shit and we'll go."

He waited for Julian, then trailed him back to the building, taking one last, long look over his shoulder. No one there.

He wondered if there ever had been.

Pussy.

"I've got your snatch right here, motherfucker," Jesse hissed, tucking the big hunting knife into his boot again. "You need to die so fucking bad it ain't funny. And you will soon enough, begging for me to end your sorry life."

Jesse might've killed him just now, gutted him like a deer. Probably would have if it hadn't been for the spic interrupting and throwing off his game.

He stood, chest heaving. Breathing the cold air, letting himself calm.

Reason returned, and he could see that his prey escaping was for the best. Wouldn't do to kill Sean too quickly—that would be like shooting his load too fast during sex. Give in to the moment and it's ultimately unsatisfying.

He'd wait, stick with his plan. Torment the bastard a little longer. Incorporate him into the big scheme.

How horrified his holier-than-thou former friend would be when he learned the truth behind *everything*.

Only then would Sean Tanner know the true meaning of betrayal.

And of long-awaited paybacks served stone cold.

11

"We need to talk, Rose." Connors approached, his gaze raking Jesse with disdain. "Tanner doesn't have to go to the captain because I will. It's about time they know what you've been up to. You're history."

Jesse's eyes glittered like a snake as he smiled. "That's a mistake you'd come to regret."

"I don't give a—"

"Connors, don't get involved," Sean said, breaking into a sweat. "Let me handle this."

Just then, one of the sergeants ran through the camp, yelling orders. "We've got some of Hussein's troops coming on fast! Let's go!"

The camp sprang to life, men scrambling for their weapons. Ready and eager to engage the enemy, send them the hell out of Kuwait. As Sean turned, he saw Jesse raise his hand, make a shooting motion at Connors with his thumb and forefinger.

"Bang," he said.

Still smiling.

Eve felt slightly ill as her friends teased her about the humongous bid she'd placed to win Sean. She shouldn't have done it, but by God she wasn't about to watch that bottle-blond ho waltz off with her man.

"Holy shit, do you have ten thousand dollars?" Kat breathed.

"Of course I do," she muttered.

"They can't really hold you to it. Can they?" This from Shea, who swung her gaze toward Grace. All eyes fell on the willowy attorney.

"Hey, I'm a criminal defense lawyer. Legally, I don't think they can, but . . ." She shrugged.

But it would look bad, and be in terrible form to cheat the families of fallen firefighters. Eve mustered a smile. "It's no problem. I'll claim it on my taxes."

I'd just better pray nothing goes wrong with my car, or no other major catastrophes happen while I spend, oh, the next ten years saving it up again.

Then the crowd next to their table parted and she found herself staring up into brilliant green eyes, into that beloved face. And she knew she'd spend every penny all over again to keep another woman from sharing so much as a French fry with the man she loved, much less an entire dinner.

"May I have this dance?" His low rumbly voice sent a shiver through her.

"You bet."

Taking her hand, he helped her up and led her to where some volunteers had cleared away the tables to create a dance floor. The DJ had switched to a slow song, something haunting and pretty about love lost and found.

Sean pulled her close against his body, practically wrapped himself around her, tucking her head underneath his chin. She snuggled into him, inhaling his clean, manly scent, and swayed with him, wishing she never had to let go.

"Chief Mitchell is watching us," he said next to her ear.

"Oh, crap." She tried to put some distance between them, but he didn't budge.

"No, let everyone look. I'm not going to hide. If he says one of us has to transfer, so be it."

Before, she was going to leave Station Five because of him. Now she knew she would leave *for* him. She didn't want to mess up any chance he might have for promotion.

Settling down again, she decided if he wasn't going to worry, neither would she. In fact, he wasn't thinking of the others at all, from the size of the erection burning her through two layers of denim.

After just a couple of songs, he nuzzled her ear. "You're driving me crazy. If we don't get out of here, I'm going to come in my jeans."

"Can't have that, can we?"

"Let's go."

As he dragged her toward the exit, she managed to wave at Kat, who gave her the thumbs-up. She knew Howard's wife would tell the others she'd left.

On the way to the parking lot, she remembered. "Damn, my car is here. Want me to follow you?"

"Or I can bring you back tomorrow to get it, since we're off. I don't mind."

She thought about it. "Let me at least drive it as far as my apartment. Then it will be there, whatever we decide to do."

"All right. I'll walk you over."

His gaze seemed to roam everywhere, searching the edges of the lot, and his pace picked up.

"What are you looking for?"

"I'll tell you later."

Instantly she went on alert. "Has something else happened?"

"Not really. I'll tell you when we get back to your place."

He wasn't eager to linger here and his caution made her afraid. She didn't argue, and was grateful that he saw her safely to her car with strict instructions to lock the doors as soon as he went to his SUV.

"I'll follow you," he said.

"Okay."

He gave her a quick kiss and she got in, hitting the locks. Nodding in approval, he jogged away and she started the car, just as anxious to be gone and she didn't even understand why. Relief blasted through her as the Tahoe emerged from the other side of the parking lot, and she pulled out, secure in the knowledge that he was behind her if something happened. Whatever that might be.

The drive to her apartment took only a few minutes and they were inside, Sean pushing her against the door, devouring her mouth. His innate dominance plucked her nipples, tightened her womb. Set her ablaze. This man did it for her like no one else.

"Tell me . . . what was bothering you," she managed between kisses.

His hand ventured under her shirt, going for the clasp on her bra. "Later. Need you now, baby."

Freeing her breasts, he bent and took one nipple between his teeth, teased it to a hard nub. She dug her fingers into his soft hair, relishing the waves of pleasure created by his talented mouth. He suckled one tip, then the other, before losing patience and yanking at her jeans. She kicked off her shoes and helped him get her naked. Then gladly returned the favor.

They rid him of his shirt and jeans, and his cock sprang free, flushed deep red and leaking with pre-cum. She was about to kneel and taste the salty-sweet drops, but he guided her to the sofa instead.

"Bend over the back and spread your legs for me." She complied, eliciting a feral moan from her lover. Fingers trailed down her spine. "God, I love looking at you. So pretty and wet for me, waiting for my cock. Do you have any idea how beautiful you are? How sensual? Stay like this."

The questions didn't seem to require an answer, but she knew she'd never felt beautiful or sensual with anyone else. Not like this. She heard some rustling, the crinkle of foil. But then he moved away and she realized he'd gone into the kitchen. He fished in the pantry and returned, set something on the floor. Then the foil ripped and she knew he'd sheathed himself.

His palms glided down her sides, rough and callused. The hands of a hardworking man, and she loved them. He ran them down to her buttocks, parted her ass cheeks.

"Wh-what are you doing?"

"Something I think you'll enjoy," he said, voice low. "Has anyone ever played with you here?"

To emphasize his meaning, he rubbed her opening. His finger was slick and cool with . . . cooking oil?

"No," she croaked.

Which apparently pleased him to no end. "Good. Relax and open yourself to me, honey. Just like that. This will feel strange at first, but it won't hurt. Only going to use my fingers, okay?"

She nodded, melting a bit at the gentle assault on her defenses, her body. Dominant as he was, he'd still asked before doing something alien to her, and it made her trust him even more.

Dribbling a bit more oil into her crease, he set the bottle aside and held her open. Began to massage her entrance in lazy circles. With each pass, he worked a finger inside slowly. The tip, the knuckle. Deeper and deeper, stretching.

The peculiar sensation eventually gave way to a bloom of heat. The heat became flame, increasing to sweep her sex, sweet torment. She bent lower over the sofa, offering herself fully, quickly becoming mindless to this new, dark desire.

"You like this, pretty girl?"

"God, yes!"

"Look at you, writhing on my hand," he whispered. "I'm going to fuck your ass and your pussy at the same time. Want me to fuck you, baby?"

"Yes, please! Sean!"

Wasting no time, he guided the head of his cock to her sex, pressed inside with a groan of sheer male satisfaction. A helpless noise escaped her throat as he filled her. So good. Naughty. As promised, he fucked her with long strokes, and the dual stimulation was almost too much.

She was oversensitized, every nerve throbbing in tempo with his thrusts. He owned her and she loved it. Her climax built before she was ready, but she was along for the ride. Nothing to do but let the explosion happen—and it blew her apart.

Her cries echoed in the small space and she barely heard him crooning, praising her. Then he stiffened with a shout, his cock pulsing hot, buried in her core. At last he kissed her back and carefully withdrew, helping her straighten.

She faced him on wobbly legs and accepted his hungry kiss. "I've *never* felt anything like that."

"Was it good?"

"Are you kidding? You're turning me into a wanton slut."

He puffed up at this. "*My* slut."

"Yours," she agreed. "Your very oily slut. Shower?"

"After you."

The water was hot and wonderful, but even better was the hunky man sharing it. The space was barely big enough for both of them and she found herself dreaming about them sharing another shower, a huge one with pretty tile and a bench seat for messing around. One that was theirs together, not his or hers.

Maybe one day. She closed the door on those fantasies for now and enjoyed letting him soap her up and rinse, and vice versa. They laughed a lot, which fascinated her because until recently, he hadn't laughed in years. Selfishly, she hoped she was part of the reason.

They dried off, and Sean stretched out on her bed naked while she dug in a drawer and pulled on an oversized T-shirt. As she admired his sexy body, for no particular reason the broken condom came to mind. How long had the incident been nagging her like a sore tooth? They were healthy, and she was on the pill. Nothing to worry about. Right?

Her lover closed his eyes and dozed. While he was drifting, she padded to the living room where she'd discarded her purse, and retrieved the minicalendar she always carried around. Opening it, she flipped to the previous month, and dread settled in her gut. She counted off the weeks since her last period. Twice.

"Holy crap."

Late. By two weeks.

Not to panic. She'd start. And if not? She'd take a test and they'd deal with it together.

Everything would be fine.

Sean flipped a couple of pancakes and the bacon, smiling as a pair of slender arms wrapped around his waist and plump lips nuzzled his neck.

"Hungry?" he asked.

"Mmm. Not for pancakes."

He chuckled. "Every wanton slut needs fuel. It's a house rule."

"Is that so? Well, I guess I'd better eat first." Fetching two plates from the cabinet, she set them on the counter and got out the forks next. "You fell asleep before you told me what was bothering you last night. Time to spill."

"Can't put it off anymore, huh?"

"Nope."

"Let's get breakfast on the table and we'll talk."

"Sounds ominous."

"Hope it's not."

Finished, he took the pancakes and bacon to the table. Eve set it, bringing the plates, forks, butter, and syrup, while he poured two glasses of milk. They sat next to each other and filled their plates, and he was gratified at her moan of happiness with the meal.

"This is great! I love breakfast."

"Me, too. Glad you like it."

"Okay, out with it."

He took a bite, chewed, thinking how best to get into this. "Remember my nightmare in the hospital?"

"About your ex-friend." She nodded. "Sure, go on."

"I had the nightmare because I thought I saw him."

She blinked at him. "Where? When?"

"In the crowd, while we were working the fire at the strip mall. I only caught a glimpse of a man with long dirty blond hair and he was gone. So quick I guess it stuck in my subconscious. I mean, the guy moved, walked, just like Jesse. I know that sounds crazy."

"Not really. You knew him for many years, practically lived together in the marines. He'd be very familiar to you."

"Not anymore, I'd think. But still, with the explosion . . . I don't know. I have no reason to think he was responsible."

"But someone was. They confirmed it was a bomb in the restroom that did the damage and started the fire." She paused. "And someone's been trying to get to you, mentally."

"That's the other thing. Considering the bomb and the cut air hoses, it might be turning physical. And that's not all—last night, I saw him again."

She sat up straight. "The blond guy?"

"Yes. During the auction, when I was onstage. It was dark, but I'm pretty sure it's the same man I saw at the strip mall, and I'm almost positive he *wanted* me to see him this time. In fact, when I changed clothes and went to put my turnouts in the Tahoe, I heard someone in the darkness moving around. Like boots on gravel. I challenged him."

"You did what!" Her fork clattered to the plate. "He could've had a gun or something."

"I know that," he snapped. "But I was certain he wanted me to know he was out there, watching, and was deliberately trying to freak me out. I wasn't going to let him get away with it, and it almost worked. I heard him coming toward me when Julian came outside and asked who I was yelling at. The guy vanished."

She let out a breath, scowling at him. "Thank God for Julian. You idiot, that lunatic could've hurt you, dragged you off, and nobody would've known where you were, or found you until it was too late."

"I'm not going to let him push me around and I let him know it! Fuck that asshole."

"Terrific. You've instigated a pissing contest with a psycho."

"Hey, I didn't start it," he defended. "But I'll damned well finish it if he comes around again."

How was the question, when he didn't know anything about the man. Why he was doing this, what he wanted.

Unless the man was Jesse.

They finished eating and she helped him take care of the dishes. He sneaked glances at her and could tell she was upset with him. Or the situation in general.

"Gonna stay mad at me all day?"

Her frown softened. "No."

"Good. I have some things to do, but I'd like to see you again tonight. If you want."

"Of course I do. I just worry about you, that's all."

"I know, baby," he said, wrapping her in his arms. She snuggled into him and he kissed the top of her head. "It's all going to be fine."

On his way home, those words echoed in his head. He hoped he hadn't lied.

The unsettled feeling in his gut nagged at him. Told him that somewhere along the way, he'd missed something. That the puzzle was missing a few pieces in the center to complete the picture.

When had his life gone from happy and fulfilled to simply existing for his children? When had he and Blair begun to drift apart? Because that was the start of his downhill slide.

Two years before the accident, she'd started harping at him. All the freaking time. About every damned thing. Blair had always been spoiled, but happy in their marriage, or so he believed. Gradually, he hadn't been able to please her no matter what the hell he did. So he began picking up more overtime.

It wasn't a conscious decision on his part, to avoid his family. But sometimes he'd needed a break from her, and he thought she'd felt the same. It never occurred to him they wouldn't get through their rough patch. He wasn't a quitter.

And then the arguments began in earnest. Blair began to work late, leave early. Her cell phone was rarely visible, and once when he'd picked it up to make a call because hers was handy, she'd nearly taken his head off.

The innuendos began, the subtle threats. Her voice rang in his head.

I don't know why I bother.

Aren't you man enough to admit when you're wrong?

Work yourself into the ground if you want. I'm going to have fun while I can.

If you can't appreciate what you have here, someone else might.

The last words she'd ever spoken, filled with venom. At the time, he'd believed she was pissed because he'd missed Bobby's game.

And now he was very much afraid those words meant something else altogether.

Bursting into the house, he found the detective's card

from his visit. Dialed the number and waited. To his surprise, the man answered on the second ring.

"Detective Kayne."

"Detective, this is Sean Tanner. You came out to my house a couple of weeks ago—"

"Tanner, right!" A pause, and some shuffling of papers or something. "My apologies for not getting back to you sooner. I've been meaning to call since yesterday, but I've been swamped."

"That's okay. You have anything?"

"Not much, I'm afraid. As I suspected, there were no prints on the box left at your house, or the contents. But we have an interesting tidbit on the suspicious call you received. The number was registered to a cell phone belonging to a woman in Chattanooga. Stolen."

That revelation hit him hard.

"I grew up there," he said quietly. *And so did Jesse.* Oh, God. Please.

"No shit? May mean something, or it may not. But also of interest is the fact that the call that was made to your number from the stolen phone was made around the halfway mark between Chattanooga and Sugarland."

"As though he called on his way here, to get me." Fuck, he was going to be sick.

"We don't have any proof he wants to harm you. The hell of it is, he has to try for us to get that proof."

"I think he may have already."

"How? Explain." To the detective's credit, he didn't sound cynical or like he was merely humoring a complainant.

"You know the bomb that went off in the restaurant at the strip mall?"

"Yeah . . . oh, wait. Your lieutenant called me about

this after you were hurt. I went out and looked at the air tanks and the cut hoses. So, you think the strip-mall bombing and the tampering with your equipment is related to the other stuff going on with you?"

"Yeah. I think it was aimed at me, at least indirectly."

"Let me hear what happened from your point of view."

Sean told him about seeing a man who looked familiar in the crowd, and how he nearly died of smoke inhalation. Howard and the team finding that the hoses to the air tanks had been cut. He added the recent events, seeing the man again at the auction last night. About challenging his mysterious stalker, who was approaching until Julian interrupted them. He left out the nightmare, and Jesse's name, related only the facts as he knew them for a certainty.

"What do you think?" he asked when he was finished.

"That you've got a bigger problem than we first thought. The question is, who is this guy and what does he want?"

"What am I supposed to do? Buy a gun?" He'd never owned one. Blair hadn't liked guns and he hadn't dared buy one after his family was killed.

"Fuck, no! In civilian hands, guns cause more problems than they solve. Does your house have an alarm system?"

"Yes, but I haven't bothered with it in ages."

"Start setting it. Even if you just go outside for a while, lock up and arm it. And until we catch this asshole or he disappears, don't go off without someone knowing where you are. Commonsense stuff."

"And then what?"

"We need more to go on to figure out who this guy is. Can you think of anyone at all who might get a kick out of harassing you?"

His stomach lurched. "I've got a couple of ideas, but that's all they amount to. I'm going to check my wife's office and I'll give you a call back."

"I remember you saying you thought she might be having an affair. Think he's still around?"

"Maybe. There's another possibility, but I'd rather get into that only if it becomes necessary."

"All right. Do some digging and call me back."

"Will do. And thanks for your help."

"That's why I get paid the big bucks."

Saying good-bye, Sean hung up and steeled himself to face what he'd been avoiding for so long. Deep down, did he suspect he'd find something incriminating in Blair's sanctuary, and that was why he'd put off going through it? Yes, if he was honest. If Blair had been involved with someone, the clues would be located where she'd spent most of her time. After all, she'd never envisioned there would come a day when she wouldn't be around to guard her secrets.

At the closed door to her office, he stood staring at the polished wood. He hated this, feeling like he was invading her privacy, even though that was no longer the case. But it had to be done, if for no reason than to prove him wrong.

He pushed inside and took a moment, letting the stillness permeate his entire being. Her computer sat on the wide mahogany desk, a neat stack of papers on the right-hand corner. Her BlackBerry had presumably burned in the accident, but he knew she was prone to jot notes first, then input information into the device later regarding lunches, meetings, and such. His wife had been meticulously organized.

No sense putting this off any longer. Deciding to save the computer for last, he tackled the stack of papers first. A glance through them showed they were all work related. Nothing that would be important now, just ideas and notes on projects that had no doubt been long reassigned. The idea made him sad; Blair had been creative, her ad campaigns innovative. Nobody could take that from her, no matter what else she'd done.

A search through the drawers turned up an array of smaller office supplies in one. Notepads in another, unused. He rifled through the typical variety of office stuff. Until the last drawer.

A notepad there had been written on, several pages of shorthand notes and scribbles that were difficult to decipher. Among those writings, however, were a few notations of interest.

Lunch with G, 12:30 p.m.
Investors' meeting, 8:00 a.m.
Dinner with G, 7:00 p.m.
Jimmy's Auto, brakes, $450(?)

Sean blinked, reread the last note. The brakes? On the Mercedes? If there was a problem, she'd never mentioned it to him. Had she called Jimmy's, gotten an estimate on some work? If so, would they remember her?

Shuddering, he laid the notepad aside to show Detective Kayne. The computer was next, and he really, really did not want to check her e-mail. But he was in for the duration, and booted up the machine. It clicked and whirred, as if protesting the sudden prod to life after a long sleep. He knew exactly how that felt.

At the prompt for the log-in and password, he entered the last combination he'd known her to use and hoped it worked. She hadn't allowed the kids to use her computer and never gave them the log-in information, but he'd used it infrequently. He supposed it would've seemed suspicious if she'd refused to give it to him.

He was surprised when the command worked, and he was in. Launching the Internet, he waited for it to come up, and then went to her e-mail program. Belatedly, it occurred to him to wonder if the account would've been rendered inactive. If she had her account set up to roll over each year, the renewal charged to their credit card, it should still be there. In his haze of grief, it wasn't like he'd checked.

The password for the e-mail proved more problematic because he'd never known it. The log-in was simply her e-mail address, but he tried several combinations for the password before hitting the correct one—Mia's birth date. Tears pricked his eyes and he ruthlessly shoved down his sorrow.

The messages came up and he was startled to find several unopened ones from addresses he didn't recognize. They struck him like a fist to the gut, almost ghostly. Remnants from a life ended too soon.

He should've expected that, but hadn't. Stood to reason that she'd get e-mails from friends and co-workers before they got word of her death. Hand shaking, he moved the mouse to the first one and began to read.

Not much there among the unopened mail. Two were spam. Three from work, regarding current projects and meetings. An off-color joke from a friend. Nothing.

He started down the list of opened mail, finding more of the same. On the fourth e-mail, however, his luck changed.

Be there Friday. Miss U, sexy. Gonna fuck U so hard U scream. –G

Sean stared at the message for the longest time. Hand on the mouse, stunned in the face of seeming proof of his wife's infidelity. The last message from her lover, dated two days before she died with their children.

Be there Friday.

The day they were killed.

G. Who was he?

Numb, he checked the incoming e-mail address. From one *Gsparks*. His heart pounded in recognition. Where had he heard that name before? Where? And then it broke over his head like ice water.

"George Sparks," he whispered.

Amelia Marshall's new neighbor. The one who'd just moved here.

What the fuck? What the fuck?

Whipping out his cell phone, he scrolled to Kayne's number and punched it.

"Detective Kayne."

"It's Sean Tanner again. I need to show you something, right fucking now."

Kayne's voice perked up with interest. "Whatcha got?"

"Not over the phone."

"I'm here. Just come to the front desk and tell the officer there I'm expecting you."

"See you soon."

Holy God. What in the fuck was going on?

He had a bad feeling more puzzle pieces were about to fall into place.

12

Sweat streamed down Sean's face as he fired. Took down the enemy, one by one.

Over the next rise, Connors was busy with his own fight. Doing pretty well.

But he didn't see Jesse sneaking up on his five o' clock.

Sean ran.

The pounding on her door caused Eve to start. Cautiously, she approached, peered out the peephole, and let out a breath.

"You've only been gone a couple of hours," she said as she swung the door open to smile at Sean. "Miss me already?"

Instead of the happy greeting she expected, he was fidgety, out of sorts. "Would you come with me to the police station?" he asked hoarsely. "I need you."

His urgency, the look on his face, forestalled her questions. "Hang on. I'll get my purse." She fetched it quickly and locked up behind them. He took her hand, gripping it like a lifeline as he practically dragged her to his Tahoe.

"Thanks," he said as they jumped inside. "You're the only one who knows everything that's going on with this bastard who's harassing me. Blowing up buildings. God knows what else."

"What's happened?"

He fired up the SUV, pulled away from the curb. "I went through Blair's office. Her desk, computer. She was having an affair. Shit, I can't believe this."

"But you already suspected she was," she pointed out gently.

"Yes, but it's not the *what*—it's the *who*."

She studied him, trying to make sense of what had him so agitated. "Who she was seeing, you mean?"

"Yes. I found e-mails," he said breathlessly, grabbing a sheaf of papers from between his seat and the console. "Look."

She took them, scanned the sender's and recipient's addresses, and began to read. The sleazy contents both sickened her and filled her with sadness for him. Sean was a hardworking, good, and loving man. And the bitch had been cheating on him. She hated to think ill of the dead woman, but he hadn't deserved to have his wife sleeping around.

"I'm so sorry," she said, looking at his stark profile. "This is bad, but I still don't see, why the police?"

"Check out the guy's name."

"He signed them G. That doesn't tell me anything."

"No, look at the top. His e-mail address."

"*Gsparks at . . .*" The name teased her brain. "That sounds familiar, but I don't know why."

"George Sparks." She stared at him blankly. "Your mother's new neighbor."

Instantly, she felt the blood drain from her face. "Oh

my God! She was seriously freaked-out by that man! But she said he just moved here. How could it be the same guy?"

"Sparks just bought her neighbor's place, but that doesn't mean he wasn't in the area before then." He blew out a tired breath. "You're right. He could be a different G. Sparks, but what are the odds? Either way, Detective Kayne can find out. I hope."

"Even if he is the same man, that doesn't mean his being here indicates anything sinister. He could simply be her ex-lover, nothing more."

"There's something else that gets me. From the stack of e-mails, this affair went on for almost a year," he said tightly. "It was hot and heavy, right up until two days before—before she died." The last he got out with difficulty, and cleared his throat. "After her death, the e-mails stopped. Just like that."

"I'm not following."

"If you're having a clandestine affair and your main communication is e-mail, and your lover suddenly dies, would you necessarily know of the death right away? Wouldn't you keep sending messages until you investigated and finally learned what happened? Where are his e-mails saying, 'Hey, I haven't heard from you'?"

A chill went through her. "That would seem logical. So, if his messages stopped immediately, it might be because he knew right away that she was gone." This kept getting more horrible by the day.

"That's what I'm thinking." He banged his fist on the steering wheel. "This whole thing has a gaping hole in the middle and it doesn't make sense."

"It will." She laid a hand on his thigh. "We'll get to the bottom of this."

"I don't know if that's good or not."

At the police station, they hurried inside and Sean politely asked for Detective Kayne. They were told to wait because something had come up, but he'd be with them as soon as he could.

Sean paced the lobby like a caged tiger, papers in hand, glancing at every cop that came in or out. She was about to urge him to sit down when a familiar face walked through the door. Sean stopped his pacing and actually smiled, approaching the man and sticking out his hand.

"Shane, it's good to see you."

She recognized him as Detective Shane Ford, Shea's twin brother. The man Tommy had gotten to help them with Sean's problem.

"Same here," the man greeted him good-naturedly. "You're not here regarding that matter Tommy called me about, are you?"

"Afraid so." He gave Shane a condensed rundown of his suspicions about the bombing, the continued harassment. When he was done, the cop shook his head.

"Damn, that's frickin' creepy. And I'm guessing something else has happened or you wouldn't be here?"

"You could say that. Not sure what it means, though." He hesitated. "I'd better talk to Kayne first, though. I'm sure he can fill you in."

"No problem. I hope this gets solved, soon."

"Me, too. And thanks for getting him to look into all of this. He's a stand-up guy, seems to be taking this seriously."

Shane nodded. "You can count on him." He paused. "How are you doing, man? Personally, I mean."

"I'm sober, feel better than I have in years. I've got a good reason to stay healthy, too." He threw a grin at Eve, and her face flushed as the cop smiled knowingly.

"You don't say. I'm happy for you."

"How's your future brother-in-law doing in Arson? We miss him at the station."

All three of them were very aware that Sean was a big part of the reason Tommy's firefighting career was over.

"Doing great. He's really taken to investigating fires and all the other stuff they handle. He and Shea are truly happy."

"That's terrific. I—"

"Mr. Tanner?" the cop behind the desk called out. "Detective Kayne says you can come on back."

"I'm going that way," Shane said. "I'll walk with you."

Eve followed the men, feeling a little in the way. She wasn't sure what she could do to help, but being here for Sean was the important thing.

"Hell of a mess Tommy got himself into with Forrest Prescott," Sean commented as they walked. "He and your sister were very lucky, and so were you."

Shane's voice turned grim. "Yeah. Too bad that bastard's dead. I'd sure love to kill him again, slowly. You heard about him skimming money, didn't you?"

"Not the details, but I heard he was crooked as a snake."

"Yeah, that's a long story best told over a beer— shit, I'm sorry."

"No worries. I want people to forget around me." He waved off the detective's blunder. "Anyway, what went down with Prescott—I heard the FBI got involved."

"In a big way. They believe he was funneling money to a homeland terrorist group run by a real nasty guy. One of the agents left a photo of him. You've seen it, right?"

"No, I was in rehab when all of that went down," Sean reminded him.

Shane ducked into an office and waved them in. "The picture is in my stack. Give me just a second." He tackled a stack that bore a resemblance to the Leaning Tower of Pisa and finally produced the eight-by-ten glossy he sought. "If you see this guy, we're to call the FBI right away. The agent said if he's in the area, something bad is going down."

He handed the photo to Sean, who took it, looked down . . . and went white. "Jesse Rose," he whispered. "Jesus fucking Christ."

Shane rounded his desk, expression excited. "You know him?"

"I did. A long time ago." His knees buckled and he sat hard in one of the guest chairs. "I might have seen him in town, twice. In fact, I think he could be the one who's been harassing me."

"Shit. I think you need to start at the beginning. And Kayne needs to be in here for this, too. Hang on."

Shane disappeared and Eve took a seat beside Sean. His pallor was awful and he looked like he'd seen a man literally rise from the dead. In a way, she guessed he had. She put her arm around him, glad when he leaned into her, soaking up the strength she tried to lend him. He didn't speak or take his eyes off the photo until the two detectives rushed into the room, followed by two more men. Eve recognized one as the police chief; the other she didn't know.

"Given that this man is a serious threat to homeland security and is wanted by the FBI, I've also brought Chief Browning and Captain Craig with me," Shane said. The two shook hands with Sean and said a polite hello to Eve before Shane went on. "We need for you to start with how you know Rose and go from there. Leave nothing out."

The men settled around the now crowded office and listened with rapt attention as Sean began.

"Jesse and I were best friends in high school. We went into the marines together."

For the next twenty minutes or more, everyone listened to the sad tale of two young men who were inseparable, fought side by side. How eventually it became slowly, painfully obvious that one was a bad seed. Sean's discovery of Jesse's illegal activities and his agony knowing he must turn in his best friend.

How it all came to a head and met with a bloody end during Desert Storm.

This last was the part Sean hadn't told Eve the other day, and she listened intently.

"You turned down Rose when he asked you to be his right-hand man."

"Yes."

Kayne leaned forward. "Then what happened?"

"I agonized over the decision for a few days, but after Connors confronted Jesse, I knew I couldn't put off speaking with our captain any longer. I went to see him, but he was busy. I left a message saying I needed to meet with him and that it was urgent. In the long run, that's part of what saved my ass from being dishonorably discharged or worse."

"Then what?"

"We were engaged by the enemy and a nasty firefight ensued, and my chance to get Jesse taken into custody without further incident was lost, though I didn't know that at the time."

"Let me interrupt with a question," the chief said.

"Did Rose know you were going to turn him in that day?"

"No. In fact, he was confident I wouldn't, that I would even change my mind about joining him. His faith in me was the one unshakable absolute in his life at that time. That's the part that hurt most—his actions were those of a traitor, but he truly loved me like a brother, as I did him." Sean's face was miserable with the memory.

The chief was brisk, but not without sympathy. "I can imagine how that must've affected you. Go on."

"Anyway, there was a soldier, Connors, who'd overheard me arguing with Jesse over all the illegal stuff he was involved with. Connors knew I wanted no part of it, but he also knew how conflicted I would be about turning on Jesse. Connors confronted Jesse and said he was going to report him. Like me, he didn't get the chance before we were engaged in the fight. I saw Jesse circling around on Connors, getting a good bead on him. I knew then that he planned to take Connors out. Hell, it was war. Who would know, except me? Like I said, Jesse never thought I'd turn on him."

Sean's voice was low, the recollection still painful. Kayne urged him to take his time.

"Jesse brought up his gun to shoot Connors . . . and I shot Jesse. In the chest. Just took him down like a dog." He cleared his throat. "As long as I live, I'll never forget the look on his face. Stunned, betrayed. Grief-stricken."

No one spoke, letting him finish at his own pace.

"I had to tell the truth, and plenty of the other soldiers backed me up. They placed him in custody in the military hospital while he fought for his life. When he was finally well enough for me to see him, I went under escort. Guess they didn't trust me. Or him." He paused.

"I needed to talk to him about everything we'd been through, explain that I had no choice but to act when I saw him draw down on Connors, and he wasn't having it. The last thing he said to me was that no man stands against Jesse Rose, and if it took the rest of his life, I'd learn that lesson well."

"You're on the hit list of one of the FBI's most wanted terrorists," Kayne muttered. "Fucking fantastic. That sure shines a big-assed spotlight on recent events in our fair city. Any other revelations you'd like to disclose?"

"Maybe. I don't know if this is related, but look at these." He thrust the sheaf of e-mails at Kayne. The detective read a couple, brows rising to his hairline. After giving Sean an inscrutable look, he passed a couple to Shane and the chief.

Eve winced inwardly, thinking how much it must hurt to have his dirty laundry aired in a roomful of cops.

Shane spoke first. "Blair Tanner. Your deceased wife?" At Sean's terse nod, he continued. "She was having an affair, it seems. I'm sorry to hear about this, but what does it have to do with Rose or whoever is harassing you?"

"With any luck, nothing. But this man, G. Sparks, was having an affair with my wife right up until she was killed. Then the e-mails stopped. Nothing, not even an inquiry as to where she'd suddenly gone. But Blair had other e-mails on her computer, from friends and coworkers before they heard she was dead."

"Okay, I see where you're going with that. Strange, but?"

"Eve's mother, Amelia Marshall, has a new neighbor just outside of town. His name is George Sparks. She went to visit him the other day and he made her really nervous. Said there are trucks rumbling up and down her road at all hours, yet his place is dead. No animals, no other people in sight. But there should be people around with all that activity, right?"

"I'd think so," Kayne said. "But even if this George Sparks is the same as the man in the e-mails, that just tells us he decided to purchase a new place and move in."

"There's also the fact that he had one framed photograph in sight, of him and some buddies in the military. And with the other shit that's been going on, I think Mr. Sparks warrants a look. What if he's someone who works for Jesse?"

"Won't hurt to check out Sparks," the chief said. He addressed Eve. "Do you think your mother would be willing to come in, give a description of George Sparks, and take a look at the photo?"

"I'm sure she won't mind. I'll call her now." Eve rose and stepped into the hallway, not the least bit happy to involve her mother in this. Still, she might have important answers. She fished her cell phone from her purse and made the call.

"Hey, my sweet girl! What's up?"

"Mama, remember what you told me and Sean about George Sparks, your new neighbor?"

"How could I forget?" she said, her distaste evident. "Why do you ask?"

"The police are interested in Mr. Sparks and they have some questions. Since you've met him, they'd like for you to come down and give a description."

"Oh, boy. They think he's done something criminal?

I wouldn't be surprised. Listen, I'm leaving the gym and I'll come straight over there, if they want."

"That would be great, Mama. Thanks."

"Why are *you* there?"

"I'll explain later."

"You'd better."

"Promise. See you soon." Returning to Shane's office, she said, "She'll be here shortly."

Sean and the detectives spent the next few minutes filling in the chief and captain on Sean's harassment. The officers had to admit that the entire story made for some very damning and frightening conclusions. The mood in the room was tense, on edge.

Her mother was shown in about twenty minutes later. Eve jumped up and gave her a hug, clinging briefly before relinquishing her to the officers.

"I understand you gentlemen want a description of George Sparks for some reason? I'd like to get this over with so I can get home and watch *Ellen*."

"Yes, ma'am. If you don't mind," Kayne said. "This shouldn't take long."

"Okay, well, he's sort of tall, a little over six feet. Lean. Long blond hair that he wore pulled into a ponytail. The deadest eyes I've ever seen, too."

Sean's fingers tightened on the arm of his chair.

"Any distinguishing marks on Mr. Sparks that you can remember?"

"Oh, yes. I thought it very odd that a man would want to sport a tattoo of a rose, but to each his own."

"Oh, God." Sean looked like he was about to throw up.

"Where is the tattoo located, Ms. Marshall?" Kayne asked calmly.

"On his neck, here." She pointed to the spot.

Shane handed her the photo. "Can you name this man?"

She studied the photo for a moment and then looked back at Shane. "Of course. That's George Sparks."

Silence followed this announcement. The detectives and their bosses shared some looks that went beyond concern to fear.

Eve felt that same fear wash over her and become terror. That monster had been alone with her mother.

Amelia glanced between them all, confused. "Why? What does that mean?"

The chief recovered first. "It means," he said, "that you're going to miss *Ellen*."

Sean sat drowning in emotions as someone called the FBI, an agent named Westfall, he thought. His head was too busy ringing, his brain screaming in protest at having his worst suspicions confirmed.

He's come back for me. Whatever his plans for this town, he means to see me dead.

Not happening. And he wasn't going to live in fear of what Jesse might do.

"He wanted me to know he was coming, and when he arrived, that he was here," he said to nobody in particular. "He knew we'd learn the truth. He's flaunting it in our faces."

"I agree," Shane said. "But we're going to call in the big guns and let them handle Rose. They'll do surveillance or whatever they need to do, and Ms. Marshall is going to decide to go visit relatives. Immediately."

"That's a good idea," Eve said, expression scared. "I don't want Mama anywhere near Sugarland with that man here, now that she's met him."

"I can take care of myself," Amelia protested.

"You can under normal circumstances." The chief shook his head. "But this man is extremely dangerous—FBI's most wanted. Despite his scrape in the military, from what I gathered from the Feds when they were here before, they've never been able to prove his activities on the major charges. The FBI had a man inside their organization, and he turned up dead a few months ago. No one can get close to them without getting killed."

"Mama, why don't you go visit Aunt Felicia in California for a while? She's been after you to visit and it's nearly Thanksgiving. You know she'd love that."

"But what about you? I don't want to leave you alone for the holiday."

Eve gave a tremulous smile. "I won't be alone, and besides, we have to work that day. I'll feel better knowing you're off that monster's radar."

Sean was saddened. There was a time when Jesse wasn't a monster—just a gremlin in training. He'd been a good friend, once.

Why did you go down that path? Why?

Why does anyone?

Amelia relented. "All right, I'll go. But I wish you'd come with me, baby."

"I'll be fine. I need to stay here."

"You should go with your mother," he heard himself say. "It'll be safer and—"

"Forget it," Eve replied flatly. "I'm not leaving you."

That made him feel pretty damned good, and scared him at the same time. He'd have to be on his guard with Jesse around. Still, he reminded himself, the man had waited all these years to make a move. The FBI would probably have him in custody before he could step up his campaign to drive Sean crazy.

That prompted a question. "Besides me, why is Jesse here? Don't tell me you don't know, because the FBI wouldn't be on your friggin' speed dial if you didn't."

The chief pinned him with a stern gaze. "Let's just say that if his reason for being here got out, there would be panic."

"Christ, what's he planning?" he asked quietly.

"To blow up something big that would turn this entire region of Tennessee into a wasteland . . . Chernobyl-style. And he's rumored to have the resources and the contacts to pull it off, thanks in part to the dearly departed Forrest Prescott. You follow?"

Sean was speechless. This was far beyond any horror he'd thought Jesse capable of perpetrating.

Shane broke in with more questions. "Since you and Rose were once so close, how come he and Blair never met? Assuming she was innocent of working with Rose at the time of her death, why wouldn't she have recognized him?"

"Blair and I met toward the end of my time in the marines," Sean said. "I found out she was pregnant with our son, married her, and then was immediately sent to Kuwait along with Jesse. We were stationed there for over a year, serving in Desert Shield and Desert Storm after that. Blair never had a chance to meet Jesse before my falling-out with him." Obviously that had changed at some point in recent years when Jesse posed as Sparks.

"Rose didn't come to your wedding?"

"No. He claimed he couldn't make it, but by then things were tense between us. I'm pretty sure now that he spent all his leave time involved in his illegal dealings."

"Makes sense," the chief commented.

"The FBI will be here in about three hours," Kayne interrupted, hanging up. "My suggestion is to take Ms. Marshall home, help her pack, maybe get a bite to eat. Then come back here so Sean can tell his story to them, and she can identify Jesse, aka George Sparks. After which Ms. Marshall is on the first plane out of here to enjoy Thanksgiving in California. Everybody got that?"

A round of agreements followed and everyone rose to leave. Sean thanked the officers and escorted Eve and her mother to his SUV. He cut off the older woman's protests when she insisted on driving home.

"Leave your car here. It'll be better if it looks like you're not home, in this case. That way Jesse won't be tempted to drop by and make trouble."

She relented, but didn't like it.

At Amelia's house, Eve helped her mother pack everything that was necessary for an extended stay, and called her aunt. Amelia then called her boss. On his own phone, Sean booked her flight. When she was packed, she suffered a few anxieties about small things like bills, her plants, and the newspapers. It took both him and Eve to fend off her arguments until she didn't have a single one left.

They drove back to the police station just over three hours later, and the Feds were waiting for them. One was a big, dark, dangerous-looking agent named Nick Westfall, the other his redheaded, freckled partner, Jack Coleman.

Amelia kept her cool, though Sean realized she was frightened. She positively identified Jesse as being the man who'd called himself George Sparks, and they thanked her, appearing very excited about this break in the case.

Sean went next, going through the whole saga again. Amazing how the more he related it, the more numb he became. Had to be shock or something. He would've been content to go his whole life without ever being involved in a homeland-terror case. Especially when he knew the man responsible.

God, he hoped the papers never got wind of this.

He shook hands with the agents.

"Don't leave town," Agent Westfall said. "We might need you again."

"I'm not going anywhere, Agent. I want to see the end of this as much as you do. Trust me on that."

"I believe you do," he said. "Here's my card. Call if Rose shows up, if you think of anything, or have any more trouble out of him."

"I will. Thanks."

After sticking the card in his wallet, he and Eve drove Amelia to Nashville Airport. The women hugged fiercely outside the security checkpoint, like they'd never see each other again. Both were teary-eyed and he figured the stress of parting so abruptly, and the reason why, was getting to them. Things would be better after Amelia was safe.

"Thanks for taking care of my mother," Eve said once they were on their way again. "Mama means the world to me, and if anything happened to her, I'd be lost."

"I understand the feeling. It was the same for me when I lost both my parents." He squeezed her hand. "There's no way I'd allow Jesse anywhere near her. I just wish you'd gone, too."

"Really?" She arched a brow.

"Okay, the selfish part of me is glad you're here. But it worries me, baby. If Jesse so much as looks at you cross-eyed, I'm putting you on the first plane."

"You can try."

"Stubborn woman."

"Yep. And you're a stubborn man."

"This could make for some sizzling arguments in years to come."

She beamed at that. "You still want to argue with me years from now?"

"Why not? Making up is fun." He knew what she was getting at—the "years" part. "And yes, for decades."

She snuggled into his side and he put his arm around her, held her close. Being with her was about as perfect it got. He couldn't wait to see what the future held in store for them.

As soon as he figured out a way to rid his life of Jesse for good.

13

"Connors! Jesse, no!" Sean screamed. But the man either didn't hear or didn't care.

He was going to shoot Connors in cold blood. One of their own.

Jesse raised his rifle as a startled Connors jerked his head in Jesse's direction.

Sean raised his a split second after . . . and got his shot off first.

His armor-piercing bullet ripped through Jesse's flak jacket with a sickening punch, sending the man backward. Darkness bloomed on his chest, his expression shocked as he fell.

Jesse hit the ground on his back and Sean lowered his rifle. Could only stand there, numb, as the fight raged around him. Could only watch his best friend bleed onto the desert sand. Eyes accusing.

"Oh, God. What have I done?"

"Saved my life, man!" Connors yelled. "Now get your ass down before we end up the same."

But he couldn't take cover and leave Jesse to bleed out. He had to believe the man had some good in him, still held on to some thread of the boy he'd known.

Crawling over to his friend, he hooked his arms under the

man's middle, and began to drag him to a waiting medic unit.

"Heard Chief Mitchell is retiring at the end of the year."

"No shit? Damn, I hate to see the old fart go."

"Yeah. Can't say I blame him, though."

Eve plucked a paper towel from the dispenser and began to dry her hands. Wasn't like she was trying to eavesdrop on the two C-shift firefighters who were going off duty, but their deep voices carried from the hallway outside the women's restroom.

"Gonna be interesting to see who falls in line for the promotions."

"Heard through the grapevine that Tanner is up for battalion chief. That would rock."

Eve smiled, dried her hands more slowly.

"Yeah, he deserves it. I mean, if he can just keep his dick in his pants."

Her smile faded as she tossed the paper towel into the garbage.

"Word, man. Hasn't he had enough bullshit without banging one of his own team?"

"Fuck, it ain't his fault. I'd jump, too, if she wiggled that tight little mocha ass at me."

"Guess you're right. Still, I never figured Marshall for a slut. What kind of bitch puts her captain's career on the block?"

No fucking way.

Eve's temper exploded like gasoline and a blowtorch. Heedless of anything except her targets, she stormed to the door and yanked it open, taking in two very shocked male faces. Wyatt and Green. Catching them off guard with their figurative pants down made her inner bitch chortle with glee.

"First of all, my tight little mocha ass wouldn't want your limp, shriveled excuse for an appendage if you dipped it in gold!" Wyatt blanched, stammering a response that wouldn't quite emerge. A couple more firefighters paused in the hallway, observing from a safe distance. Ignoring the gawkers, she went for the kill. "Second, this slutty bitch would *never* do anything to put the captain's career in jeopardy, and you need to give him some credit for being man enough to handle his personal life. And it *is* just that—personal."

"I—I—that is, we—"

"Furthermore, I'm well aware of the department policy regarding relationships within the same station. Do you honestly think I enjoy being the subject of ridicule? Nobody *plans* to fall in love. It just happens." Shit, that wasn't what she meant to say—and she had no idea whether Sean's feelings ran as deep. Swallowing the blunder, she went on.

"I didn't plan to make our work environment uncomfortable for anyone, and I'm well aware I'm facing a transfer. Until then, I'd appreciate some understanding, and for our 'family' here to practice the same discretion I'm trying to use."

"I . . . goddamn, I'm sorry, Marshall," Wyatt muttered. "Was just talkin' out my ass, ya know? Guy shit."

Green nodded emphatically. "Same here. We're not spreading anything outside the station, I swear. It's just that we've got eyes, that's all. Discreet as y'all are tryin' to be, a guy would have to be a moron to miss what's going on when you look at each other."

"We just don't want anyone to get hurt if you two

are distracted. And I apologize for disrespecting you," Wyatt finished sheepishly.

"Me, too."

"Fine. Apology accepted." She thought about apologizing for saying Wyatt's dick was shriveled, but decided to let it go. As far as she was concerned, they were even. "You two have a problem with me from now on, say it to my face. Believe me, I'd have no qualms about stating mine to yours."

"You got it," Wyatt said, and Green chimed an agreement.

She left them standing there with their mouths hanging open and walked away as normally as possible. Wouldn't do to appear desperate to find a corner to slink into and hide. In short, good acting was required.

Rounding the corner to cross through the kitchen, she ran right into her team, who were, to a man, staring at her wide-eyed, expressions varying from amused to worried. Sean leaned against the counter near the coffeepot, red flags on his cheeks, an emotion she couldn't pinpoint in his gaze.

"Great," she said sharply. "Since the gang's all here, why don't we just hunt this issue down and shoot it, hmm?"

"This isn't our business, Eve," Zack said. "Besides, you know we support you two one hundred percent, as long as you're happy." A round of agreements met his words.

"I appreciate the sentiment, and I love you guys for it. But as much as I hate being gossiped about like I'm the Whore of Babylon, Wyatt and Green have a valid point." She held her hand up, cutting short the angry outbursts fueled by the C-shift firefighters' disrespect.

"If any of us screw up on the job, whether or not it's related to me and Sean being involved, we're opening our team to scrutiny, nasty rumors, and even lawsuits. Especially now that our relationship is out in the open and we can't deny it."

This sobered their friends and they fell silent, thinking.

She sighed. "I think the best solution is for me to transfer before the brass comes to me and slaps my wrist."

"I disagree," Julian said. "We all know Sean is on the promotions list. I say wait—why lose two good firefighters from our team when we might only have to lose one? Besides, even if the brass knows about you two, if they're truly planning to move Sean up, they won't say anything, because they'll know he's going to leave anyway."

This met with approval from the gang, and Eve smiled despite the crappy start to their shift. "Have I told you all lately how much you mean to me?"

"Oh, God!" Clay cried in mock distress. "Tissue alert at twelve o' clock! Let's go, boys, before she has us all PMS-ing."

They scattered, laughing, all except for Sean, who hadn't moved. He watched them go, a content expression on his handsome face.

"Idiots," he said fondly. "If I do get the promotion, I'm going to miss the hell out of this. The camaraderie, the sense of family. They're the brothers I never had."

"You'll visit." She was pretty sure he'd get the promotion. A lump formed in her throat.

"It won't ever be quite the same, though." He pushed

from the counter. "Hey, no long faces, right? Nothing is ever a done deal."

"Any of us would kill to be on that list. Don't you want it?"

"Sure I do! I need a new challenge. If I don't get the position and one of us has to leave, I'll probably retire."

"What?" Her mouth fell open. "You're too young to retire! What would you do?"

He shrugged. "Open a business, or invest. Raise horses. Who knows? Doesn't matter, because the most important thing is standing right in front of me."

Her heart fluttered, and she let out a big sigh that she kept to herself. "That's sweet, but you'd lose your retirement money. Your nest egg."

His lips curved into a rueful smile that held a hint of melancholy. "No, that would be the money I inherited from my parents and Blair. As long as I'm smart about managing it, I'm pretty much set."

"Oh."

Jeez, how much money did he have? She'd love him even if he didn't have a cent, but the man was a continual surprise. With that fabulous house and land, she'd known he couldn't be destitute, but that didn't necessarily mean a supply of ready cash. Her tongue burned with the need to ask how rich he was, but she refrained. With great difficulty.

She was only human, for cryin' out loud.

On the heels of that thought, she was ashamed. Whatever his wealth, it was gained due to great personal loss. She vowed not to broach the subject unless he found it necessary for her to know.

"I've got some things to do in my office," he said. "Do an inventory of the medical supplies on the ambulance, if you don't mind."

It really wasn't a question, but an order. Ever the alpha.

"Got it."

As she attended to the task, her mind drifted from challenges within the station to those without. Somehow, she'd have to find the courage to address one other issue that might not make him very happy. But they were a couple now, or so she believed, and they'd work through it. Together.

After a load of heartache and fear, the worst had to be behind them.

Eve straightened the living room, checked the chicken parmigiana in the oven, tossed the salad. Paced. She hadn't seen Sean since they'd gotten off shift this morning, as they'd both had stuff to do.

They weren't in each other's pockets. Still had their own separate lives.

Yeah, that might change. Real soon.

A knock made her jump, and she looked before opening the door. And finding herself swept into a pair of muscular arms.

"Damn, what smells so good?"

"Chicken parmigiana."

"Mmm, no, I think it's you." He kissed her soundly, then made a show of nuzzling her neck until she squirmed, laughing.

"Stop! It's definitely the food, not me. Want some tea or soda?"

"If I can't have you, then I suppose so." His eyes twinkled with humor. "Soda, please."

"And me later."

His proximity did nothing to quell her nerves. She had no idea how to broach such a momentous topic, and nothing seemed quite right. Before dinner? During? How did a woman blurt out something that would alter a man's life?

She fetched a can of Coke for him, pouring it over ice. Handed it to him and busied herself removing dinner from the oven and setting it on top of the stove.

"Here, let me get that." Using the pot holders, he took the dish from her and put it on the table, which was already set.

Fetching the salad from the fridge and grabbing the bowl of spaghetti, she joined him and put the rest of the food on the table. She had to admit it smelled good. Too bad she was much too wigged-out to enjoy it.

"Eve? You're awfully quiet."

"Oh, just a lot on my mind. What did you do today?" she asked as they took their seats. Nothing like a diversion while she gathered her wits.

"Worked with Elvis and the girls for a while, then started on a landscaping project out front of the house. I'm making a planter around the big tree on the left side of the driveway."

"That's cool. I could help if you want." She dished up his plate, keeping her hands busy.

"I'd like that. It's fun working with plants, flowers, bricks, and wood, making the outdoors attractive. I'd forgotten how much I enjoy it."

"I'm not surprised. You've always been an outdoorsy type as long as I've known you."

They ate in silence for a few minutes, or at least she'd thought she was eating, until he laid a hand over hers.

"That chicken is dead, baby. Are you going to eat it or keep mutilating it?"

"Oh." Crap. She'd picked her meal apart, hardly touching a bite. With a sigh, she put down her fork.

"What's wrong? You always make me talk, so out with it," he said gently.

His tone was encouraging and she took a deep breath. "I have a doctor's appointment tomorrow."

"What's wrong? You look fine." His brows drew together in concern.

"With my ob-gyn."

Concern slowly became understanding, and denial. "I don't . . . you mean . . . you're on the pill."

"One of the condoms broke," she reminded him. "And the pill isn't always one hundred percent effective."

"You said it would be safe. You . . ." Color slowly drained from his face. "I'm sure it will be negative. Nothing to worry about."

Her heart plummeted. "So you want it to be negative?"

"We took precautions! This isn't supposed to happen." He pushed his chair back, running a hand through his hair.

"Tell that to the little pink line on the stick."

"What? What!" Shoving out of his chair, he prowled the room, looking very much like a man awaiting execution. "How could you let this happen?" His voice rose, sounding more upset by the second.

"Hey, this wasn't all me. It was your cock fucking me, wasn't it?"

He didn't even appear to have heard her. "God, I can't do this."

"You don't have to *do* anything if you don't want. He or she would be my baby." Tears pricked her eyes, burning. She would not let them fall.

"How could you do this to me?" he whispered, voice breaking. "I had two beautiful children and I lost them. I watched them burn. It was my fault. Mine."

"No, it wasn't! Sean, we can start a family together—"

His face morphed into a mask of fury. Agony. "You think I can just *replace* them?" He was shouting now. Losing it completely. "Like a broken glass or a lost puppy? My babies died, but it's okay because I can make more? *I wanted to die with them!*"

She stood and took a step toward him, legs shaking, reaching out to him. "But you didn't." Her voice broke on a sob. "Sean, please—"

"No child will ever take their place! I didn't deserve them. I can't . . . can't . . ."

Clutching his chest, he swayed on his feet.

Then he lunged for the table, grabbed his keys, and bolted. She screamed his name as she ran after him, but he didn't stop, kept running. Jumped in his Tahoe. Squealed from the parking lot at a dangerous speed, barely missed a car turning into the complex.

She stared into the waning afternoon, numb. Heartbroken. Happiness had become a nightmare so fast her head spun. All the shouts he'd hurled replayed over and over. But the one she recalled the most was the one that eventually dried her tears.

I didn't deserve them.

Guilt.

The more she recalled how he'd said the words, the more she heard the grief and reproach in them. Deep down, he felt guilty for moving on. He hadn't dealt with the last of his grief, and until he did, they had no future.

His meltdown, she realized, had very little to do

with her at all. Their relationship and possible pregnancy had been merely what brought his emotions to a head.

How long since he'd gone? About twenty minutes. She had to talk to him, make certain he was all right. A few calls to his cell phone and his house yielded no results. She left messages anyway, asking him to please call. Let her know he was all right.

She put their abandoned dinner away, scouring her brain. Where would he go?

She tried the station, but no one had seen him. Called Six-Pack and the other guys, though the lieutenant was the only one she told what was going on. Same deal—no one had seen or heard from him. Then Six-Pack called back, and gave her an idea, bless him.

"Eve? It's me. Hate to say this, but try the cemetery."

The blood drained from her face. "Howard, you don't think he would try to hurt himself, do you? God, I'm losing my mind."

"No, I don't think so, but—shit, I'm picking you up and we'll go together. I don't want you going out there by yourself. Be there in fifteen."

Before she could argue, he hung up. Truthfully, she was grateful for his coming to the rescue, especially when she didn't know what she'd find. She didn't think Sean would harm himself, either, but the cemetery was isolated, and with this Rose guy on the loose, going out there alone would be stupid.

Waiting for Six-Pack was the longest fifteen minutes of her life.

Please, let him be all right.

Sean tore out of the parking lot, down the street, dodging other cars. Ignoring honks. All he knew was he had to escape the agony searing his chest. Constricting his lungs. He drove endlessly, for how long he didn't know.

He'd had children. They were gone.

He needed to be where his babies were.

Before he realized where he was going, he pulled through the old iron gate. Drove the Tahoe over the rutted drive, down the grassy path worn with tire tracks. Past a sea of headstones. Loved ones. Waiting for someone to visit, to care.

Or maybe the living just needed to believe there was something left of their spirit.

At the end of one lane, he threw the truck into park and stumbled out. Wove through more stones, careful not to step on the graves. Bad luck to do that. God knew he didn't need more.

At the end of the row, three neat granite stones rose from the trim lawn. Together, yet alone. Forlorn. Staggering to a stop, he stared at the words.

BELOVED WIFE.

BELOVED SON.

BELOVED DAUGHTER.

"Daddy, look at my collage! It's for you. Do you like flowers?"

"Come on, Dad, math sucks. I'll do better next time. Can't you loosen up?"

"Daddy, where do babies come from?"

"Hey, Dad! I'm the starting quarterback tomorrow night! Woo! Can you come?"

Gone forever. *Forever.*

"No," he moaned. "No."

A huge hot bubble expanded in his chest. Stretched his skin, expanding, tearing him apart. He'd stopped this feeling, numbed it with alcohol, many times before. But now there was no buffer for the grief consuming him. Swallowing him whole.

A sob escaped, and he sank to his knees in the grass. Doubled over clutching his chest. Tried, so hard, to keep the devastation locked away. As he always had.

"No," he rasped. "No, no, no . . ."

Another sob ripped from his throat, and another. From the depths of his soul, turning him inside out. The pain was not to be believed. He couldn't survive the onslaught. Didn't want to.

The sobs were deep and harsh. He'd never cried like this before. The force of it shattered him, left him naked and defenseless. Pouring out his broken heart to God and whoever else would listen.

"Please, no. Don't let it be true. It's not true."

But it was. He rocked, arms around his middle, tears dripping off his chin.

"Please, Bobby. I'm sorry. Mia. Baby, Daddy's so sorry. Oh, God."

Then a pair of slender arms wrapped around him. Someone there, kneeling with him, holding him tight.

"Sean, sweetheart. They know it wasn't your fault, I swear."

He knew her voice, her scent. Eve.

And he collapsed against her, clinging to his lifeline in the storm. His anchor. Her soothing words began to calm him, reach his stricken soul.

"It's all right. They know, honey. Shh, I'm here. Howard, too. We're here for you, always."

She repeated them again and again, until his cries faded to hitching breaths. Until there was nothing but the two of them. The birds, the grass, the soft evening sounds in the waning light.

"They're not here," he whispered.

"I know. They're in your heart, and that's where they'll always be." She sniffed, holding him tighter.

Wetness soaked his neck, the collar of his shirt. She'd been crying, too, he realized. With him. Sharing his grief.

And he knew in that moment, for a complete certainty, that he loved her.

A few minutes ago, he could have sworn that white-hot ball of agony had blown a hole in his chest. Now, slowly, a golden glow, an incredible sense of peace, filled the hollow space. Time lost all meaning as they remained wrapped around each other. The glow encompassing them both in a tangible bond.

Finally, he pulled back enough to wipe his face, look into her eyes. "I'm so very sorry for the awful things I said to you. Can you forgive me?"

She gave him a watery smile, blue eyes shining. "I love you. There was never a question of forgiveness."

He ran a finger down one beautiful cheek. "I love you, too. I have for a long time, and I just didn't know it."

"Oh, Sean."

"What's more, I'd be honored to be the father of our child, should that be the case."

"You don't have to say that if you're not ready."

"No, I am. I said before my family would've wanted me to be happy, but now it's different. This time I *know* it."

"I'm so glad for you. Us."

"Don't get me wrong. I will always miss my children, and missing them will hurt. But I can live my life now." He placed a gentle kiss on her lips. "I want to live it with you."

"I—I want that, too." She hugged him again, fiercely. "Why don't we go? I think Howard is about to wear a rut in the trail over there, worrying about you."

"Sounds good."

Pushing to his feet, he gave her a hand up and paused, his gaze roaming over the three headstones once more. He loved them all and always would, but he had to let go. Had to live. "Good-bye," he said quietly.

Taking Eve's hand, he led her from the lonely site. To where his best friend stood watching them approach, anxiety etched on his face. Sean walked up to him. Hesitated.

Then found himself wrapped in a tight bear hug, big fists gripping the shirt at his back.

"Scared the fuck out of me." For Howard, that was strong language.

"Didn't mean to. I'm sorry."

"That was a long time coming, my friend."

"Yes. And I'm okay now, really."

His best friend pulled back and studied him, apparently judging for himself. "I think you might be right."

"I am. I'm the luckiest man to have a second chance, and to have a friend like you."

The big man released him and smiled. "I'm lucky, too. So, before we get too mushy, I'm going to head out, since it seems you're in good hands."

"Thanks, Howard. For picking up Eve, and coming for me."

"Anytime."

His friend gave Eve a quick hug, and started for his truck. Sean watched him leave, and then he and Eve made their way to his Tahoe at the end of the lane. Suddenly, he was exhausted.

"Stay with me tonight? Then we'll go to your appointment tomorrow, together. Whatever the news, we'll face it as a couple."

"I'd like that."

He took her by her apartment, where she packed a small bag, and then they were on their way to his place. As he pulled down the long driveway, he made a decision.

They would hunt for a place of their own. A haven to put their stamp on, together.

In his bedroom they stripped to the skin and slid into bed, spooning with her back to his front the way he loved. Reaching back, she stroked his hair. Soothing, comforting.

Loving.

He drifted into sleep, letting love surround him.

And work its healing magic.

14

"Son, do you realize the import of what's happened?"

Sean swallowed hard, staring at the colonel. "Yes, sir."

"If your story about Rose and his activities is proven true, you've helped weed out a traitor. You're already being hailed as a hero for saving Connors' life when Rose drew on him. Several of the men witnessed the incident."

Incident. Such a nice, pleasant word for an event that had just changed life as he knew it.

"I don't feel like a hero, sir. I feel sick."

"That's to be expected," he said, not without sympathy. "But it's done, and you did the right thing by coming to me. Turning in a comrade is never easy, especially when you're as close as brothers. If the other men had done the same the moment they heard the rumors, this might not have happened."

True, but that applied to Sean as well. He still felt guilty.

The colonel considered him for a long moment. "You've learned a valuable lesson in what happens when our humanity must make war with our duty. This will make you a better soldier."

"Yes, sir."

"Carry on, Sergeant."

He left, unsure how he'd finish this tour of duty. He'd much rather save lives than take them.

But when he did finish, in a few months, he was out of the military for good.

Eve glanced at Sean's profile as he drove them to her doctor's appointment. He looked a little tired, but he seemed okay. She hoped so, because she never again wanted to see him like he was yesterday—on his knees, the picture of total devastation. His sobs had ripped her in two, and she'd been terrified he wasn't going to come back from the edge.

Thank God he had, but the much-needed emotional catharsis had left him drained.

"Here we are."

Giving her hand a reassuring squeeze, he walked her into the one-story office building and down a hallway to a glass door marked with the name of her ob-gyn. After she signed in, she and Sean sat in the waiting area for about twenty minutes, making small talk about everything under the sun, mostly to ease anxiety.

"Eve? Come on back."

She followed the perky nurse to an alcove where another nurse weighed her and took her blood pressure. Then she was handed a cup.

"Write your name on it and leave us a urine sample in the little window." The girl beamed at her like this was the most fun thing in the world.

"I know the drill, thanks." But never for a pregnancy test. Brand-new, frightening territory.

She did the deed, which always required a certain amount of acrobatics, and left the sample. After washing her hands, she emerged from the restroom and was directed to sit in a chair near the alcove where a couple of nurses were bent over the sample, perhaps anticipating telling her joyous news.

Her breakfast threatened to rebel.

The nurse who'd brought her back there stopped and addressed her, still smiling. "The test will only take a minute. They're pretty fast these days. If it's positive, the doctor will see you to discuss basic health and scheduling your checkups."

"Okay."

When the nurses turned to her and approached wearing pleasant but neutral expressions, she wasn't sure what to think.

"Miss Marshall? The test came back negative."

"I—oh. Wow. I wasn't sure—I mean the home test was positive and those things are usually accurate." She stared at the nurses, feeling strangely bereft.

"That happens sometimes," she said, voice sympathetic. "I saw your gorgeous man out there, being so sweet to you. Are you two trying for a baby?"

"No, the positive test took us by surprise." Boy, there was the understatement of the century. She rose to leave. "But I'd kind of gotten used to the idea."

The nurse gave her a quick hug. "Don't worry. There will be another time."

"Thanks."

One showed her the way out even though she didn't need directions, and she checked out, retrieving the billing slip without really being aware of what the lady said. Something about insurance, like she cared at the moment.

Sean rose when she walked into the waiting room,

his eyes anxious. But full of love. When she shook her head, he opened his arms and she walked straight into them, burrowing close.

"You're disappointed," he said into her hair, kissing her.

"Yeah, I am. But I didn't know I would be until about two minutes ago."

"We'll try again."

"One day. I know we weren't ready, but still."

"I know, baby." Pulling back, he tipped her chin up. "Why don't I treat us to dinner and a movie? Let's enjoy our day together and forget all our troubles for a while."

"Sounds like the perfect plan."

"Grimes is set. He's practically makin' love to that reactor—he's so close." Hammer smiled, showing off a perfect set of white teeth. "I still can't believe you got him a Red-Level badge clearance. How'd ya do it, boss?"

Jesse straightened from his bent position, loading supplies in a stolen van. "Did you really just ask me that question? Guess you *are* as dumb as you look."

Hammer was unperturbed, and chuckled. "Friends in the right places, ones who are sympathetic to our cause."

"You've got that half right. Not friends," he said coldly. "We've got people we use and people who use us. Never friends."

"Right. Figure of speech, that's all."

He eyed the big man. "You'd sell me out for the right price, wouldn't you?"

"Sure. Price has never been high enough."

Taken aback for a second, Jesse stared. And then laughed. Big bastard had probably been offered plenty to nail Jesse's hide to the wall. "I doubt it ever will be. But if it is? You've only got one shot." He patted the man's cheek, hard. "Make it count."

As the man ambled away, Jesse considered his own advice. That was how enemies were defeated—they failed to make the most of their shot when they had it. They allowed their emotions, other tangled-up shit in their heads, to fuck with their perception.

Failed to make the kill.

And then the prey became the predator, ripped out the enemy's throat.

"I'm coming for you, Tanner. Can you feel me? Real soon, you can join your precious little family in their dirt nap."

Everything was accounted for, the last of the charges loaded and ready to be placed. But they weren't loaded in *this* van. This one would serve as the decoy. Disappear, and reappear at a very different destination.

It would carry Sean to meet his fate.

And then his former best friend would scream in terror as the town he loved came crashing down. With Sean buried underneath.

In a surveillance van a mile away, on a rise, Special Agent Nick Westfall turned in his seat to one of the tech guys. "Get all that?"

"Yep. Think Hammer will come through with the names?"

"Let's fucking hope so, and before he gets his ass killed like our last man."

"God, I don't know how you guys do that undercover shit, especially a gig that lasts years. If I was Hammer, I'd go nuts hanging out with those slimeballs twenty-four-seven."

"Some do. And some eventually buy into their role, become what they hated most." It was why Nick had gotten out of deep undercover work. Too many monsters.

People had absolutely no idea how real they were.

"Better them than me. I just record the shit."

"I'll bet you've seen and heard a lot."

The techie snorted. "Stuff that would turn your hair white. I've got a ringside seat." He shrugged. "But you've seen more than me, and up close."

You have no clue.

He shook himself back to the present, swiped a hand down his face in frustration. "We need to find out where he's going with that last load of C-4. Dammit!"

"Hammer doesn't know?"

"Rose is keeping his side project close to the vest. He's going for Tanner, but we don't know where or how."

"All we can do is keep watching and listening. Hope we get something, or Hammer does. Why don't they just put this Tanner guy into protective custody?"

"Come on, you know better." He gave the techie an arch stare.

"Oh, right. He's the bait. You need Rose to come out and play."

"Exactly. Every criminal has an Achilles' heel, and Tanner is his."

And when Rose showed his face, Nick hoped like hell they got to the bait on time.

A cough shook him, and Sean covered his mouth with his napkin. The irritation in his lungs hadn't gotten much better, and at first he'd blamed it on the smoke inhalation.

"You've been fighting that cough for a while," Eve said, frowning. "Maybe you should go back to the doctor."

"I think I'm getting a chest cold." Another cough shook him, and he shuddered.

She leaned over the table and felt his forehead, his cheeks. "You're really warm. Want to skip the movie?"

"No way. I want to show my girl a good time, and that's what I'm going to do." He smiled at her to cover the fact that he'd been feeling worse by the hour all day. But he wasn't down yet and certainly not out. His baby deserved to be spoiled.

She didn't look convinced. "Okay, but if you feel any worse, I'm taking you home and putting you straight to bed."

"Oh, promise?"

"Pervert."

"You love me that way."

"True."

They finished their dinner, chatting about work and their friends. Balancing their lives together, becoming them. The perfect opening presented itself and he sat back in his chair, regarding her, hope blooming in his chest.

"I was thinking. . . . Remember when I said I might sell my place, buy something else?"

"Sure. That sounds like a great idea. New start and all that." She took a sip of her iced tea.

"I know this is soon, but what would you say if I suggested we look for a new place together? One that's ours?" Her blue eyes widened and her lips parted in surprise. Was that good or bad?

"*Is* that what you're suggesting? You want us to make a home, you and me?"

"That's exactly what I want. I love you," he said quietly, heart pounding. Reaching across the table, he took her hand. "I want a total second chance, with you. Love, marriage, children. The whole deal. What do you say? Or do you need more time to decide?"

"Y-you want to marry me?" she squeaked.

"Smooth how I sort of slid that in there, don't you think?" He chuckled. "You know me, Eve. I'm not a man who wants or needs a lot of fanfare."

"Well, perhaps *I'd* like a little bit of fuss," she said, nearly bouncing in her chair. "At least a small party horn or a sprinkle of confetti."

"Forgive me. I'm an idiot." Smiling, he rose from his chair and walked around to her side of the table. Got down on one knee next to her.

"What are you doing?" With a muffled laugh, she glanced around at the other diners, who were starting to take notice.

He cleared his throat. This was the last time he'd ever do this, so he'd better get it right. Loudly, for all in the vicinity to hear, he said, "Eve, I can be a bastard. I'll probably fight against the bottle all my life. I'm hardheaded, arrogant, and I like to have my way. I like to get dirty, and then leave my muddy boots and clothes all over the floor. I snore. In fact, I don't have much to recommend me at all. Hell, you'd be better off getting a dog."

This earned a few laughs from the delighted diners. Eve was beaming like the center of the sun.

"The only thing going for me is that I love you more than my own life, and that won't ever change. Eve Marshall, will you marry me?"

"Yes, yes!"

threw herself into his outstretched arms and

he caught her, standing and kissing her senseless to a round of applause. So much for taking things slowly.

He pulled back, grinning. "Is that enough confetti for you?"

"Until the wedding, yes. Oh my God, Mama's going to be thrilled! She'll invite half the countryside, her friends at church, and then there's all of the fire department—"

He faked a put-upon groan and she giggled.

God, he was happy. At last.

"Whatever you want, baby, that's what you'll have."

"See, you don't always have to have things your way," she teased. "You're a softer touch than you like for people to know."

He actually felt his face heat. "Nah, I'm a porcupine."

The waiter came by and handed him their bill. After he'd paid, the movie theater was next. Outside, the weather had turned cold and drizzly, the sort of dampness that made his lungs ache. Determined not to complain, he drove them into Nashville for a change of scenery, stretching out the evening.

The movie Eve picked was one of those tragic romances, the snively girl crap he usually avoided like the plague because just being in its vicinity might make his balls blacken and fall off. But Eve sniffed and dabbed all the way to the bitter end, heaving a sigh as the houselights went up.

"That was so sad. They were doomed never to be together."

"What a melodramatic piece of crap," he grumbled. "I prefer happy endings, thank you very much."

"Aww, you softy. Prefer the hero alive at the end, do you?"

"If I was the hero? Not much of a contest."

"You're *my* hero."

"And you're good for my ego, you know that, lady?"

"I try."

Laughing, he hooked his arm through hers and they headed out into the rain. When she jumped with both feet into a puddle and doused their jeans on purpose, he mock-growled, "You are so going to pay for that."

Around the side of the building and through the back parking lot, a game of puddle wars ensued, the two of them getting nice and soaked. Which was going to help his cold immensely, but screw it. He was having fun.

"Isn't that fucking cute? So precious I could hurl."

Snapping his head up, he stopped dead in his tracks. Leaning casually against the side of his Tahoe in the lamplight, legs crossed at the ankles and hands in his pockets, was Jesse.

Pushing Eve behind him, Sean approached slowly, taking in the sight of the man who was once like a brother to him. The years had not been kind to his natural good looks.

Jesse's square face was lined with every one of his years and then some, his blond hair long and stringy. It was pulled into a ponytail, revealing the rose tattoo they'd gotten him in Thailand, in a lifetime he'd rather forget.

"Why a rose, man? They've got all sorts of cool designs. Celtic, dragons, whatever."

"Besides my name? So my enemies will remember that if they touch me, I'll make them bleed."

"Jesse." He was shocked he had a voice, and that it sounded even. Calm.

"Sean." His name came out almost like a taunt. Jesse

pushed his lean body from the SUV, strolled forward, his gait unhurried. "Good to see you, old friend."

"We haven't been friends since the day you tried to murder one of our own men in cold blood." Anger began to take over from shock.

"He was going to rat me out, but you did that for him, didn't you?" His eyes glittered like onyx. "But that's ancient history."

"Why are you here, Jesse?" His muscles tensed, ready for a fight. He hadn't had to engage an opponent hand to hand in almost twenty years. Some lessons, he hoped, were ingrained too deeply to forget.

"You mean, other than to fuck your wife?" he asked pleasantly. "Blair sure was a wildcat in bed, but you know how it is with bored, unsatisfied wives."

"Did she know who you were?" He kept his anger in check, because he had to know for sure whether Blair had full knowledge that George Sparks and Jesse Rose were the same person. Blair had heard him talk about Jesse before and after their marriage, but she'd never met him—that he knew of. After Jesse's court-martial, Sean had told her what happened and they'd never mentioned it again.

"What if she did? Whoo-boy, that would be a real kicker, huh? To know your fancy wife threw in with me? That her knowledge got her killed?"

A sudden surety settled over him, and gave him peace in this, if nothing else. "Blair might've slept with George Sparks, but she would never have knowingly put our children in danger."

"Know about George, do you? Guess you found the e-mails. Knew you would, eventually. That was part of the fun."

"I'll repeat, what do you want?"

"How're those adorable kids, too?" Then he snapped his fingers as though just remembering. "Oh, my bad. I think I read somewhere they were toasted like marshmallows, along with your wife. Damned shame."

Did you ever ask yourself . . . what if it wasn't an accident?

The anger he'd tried so hard to keep in check flared into rage. With an inhuman roar, he charged, barreled into Jesse with all his strength. Dimly, he heard Eve shouting for help, asking someone to send the police. He didn't care. All that mattered was tearing this bastard apart.

Too late, he knew that was just what Jesse intended.

They rolled on the asphalt, each struggling for the upper hand. Sean was losing ground, fast. Emotion clouded judgment, and his nemesis had a definite lack of feelings to get in his way. As a terrorist, he'd no doubt kept his fighting skills in prime shape, something Sean hadn't done in years.

Firemen saved lives; they didn't take them. The very fact that had drawn him to the fire department after he left the marines.

In brief, he had his ass handed to him. He got in a few good punches, but got back twice what he dished out. Head, back, ribs. Jabs and kicks landing with crushing force, honed by a rogue soldier who'd never given up the war.

As Sean lay panting, the bastard whispered in his ear.

"You're going to die, soon. But it'll be a shitload bigger than this. Nothing mundane for you, old friend." He patted Sean's cheek. "Until later."

Footsteps receded and someone dropped to his side.

"Oh, God! Are you all right?" Hands skimmed his face, his torso.

Wincing, he struggled to sit up. "Bruised. I'll live."

"You're bleeding!" She tried to dab his mouth, but he pushed her hand away.

"I'm fine. I just want to get out of here."

"Um, that's going to be put off for a while."

"Why?"

"The police are here."

"Dammit! This explanation is going to take too fucking long." At her hurt look, he relented. "I'm sorry, baby. You did good, getting help. But our story is that a man fitting Jesse's description demanded my wallet and I wouldn't give it to him. Let me do most of the talking, okay?"

She nodded, not appearing convinced.

"Good. Soon as we get rid of them, I'll call that FBI guy and tell him what happened."

This seemed to relieve some of her anxiety. "All right. Can you stand?"

"Yeah." Even with her help, it was easier said than done. He ached all over and was dizzy. Whether from his cold or the fight, he wasn't sure. Maybe both.

A Nashville cop pulled up close to them, got out. "Evenin', folks. Got a call about a dispute? I'm assuming you're the ones who called."

"I called," Eve said. "A man jumped my fiancé and demanded his wallet."

The cop crossed his arms over his chest. "He jumped and *then* he demanded the wallet, or the other way around?"

Eve looked to Sean, expression slightly panicked. Shit.

"I can explain," he said with an effort. "We just left a movie and came out to my SUV. We were almost here when a man approached, holding a knife. He yelled at me to hand over my wallet, but I told him to eat shit."

"It's safer to just let those types of criminals have the wallet, sir," the cop scolded. "You could have been stabbed."

"Yes, I know. In hindsight, what I did was stupid, but at the time I saw red. I didn't want to let him walk off with my money and credit cards. I was pissed. We fought and he took off when he realized you were coming."

The cop sighed, as though this was the umpteenth time he'd heard a variation of this story lately. "Give me a description and I'll file a report of the incident. If he's picked up in the future for something else, your report could help put him away on more charges."

Oh, I think homeland terrorism is a tad out of your league.

"Thank you, Officer."

He gave a description, answered a few more questions that didn't tell the policeman any more information than before, and tried a smile when the cop asked if he needed medical attention. Like he was going to call in the paramedics and risk this spreading back to his own department.

"No, thanks. It's nothing a little rest and TLC won't cure." To get his point across, he put an arm around Eve's waist and pulled her close, winking at the cop. Who finally cracked a smile.

"Right. Wouldn't turn down a little of that brand of TLC myself. You have a nice evening."

After the cop drove off, Sean sagged against Eve. "Would you mind driving?"

"Mind? I'm not letting you. Give me the keys."

He handed them over and climbed into the passenger's side, hissing in pain. The bastard had done a number on his ribs in particular. Taking out his phone, he left a message for Nick Westfall and hung up.

"He must have been following us tonight for no telling how long, waiting to confront you," she pointed out, sounding pissed. "Otherwise, how could he have known where we were?"

"God, you're right." If he hadn't been so caught up in their reunion, he would've noticed. "Honey, I know you don't want to hear this, but I think it would be best if you join your mother at your aunt's house. Just until the FBI arrests Jesse."

Her lips thinned into an angry line. "Which will be when? Next week? Next year? He's apparently been waltzing around playing his games however he wanted for as long as you've known him. What makes you think he'll get caught now?"

"He will. He's been working toward a big finale, a horrible act that will put his name down in history, and this is it. One way or the other, his games are coming to an end. And I don't want you here when he decides it's showtime."

She was silent for a long moment. "I'll think about going to California, but I'm not making any promises. That's the best I can do."

"Knowing you're safe would ease my mind, baby." He knew when not to push Eve. If she said she'd consider going, she would.

It was tough getting comfortable on the drive home, and he wished he hadn't suggested going all the way to Nashville for their movie. But he couldn't regret the wonderful evening they'd had, until Jesse ruined it.

Christ, he was getting remarried. The idea was wonderful and scary. But he and Eve would make it work.

"Sean? We're here."

The road, the bounce of the Tahoe, must've lured him into a doze. He blinked to find they were in his driveway. "Sorry, I drifted off."

"You need sleep. Let's get you inside and in bed."

"Sounds good." No innuendo this time. He doubted he could get hard even if she stripped naked and straddled his face.

Well, okay, maybe then, but . . .

She prodded him upstairs and into the bathroom, made him strip to his boxer briefs and sit on the lid of the toilet. Wetting a cloth in warm water, she washed his cuts and bruises, her touch light. Gentle. It was so nice he almost fell asleep.

"You're really hot," she said, feeling his forehead. "Do you have any Tylenol or cold medicine in here?" Setting the cloth aside, she began to rummage in his bare bathroom cabinets.

"I'm not sure. I tossed almost all the medicine in the garbage when I came home from rehab, over-the-counter or not. I went overboard, I know. I don't really want to take—"

"You need something or you're going to be miserable! Don't argue with me on this—just get in bed and rest."

He wasn't in any shape to argue even if he wanted. She marched him to the bed and tucked him under the covers, and he cooperated, docile as a lamb. He wanted to tell her not to expect him to take orders on a regular basis, but figured she knew.

He was dead to the world before her footsteps faded down the hallway.

* * *

Sweet Jesus, what a week.

Sean was fast asleep, but Eve was tossing and turning. In the course of a couple of days, she'd been maybe pregnant, helped her lover through a terrible crisis, been not pregnant, then engaged, and overjoyed. And after that, two days ago, she'd been terrified her new fiancé would be killed by his archenemy.

Eve threw on her clothes, tiptoed out of the bedroom to the living room, and flopped onto the sofa. If Sean had any wine in the house, she'd pour herself a huge glass. Just as well he didn't.

These were the times when a girl needed to talk to her mother. Problem was, she didn't want to worry Mama with all the goings-on and she sure didn't want to announce her engagement over the phone. If she called, Mama would employ her use of super radar and have her confessing every event of the past couple of days in nothing flat.

Crap. So calling Mama was out. In a few days, perhaps things would be more settled and she could at least sound normal on the phone. Might as well get going to the store and pick up some medicine for Sean. He really needed some cough medicine for his nasty cold, and they were out of Tylenol for the aches and pains from his fight with Jesse Rose. She'd like to cut off Rose's balls and serve them to him over pasta.

Stuffing her phone into her purse, she fished out her keys and headed for the front door, glad Sean had given her a key to use, enabling her to come and go. She still needed to learn his alarm code, and that she didn't know it yet made her nervous about leaving him here. But she'd be gone twenty or thirty minutes, tops.

On the porch, she turned to slide the key into the lock when a scraping noise made her start. Spinning, she peered to a spot at the edge of the porch where the light from the bulb overhead faded into the darkness. Another scrape. And a footstep.

In a panic, she shoved the front door open again, her only goal to get inside and lock it before—before what, she couldn't think. She scrambled, panting, slammed it closed.

Pounding feet. Lots of them.

Oh, God.

And the heavy door immediately burst open, knocking her backward, to the floor. Her purse and keys skidded away and she looked up, eyes wide, as several men ran inside, dressed in fatigues. One reached for her and she screamed, the sound cut short as his fist connected with her jaw.

Her head spun, vision going white as the pain exploded in her face. When the room came back into focus, a couple of men had her pinned. And Rose's smirking face hovered over hers.

"Where's lover boy?"

She glared at him, torn between screaming to alert Sean and trying to convince Rose that Sean wasn't here. The latter ploy she doubted would work.

"Fuck you, dirtbag," she snarled. "Sean! *Sean!*"

With a curse, Rose reached out, pinched a spot at the base of her neck.

And the world went dark.

Sean!

He blinked, the fog of sleep wafting in his brain like cobwebs. What had awakened him? A scream. Just another nightmare.

But the pounding of boots coming closer was definitely no dream. Bolting upright in bed, he didn't have time to move as the door slammed against the opposite wall and four men rushed in, dressed in fatigues, M16s over their shoulders.

"What the fuck—"

Four pairs of hands dragged him from the bed, wrestled him to the floor. At one time he'd been trained to take on several men alone, but those days were past. He put up a good fight, got in some licks, to no avail. His struggles ceased when Jesse walked in, expression smug.

"Now, that's a shame, seeing such a good soldier come to this. Brought down in your underwear, no less." Spying Sean's jeans on the chest at the end of the bed, he grabbed them, tossed them onto his lap. "Put these on. We're going for a ride."

"You bastard," he seethed. "Where's Eve?"

"Taking a little nap at the moment. Don't worry. You'll be together soon."

The way he said it, Sean didn't doubt that meant in death. *God, please let her be okay. Get her away from this lunatic.*

Pulling on the jeans, he refused to wince at the pain from his bruises. His enemy was getting far too much satisfaction from having the upper hand for him to show weakness. After he had the jeans on, he stood waiting, fists clenched.

"This, too."

A T-shirt hit him in the chest, and he caught it, yanked it on.

"Let's go."

The four goons hauled him out of the house, into the night. On the way, he saw Eve's purse and some of the contents scattered on the living room floor, and his gut clenched in fear. If he lost her, it didn't matter what Jesse did to him. He'd rather be dead than go through that hell again.

Outside, he was dragged a fair distance down his driveway, as far as one could get from the house and still see it. Abruptly, he was pushed to his knees in the grass facing the house, and he thought for a dizzying moment that he was going to be shot execution-style in his own front yard.

He should have known Jesse wouldn't settle for something that simple.

"Nice place you've got there, old friend," Jesse called loudly. "But I think it's time to renovate, don't you?"

At the flick of his hand, one of the men stepped forward, a small device in his hand. And, before Sean could yell, pressed a button.

And his house exploded with an earth-shaking roar, engulfed in an orange ball of flame. He stared in disbelief as shrapnel rained down, pelting the trees.

His home, gone. Destroyed.

He looked up, locked gazes with Jesse, who sneered at him. "Before we're done, you'll burn, too."

Snatching a rifle from one of his goons, Jesse flipped the butt toward the ground and slammed it into Sean's skull.

15

"It was an honest mistake," Jesse rasped. His tan hand with the IV rested on his chest, stark against the white bandages. "I was confused. Didn't mean to draw down on Connors. Tell them!"

"You're asking me to lie." Sean swallowed, sick at heart. Mired in endless hell. Little did Jesse know, he'd already told the truth.

He'd find out soon enough.

"I'm asking you to have my back. You owe me."

"I owe you nothing. I know what I saw, and I did what I had to do."

Jesse stared at him a long moment before his gaze slid away, suspicious moisture in his eyes. When he spoke, his voice was barely audible. "You said I could always count on you."

Oh, God. "That was before I knew about the drugs, the weapons. Before you tried to murder one of our brothers in cold blood." He backed away, toward the door. Had to run, far from this pain. "You made your bed, Jesse. I'm done."

And then he did run, as though he could escape the agony rending his chest at Jesse's hoarse declaration.

"No man stands against Jesse Rose. If it takes the rest of my life, that's a lesson you'll learn well."

Plink. Plink. Plink.

Consciousness returned in slow degrees. With awareness came pain. With pain, the knowledge that he was still alive. Alive and cold. Shivering.

His arms and legs were frozen. No, that wasn't right. He tried to move them and realized they were bound and his feet were submerged in frigid water. With his movements, he also became aware that there was someone next to him. Leaning against his body.

Cracking open one eye, he took in his surroundings. A halogen lamp hung on a concrete wall, throwing eerie shadows on his tubular prison. Tubular? What the hell.

A tunnel. A man-made one. Where the hell was he?

A groan brought his head around to look at his fellow prisoner. His pulse lurched. "Eve? Can you hear me?"

"Sean? What . . . ?"

She raised her head, gazed into his eyes. He'd never beheld a more welcome sight. A secret part of him was terrified she'd been in the house when Jesse blew it sky-high.

"Listen, baby. We're in a tunnel of some sort. I'm going to—"

"Jesse got me when I tried to run back inside. I wasn't fast enough. I'm sorry," she whispered.

He wished he could hold and reassure her. "There's nothing you could do. He was going to get inside one way or the other. The important thing is getting out of here."

A metallic scraping noise from above echoed loudly

through the tunnel. A manhole cover being moved aside? Footsteps descended down the rungs, legs coming into view. The body crowded past where he and Eve were bound to the metal ladder, and jumped into the knee-deep water with a splash. Jesse regarded them with a smirk.

"Good, I see you're awake. I much prefer you to be fully aware of what's going to happen to you and your lovely town."

"And I suppose you can't wait to tell me."

"How'd you guess?" He waved a hand at the tunnel wall behind him. "See anything special? Look high."

Sean squinted into the gloom. The light from the lamp didn't quite reach the top, but now that he knew to look for something, he spotted what had Jesse so pleased with himself.

"You sick fucker."

C-4, stuck to the walls. Wired to blow.

"Like my masterpiece?"

"Where the fuck are we?"

"In the drainage system underneath downtown Sugarland. These tunnels go for miles, did you know that?" He chuckled. "But I won't need that much to turn the whole city into a smoking crater."

"You'll kill innocent people," he hissed. "People who have done nothing to you. It's me you want. So why don't you take me somewhere away from here, settle this privately?" Beside him, Eve made a small sound of distress.

"But that would be too anticlimactic. This is payback, old friend. You have to die knowing that your betrayal of me came at a high price." He stepped forward, his face in Sean's. "And my enemies will be reminded that I'm a man of my word—anyone who stands against me will learn a valuable lesson. No matter how long it takes."

With that, his fist slammed into Sean's stomach, taking his breath away. He bent as far as his bonds would allow, gagging. When the waves subsided, he straightened and glared at Jesse, determined not to let him win.

"All I've learned is that the young man I loved like a brother never existed. He was a pale imitation of a man with character who threw a good life away for hatred and power. God, I pity you."

Jesse snarled in outrage, delivering a few more punches to his stomach as Eve cried out desperately for him to stop. Sean's knees sagged, pulling against his bonds, and his head hung forward. A fit of coughing made him sick, but he managed not to throw up. Barely.

Jesse stepped toward the ladder. "I'll be back, and when I return, me and your pretty lady here are gonna have some fun before I send you both to hell."

He climbed up the ladder and was gone. Sean couldn't hear much over the roaring in his ears.

"Did—" He gasped in pain. "Did he replace the cover up there?"

"No, I don't think so," she said, voice wavering.

"Okay. I'm going to work on these bonds and get us loose. Then I'll tell you what to do."

"Hurry."

The ropes at his wrists were damned tight. He struggled, twisting, working them for what seemed forever. Loosening them, a millimeter at a time. His wrists burned, became slick with what he assumed was blood. But if he didn't get these off, a few scars weren't going to matter. Ignoring the pain, he pushed on, rubbing them raw.

Finally, one hand came free and he shouted in triumph. "I'm loose!"

"Good! Hurry!"

Quickly, he shook the other one free as well and bent to get his feet. Grimacing, he plunged his hands into the murky, smelly water and knew a round of antibiotics was in his near future—from his chest cold not to mention whatever bacteria lurked in the sewage.

Freed, he went to work on the ropes at Eve's wrists. "Don't worry, honey. Almost done." Her whole body was shaking with cold and terror.

He got them loose and then worked on her feet. When that was done, he gave her a fierce hug and kiss. She clung to him for a few seconds, then pulled away.

"Let's get the hell out of here!"

"You're going without me. I need for you to call—"

"What? No!" Her eyes were huge in her face. "I can't leave you down here!"

"Listen to me." He took her hands. "I need for you to climb up the ladder and get help. Find a phone, call Nick Westfall, and tell him what's happened. Tell him about the tunnels and to get here, fast."

"But you have to come with me! That lunatic is coming back!"

"Yes, and if he finds us gone before the Feds arrive, he'll blow the charges. I know him. I still remember enough of my military training to disarm them. They're pretty simple."

"Sean, please come with me," she pleaded.

"Scoot, baby. I don't have time to argue about this. I'll see you soon, okay? At the police station. We'll meet there. Go!"

Tears welled in her eyes. "I love you."

"Love you, too. Now go before he comes back."

She turned and shimmied up the ladder. He didn't rest easy until she called down, "All clear up here. We're near the diner. I'm going there to use the phone."

"Got it!"

Adrenaline rushing through his veins, he surveyed Jesse's sinister handiwork affixed to the walls. Shit. He wasn't nearly as confident about handling explosives as he'd been twenty years ago. Dealing in death hadn't been in his job description in a very long time.

Now was perfect for a crash course.

He set to work, as quickly as he dared without unwittingly bringing about the end himself. While he dismantled the explosives, his mind focused to a laser point on how to turn the tables on Jesse.

And staring down at a wire in his hand, the solution became very clear.

Jesse Rose, along with his campaign of terror, was about to be history, as he should have been long ago.

"What do you mean, his fucking house blew up?" Howard shouted into his phone. Kat, who'd been lounging in her robe watching the news and patting her pregnant belly, rose with an effort, eyes wide.

"What I said! It blew up," Captain Lance Holliday yelled back. "Burned to the ground. I'm standing right here in the front yard watching it burn, and there are police and fucking FBI everywhere, man! *FBI?* What the fuck! I don't know what the hell is going on!"

Oh, God. "Was he home? Tell me he wasn't!"

"His Tahoe is here, Howard. I'm sorry."

"I'm coming over there."

"See you."

He hung up and faced his wife. "Sean's house just burned to the ground," he choked out. "Lance said it blew up. His truck is there."

"Oh my God!" she gasped. "I want to go with you."

"Not a chance, angel. I don't want you anywhere near there. Just lock up behind me and I'll call you when I know something." He paused in the act of grabbing his wallet and keys off the kitchen counter. "You can do something for me."

"Anything, you know that," she said softly.

"Call the team and let them know."

She nodded, face pale. "I will."

He rushed out, moving fast.

And prayed his best friend hadn't been home.

Breath hitching, Eve ran away from the manhole, shoes squishing. Nearly faint with panic, she ran toward the town square, toward the lights. Toward help.

Every step away from Sean was a stab wound to her heart.

He should've come with her, not stayed to play hero down in a dank tunnel full of explosives. He was sick and injured. If Jesse came back—

No. She couldn't allow herself to think that way. She'd get help, bring them here. Everything would be fine.

Reaching the diner, she nearly fell over with relief. She burst inside, heedless of the startled glances of a few folks having coffee and dessert. The dinner hour was long past.

Barely able to catch her breath, she grabbed the hostess by the arm. "I need to use your phone. It's an emergency."

The girl's eyes widened. "Hey, sure, no problem. There." She gestured to a phone sitting by the register.

"Thank you."

Stumbling over, Eve snatched it up and dialed 911. Waited.

"Nine-one-one, please state your emergency."

"I need the police downtown, at the Sugarland Diner," she panted. "No, not just the uniformed ones. Detective Shane Ford and, um, Kayne. T-Taylor Kayne. The chief. Hell, send everyone!"

"What is your name, please?"

"Eve Marshall, Sugarland Fire Department." That would help give her call, which was going to sound like a wild tale, more credence. Get them moving faster. She hoped.

"Can you tell me what's happening?"

"Jesse Rose has wired the drainage tunnels under downtown with explosives! He's going to blow up the whole damned town!"

"Jesse Rose, you said? And you're saying this is a terrorist threat?"

"Yes! I need the FBI, too. There's an agent here working on this case who'll know exactly what's going on. Nick Westfall. Someone has to call him. Now, please!"

"All right. I've got units on the way to the diner now. I'll notify the detectives of your call, and they will notify Agent Westfall if necessary."

"Believe me, it's necessary. Send lots of units. Downtown will have to be evacuated. We'll need the fire department here, too, to block off the streets."

"All right, Ms. Marshall. Stay on the line with me until our units arrive, okay?"

"Yes, fine. Just hurry."

Within two minutes, a police car pulled up and parked in front of the diner. As Eve stared, incredulous, one cop got out.

"Okay, the unit has arrived, so you can hang up," the dispatcher said. "Good-bye."

"Wait!" The click sounded in her ear and she nearly screamed in frustration. Pushing out the door, she met the cop on the sidewalk.

"Eve Marshall?"

"Yes. I call in a terrorist threat and you're all I get?" she hissed. "Someone's ass is toast for this!"

The look he gave her said, *Speak slowly and calmly to the crazy lady.* "Ma'am, you know phoning in a fake bomb threat is a serious offense, don't you?"

"Jesse Rose has wired the drainage system downtown with explosives," she insisted. "He's a known terrorist that the FBI is here to apprehend. Get either Shane Ford or Taylor Kayne on the phone. They'll know what I'm telling you is true. For God's sake, don't you guys get briefed before every shift, especially if there's a terrorist around?"

The man paused, and his entire demeanor changed. "Jesse Rose. Shit, that's right! Hang on and I'll call this in."

"You do that. And tell them to get here, fast. My fiancée is down in that tunnel trying to disarm the explosives, and if Jesse comes back and catches him— God."

He nodded. "Be right back."

Eventually she'd have to tell the whole story of how

Jesse had kidnapped them, but there wasn't time right now. She listened as the officer sat in his car and spoke into his cell phone, but she couldn't quite make out what he was saying. He made more than one call, however, and, when he was done, joined her on the sidewalk again.

"Got hold of the chief and Detective Ford. They're sending a bunch of units out to evacuate the few businesses that are still open, and the fire department will block off the streets. Thank God it's late and almost everything is closed."

"Yes." A huge blessing.

"Ford said he'd just talked to Kayne, and the man told him a fire captain's house blew up tonight. Sean Tanner. Said he's your boyfriend. That have anything to do with this?"

"Wait a second—his house *blew up*?" She stared at the cop, trying to process what he'd just said.

"That's what Kayne told him. The place is nothing but a pile of burned rubble."

"Oh my God," she gasped. Sean's home, his children's things. His mementos. All gone.

How much more could the man take?

"Again, is that connected to what you're telling me about Rose and the drainage system?"

She shook herself. "Yes. Jesse and his men kidnapped us at my boyfriend's house tonight and tied us up down in the tunnel. When we woke up, Rose showed us the explosives wired inside the tunnel. He left, Sean got us loose, stayed behind to disarm them, and sent me to get help."

"That explains some stuff. The cops and firefighters on the scene think Tanner was in the house. I'm sure Ford will tell them, though."

She nodded, past thinking about anything other than Sean. Fear clawed at her lungs and she knew she had to get to him.

That she had to wait was driving her insane.

Nick stalked the yard in front of the captain's house, furious. Men gave him a wide berth as he made his way to his partner.

"How did this motherfucker lose us, Jack? We've been watching him for days, and he just makes like a ghost. Now he's possibly murdered a good man who was trying to help us. Fuck!"

Enraged and miserable, they stared at the glowing remains of Tanner's home. Nearby, Detective Kayne stuck close to Captain Holliday of the fire department, in case the firefighters found something in the rubble.

A Ford truck came skidding into the yard, the driver braking hard. The door swung open and one of the biggest men Nick had ever seen jumped out, scanned the area. The man's jaw clenched, his expression a mixture of dread and fear. He saw Holliday and made a beeline straight for the captain. Nick wandered closer to hear better.

"Was he home? Have you found anything? Heard from him?"

"Not yet. We'll find him, Six-Pack. I promise you."

Easy to see how the man earned that nickname. He could likely break any man here in half without breaking a sweat.

"You'd damned well better. I will *not* lose my best friend after all the shit he's been through."

"I'm trying, Howard."

"Try harder." Howard pressed into the captain's space.

"You need to back off, buddy. Calm down." Holliday placed a palm in the center of the big man's chest, though he couldn't really hold Howard if push came to shove.

The situation was saved from deteriorating further when Kayne jogged over, closing his cell phone. He waved over Nick and Jack, and included the two sparring firemen. "Listen up. Just talked to my colleague Detective Ford. Jesse Rose kidnapped Tanner and Eve Marshall earlier, then blew up the house."

Howard's face was stunned. "Kidnapped? What the fuck is going on? Does this have to do with the guy who's been harassing him?"

"Listen, because I've got to make this quick. Eve Marshall is okay. She escaped from where Rose had her and Tanner tied up in the drainage system downtown. She says the tunnels are wired to blow, and that Tanner stayed behind to disarm them. Rose had left the two of them, but said he'd be back. She's scared Tanner and Rose are going to go at it."

"Goddamn," Nick muttered. "If that ain't the meat on my clusterfuck sandwich."

Jack groaned. "Does he know anything about explosives?"

"Yeah," Howard said. "He was a marine. Did all kinds of stuff."

Kayne turned to Holliday. "They've called for all available engine companies to head downtown, block off the streets. The uniforms are evacuating the businesses."

"I've got my hands full with this," Holliday said, gesturing to the smoldering house. "But when we're sure it's out, we'll be there if you still need us."

Nick slapped his partner on the arm. "Let's rock 'n' roll."

Time to find a stinking traitor and send him to meet his boss in the underworld.

In minutes, more and more units arrived. Officers went to the businesses that were open, forcing them to evacuate. The diner cleared out and people left, some curious, others alarmed. After what seemed like hours, two cars screeched to a halt in front of the diner. Detective Kayne emerged from one, the two FBI agents from the other.

The men approached her. Agent Westfall spoke first, with the demeanor of a man who was in charge.

"Show us the manhole you escaped from."

"It'll be faster by car. I had to run from that way, across the park." She pointed behind them.

"I'll drive," the other agent said.

They jumped in, Eve riding in the back with Kayne. She directed them using the closest route she could see, and pointed to an open cover on the sidewalk. "There!"

The agent pulled to a stop beside the curb.

"Right at the bottom of the ladder is where we were tied up," she said. "The explosives were wired high on the wall of the tunnel, though I hope Sean has managed to dismantle them. I don't have a clue how much of the tunnel was set to go, but to hear Rose talk, quite a bit of it."

"Detective Kayne, would you have one of your uniforms take Miss Marshall to the police station? That will be a much safer place for her to wait."

Kayne nodded at Westfall. "I agree. I'll have one of

those guys drive her," he said, pointing to a knot of officers standing on the corner looking important.

Eve wanted to shout in frustration. *Sean, where are you?*

No way in hell was she leaving him down there, not knowing what was happening. The agents got out and jogged to the hole. One after the other, they disappeared under the street. Eve pretended to be cooperative as Kayne handed her off to the officers and left to follow the two agents.

The cops then proceeded to argue about who would drive her to the station. Seemed no one wanted to miss the action. While they were hashing it out, one of their radios squawked and an announcement ensued that from the best she could tell sounded like some of Rose's men had been apprehended. This, in turn, caused a great deal of excitement.

And allowed her to walk off unnoticed. Any moment, she expected a shout for her to stop, but none came. Reaching the hole, she hauled herself over the edge and found a toehold. Began to descend. She was more frightened than she'd ever been in her life.

But she wasn't leaving without her man.

At the bottom, she peered into the gloom. Smaller lights lined the top of the tunnel, probably for maintenance workers who might have to come fix something. But they weren't nearly as bright as the bright one Rose had had, which was gone. She heard faraway voices, but had no idea whose they were, where they were coming from, or which way the agents and Kayne had gone. She chose the right for no reason, and struck out, shoes squelching in the muck under the water, on the tunnel's floor. She didn't want to think about what was down there.

Pushing on, she began to worry. If she chose the wrong direction, got lost down here, she might never find her way out. It was right about there that the arrows began. About a foot long, drawn in mud.

Sean. Setting a trap for Jesse? Had the two of them already met up, had it out? If Sean was hurt or worse—

Suddenly, a sloshing noise sounded from an alcove to her right. She was grabbed by a pair of strong hands, shoved against the wall face-first. A hard, round object pressed into her lower back. Of course, he'd heard her coming from a mile away and he'd hidden, waiting.

"Where's your lover, sweet cheeks?" His sour breath wafted next to her face.

"I don't know. I was trying to find him."

"Liar." The gun pressed harder.

"I'm telling the truth. Otherwise I wouldn't have come back down here."

"Then let's find him together," he said, tone mocking. "Ladies first."

Pulling her from the wall, he shoved her ahead of him. Legs trembling, she started walking. "He's going to kill you."

"He thinks he'll try, but in the end? He won't be able to do it." So confident. Smug. "When we were in the service and he shot me, he was riddled with guilt. Cold-blooded murder? Sean isn't made that way. I know him better than he knows himself."

She seriously doubted that, but kept it to herself.

Rose would find out soon enough how wrong he was.

His theater was ready.

All he needed was the star of the show.

God, he was ready to collapse. He hurt all over, was

so feverish he was surprised the water wasn't boiling at his feet. Just a little longer, and this would all be over.

Splashing sounded. Someone approaching. From the noise it sounded like more than one person. If Eve had gotten help, it could be the police or FBI.

Flattening himself against the wall, he waited. As the figures drew closer, the bottom fell out of his stomach. Eve. And Jesse was behind her, forcing her to walk.

Quietly he knelt, scooped a glob of the gunk he'd been using to draw the arrows on the wall—he hoped to God it was mud—and palmed it, holding it at his side. Steeling himself, he moved away from the wall and stood in the middle of the tunnel. Eve's eyes met his, frightened, but also determined. He read the unspoken message there—she would be ready, whatever he had to do.

Jesse stopped them a few feet from Sean, his sneering, hateful voice echoing in the gloom. "You lose, old friend. I get the girl, again. But this time you won't live long enough for regrets."

"Oh, I plan to live a long time after you're dead, fucker."

With that, he charged forward, drawing back his arm as Eve dove to the side, landing in the water. Jesse, who must have thought he held a plastic explosive, shouted and threw a hand up in reflex. The mud hit the side of his face with a splat, messy but harmless. As Sean closed the distance, Jesse raised his other hand and something black and shiny glinted there.

There was a pop, a sting in his side, but his momentum carried him into his enemy in a full tackle. They went over together, and the fight for survival was on—

and he had to fare a hell of a lot better than when they'd fought in the parking lot.

Because this time, one of them would not walk away.

Sean rolled in the water and muck, struggled to grab Jesse's gun arm. They were both slippery, but he managed to grab the other man's wrist. Slammed it against the concrete wall until Jesse lost his grip and the weapon plopped harmlessly into the murk.

Jesse brought his knee up and pushed Sean's chest, throwing him onto his back. The bastard got the upper hand, sat on his chest, grabbed his hair, and forced his head under the water. Sean heard Eve scream, willed her to run and get help. He held his breath, bucking, grasping at Jesse's arms. Anything to dislodge him.

Nothing worked.

His lungs were going to explode. His brain began to grow fuzzy.

Suddenly Jesse's body was knocked off balance and Sean was able to throw him to the side. He bolted upright, gasping for air. Wiped his eyes. And stared in amazement.

Jesse was on his hands and knees, Eve standing over him brandishing a broken piece of scrap wood. From the looks of things, she'd clocked him on the head, and she was ready to deliver another blow.

Which she did, swinging like Babe Ruth for the bleachers. Jesse went down and didn't move again.

Sean pushed to his feet with an effort and staggered to her, pulled her into his arms. "That's my girl," he whispered, holding her tight.

"God, I thought he was going to kill you."

"Me, too. Guess I'm not the fighter I used to be."

"That's why you've got me to watch your back." She shuddered, peering around him at Jesse. "What are we going to do with him? We can't leave him here or he might get away."

"Oh, he's not going anywhere. I've got plans for him." Walking over to a drainpipe near the alcove where he'd been hiding, he fetched the rope he'd hooked over it. "This is what he used on us. Figure we'll return the favor."

"Then what?"

"And then I'm going to finish this for good."

16

With Eve's help and no little struggle, Sean bound Jesse, got him fixed to the drainpipe. Her anxiety rolled to him in waves.

"Sean, let's just go," she urged. "He can't get free before the agents get here to arrest him anyway."

"Soon."

"What are you doing now?"

"Giving him a choice, which is more than he gave my family. I doubt Jesse will survive in prison, and despite everything that's gone down between us—or maybe because I remember the friend he used to be—I want to give him an honorable way out."

"I get that," she said slowly. "But, Sean—"

"That's not the only reason, though. His trial will go on for years. Years while we're beginning our lives together, maybe even starting a family. And even if he *does* survive in prison, what do you think Jesse will use all that time to do?"

Her eyes widened in understanding. "He'll be plotting how to get us, perhaps even our children."

"Exactly." He paused, took her by the shoulders. "You're going to go back now. Just follow the arrows the way you came, let the agents know where to find us. This once, do as I ask and don't argue with me. Please."

She had been gearing up for an argument, but after a few moments of inner turmoil, she nodded. "This once. Please, don't do anything that you'll regret."

"I won't be the one with regrets this time." Never again. Kissing her soundly, he reluctantly let her go and pushed her away. "Go, bring the cavalry."

Though it might not make a difference to his enemy.

He set to his grim task and, after he finished, stood back to survey his handiwork. Fighting might not be in his repertoire of skills these days, but he hadn't forgotten everything he knew about explosives.

Jesse stirred with a groan, coming around. Sean moved next to him and murmured in his ear. "Don't move."

Even while he was semiconscious, the other man's instincts were honed for danger. He froze, blinked his eyes open. Visibly fought to clear his head.

"What the fuck?"

"Oh, it looks to me like you're fucked, all right. How does it feel to be helpless, Jesse? To know your minutes are numbered?"

Moving as little as possible, the man took stock of the ropes binding him. The wires threaded through the ropes. The C-4 attached to his middle, the wires ending there. Raising his head, he stared into Sean's eyes, a spark of something human that used to be Jesse flaring in the depths of his.

"You don't have it in you," he said evenly. "You're not a killer."

"No, but you are. You killed my family that night, didn't you? Ran them off the road." Cold fury temporarily took the place of fatigue. He would have this settled before the night was done.

Jesse licked his lips, a hint of fear breaking his icy calm. "I didn't do shit to them. I was following Blair's car, yes. I'd planned to meet your slutty wife later, get a little snatch. The accident was just that, and I pulled over, took a photo. Figured it would come in handy later as something to torture you with."

"I don't believe you," Sean hissed. "You caused the accident, even if it turned out much worse than you planned. Admit it."

"Believe what you want. I didn't do it." The other man was beginning to sound afraid. "Tormenting you after the fact was just a bonus."

In that moment, Sean realized he couldn't trust Jesse's word. Though he believed Jesse had a role in his family's death, he'd never know for sure whether or not the man was telling the truth.

That chapter was written. Done.

And it no longer mattered, because they were just as gone.

Jesse's pleading voice intruded into his thoughts. "We were friends, once. The best of friends. Let me go, for old times' sake. I'll disappear and never bother you again. I'll leave the country and—"

"Can't do that, Jesse. You're a thief, an arsonist. A murderer." More than ever, he was resolved to see this through to the end. "You took the lives of innocent people like the ones in the restaurant. You cut the hoses on our tanks, nearly got me killed. One of my men could've been hurt. I can only imagine how many people you've terrorized and killed over the years. It stops, here. Now."

Jesse swallowed hard. Sean saw the moment he realized there was no recourse. No way out.

"You're going down, one way or the other. What's it

going to be? You have maybe another five minutes to decide. Then the FBI will be here to take you away. Know what they'll do? Send you to death row, where you'll spend long lonely years fighting the charges, only to wind up with a needle in your arm. Zero tolerance against terrorists, you understand." His voice was nearly gone now, and so was his strength.

"And don't even think of waiting until they arrive to detonate the C-4, because I plan to warn them, and there's hardly enough there to do damage to anyone but you. So I'll ask you again—what's it going to be?" As he started to turn away, Jesse's voice halted him.

"I'll see you in hell."

He looked into Jesse's eyes, saw genuine regret there. At last. That was something, at least. "I've already been there, *old friend*. Good-bye, Jesse."

Walking away wasn't as difficult as he'd imagined. It was Jesse's choice to make, and he *had* a choice, unlike all his victims.

Sean staggered down the tunnel the way he'd come before, using the wall as support. Twenty yards. Fifty. Each second echoed with the heavy beat of his heart. Waiting.

A loud rumble from behind him told him of Jesse's choice.

It was over.

But not for him. He had to get to civilization before he passed out. Warm wetness seeped down his side. Leaning against the wall, he pulled up his shirt, inspected the wound. Appeared the bullet had simply taken out a chunk of flesh, but it hurt like the devil.

One last scar courtesy of Jesse Rose.

He wasn't sure how long he'd walked when he heard

voices calling his name. His answering shout came out a croak and he pushed on.

And was suddenly surrounded by federal agents and detectives. The tunnel was also filled with bomb squad guys, a couple commenting on the fact that the disarming had already been successfully completed. Two men put his arms around their shoulders, supporting his weight.

"Jesus, you look like something the cat barfed up. Let's get him to the paramedics!"

"Wait." Agent Westfall's face floated in front of Sean's. "Where's Rose?"

Sean hitched a thumb the direction from which he'd come. "Back there. What's left of him."

"Shit. What happened?"

"Must've tripped over his own bomb, Agent," he said quietly. "Wouldn't you say?"

After a moment, Westfall nodded, lips quirking into grim parody of a smile. "Yeah, you must be right. Shit like that happens when a dumbass plays with explosives."

Sean sagged in relief as Westfall and his partner moved past him to do whatever agents did when they had to scrape up a dead terrorist. God.

The cops got him to the ladder, where he somehow climbed to street level. Vision blurry, he scanned the faces for the one he most wanted, needed, to see.

"Sean!"

He found her. She broke away from a group of uniformed cops and ran to him, nearly toppling him over in her enthusiasm. A man in love could do worse than to have this sort of reception waiting for him at the end of the day.

"God, I was so scared!" Kisses peppered his face.

"Baby, as much as I love your kisses, I stink, and I need a shower."

"Hospital first, shower, and then sleep. In that order," she said, hands roaming every inch of him she could check. "You're bleeding."

"Missing some skin, that's all."

"What happened with Jesse?"

"He's dead, baby. He'll never hurt anyone again."

Her eyes widened in alarm. "You didn't . . ."

"Kill him myself? No. Just gave him the option like we discussed. You really don't want to know more."

Falling silent, she helped a cop get him to an ambulance parked at the end of the street. The team jumped into action, taking his vitals, starting an IV.

"You'll be okay, Captain Tanner," one reassured him. "We're going to transport you to the ER, where they'll clean and stitch that wound in your side, check the rest of your injuries, and probably get you on some strong antibiotics. They may not even keep you."

"Would suit me fine. I want to sleep in my . . ." Well, fuck. His house was gone.

"You'll stay with me." Eve smiled, stroking his hair. "We'll start over, together, like we'd planned."

The ambulance doors closed and he smiled back. Or thought he did. Things got fuzzy after that and he let himself drift to sleep, the rocking of the ambulance and the touch of Eve's fingers soothing the hurt.

Good-bye, Jesse. You'll never know how sorry I am that it had to end this way.

Me, too, old friend. Me, too.

Eve watched her lover sleep, profoundly grateful that he was here, in her bed. Warm and alive. In the past three days he'd been pretty wrung out, physically and emotionally exhausted. Yesterday he'd stirred enough to take a shower and eat a good dinner she'd made. Then he'd gone back to bed.

Agents Westfall and Coleman had been by a couple of times wanting to get an official statement from him for their reports, but she'd put them off. Sean needed rest, and besides, he was in the clear officially. However, they were coming by again today and she wouldn't be able to stall any longer.

Green eyes blinked open, regarded her lazily for a few minutes. Then the corners crinkled as he smiled at her, stretched like a big cat. "Mornin', beautiful."

"That certainly sounds more promising than the last few days." She cupped his bristly jaw, admiring the shadow. Made him look a bit dangerous, which he was. And all hers.

"Sorry I've been out of it. Make it up to you?" Those eyes glinted with promise.

She stroked his bare chest. "Mmm. Someone's feeling better."

"Much. The miracle of antibiotics. Amazing." He scooted closer, nibbling at her lips.

"Oh, yes. Very amazing, and I don't mean the drugs. Are you sure you're up to fooling around, handsome?"

"Does it feel like I'm 'up' to you?" Taking her hand, he moved it to his erection, standing hard and ready.

"Why, I believe it does."

Pushing her gently to her back, he covered her, skin against skin. Slid their bodies together, creating wonderful friction as he parted her lips with his tongue. Played, teased, and tasted, cock rubbing against her belly. Thumbed her nipples, bringing them to attention.

Nibbling his way down her body, he parted her legs

and bent. Tongued her slit and chuckled darkly when she whimpered, raising her hips.

"Patience, baby."

"All out. Please, I need you."

His mouth was glorious, suckling her sex, flicking her clit until she pulled at his hair, urging him. "Inside me."

"With pleasure." He paused, a strange light on his face. "Condom?"

"Does that mean you'd be willing to stop using them?"

"That's what it means, baby," he whispered, brushing his fingers through her hair. "Let's stop using precautions, let nature take its course. If you're ready."

"Oh, yes." Tears filled her eyes. "Make love to me."

He entered her slowly, gaze locked with hers. Pushed inside, filling her, completing them both. She'd never felt anything so right as this man making love to her, no barriers between them. Their bond, already strong, glowed as the final piece clicked into place.

Trust. Love. Hope.

They were together and this love was it for them.

Moving his hips, he thrust steadily, stroking the fires. They rode the flames together, to the edge, surging. Clinging to each other, they shattered and he poured into her, hot and sweet. Sealed their love, never to be broken. Always cherished.

"Thank you for loving me," he murmured.

"I always have."

"That makes me the luckiest man in the world."

Thankfully, they'd showered and dressed when a knock came on the door. Eve didn't have to wonder who was visiting.

"Our FBI friends?" Sean asked, looking up from his newspaper.

"I believe so." She peered out, to make sure. "Yep." Opening the door, she greeted Westfall and Coleman, letting them inside.

"Hello, Miss Marshall," Westfall said pleasantly as he stepped into the living room, his partner behind him. "Sorry to keep bothering you, but we really need to wrap up so we can get back to Virginia."

Sean spoke up from his spot at the kitchen table. "Hey, Nick. Good to see you."

Westfall spotted him, and smiled. "Tanner, you're looking good. A damned sight better than a few days ago, for sure."

"I'm feeling good." He stood, shaking both of the agents' hands.

"And mentally?" They all knew the agent referred to how Sean had ended things with Jesse.

"I'm doing okay. I feel regret, but not for what I did." This seemed to trouble him. "Am I going to face charges?"

Nick shook his head. "You're facing a commendation for apprehending one of the FBI's most wanted terrorists. I suggest you accept it gratefully and move on. Enjoy your Thanksgiving. God knows you have reason to be thankful this year."

"Sounds like good advice."

"The best. Do you mind if we take a seat? I need some notes for my final report and we'll be on our way."

"Sure. Where do I start?"

"You told us your history with Rose. I need the story of what happened the night he kidnapped you and your fiancée. Start there and take me through Jesse's demise. Leave nothing out."

Sean began to talk. Eve knew the whole mind-numbing story, until the part when Sean made her leave him alone with Jesse.

The missing piece of the tale broke her heart. For Sean. And strangely enough, for Jesse, too. When he stopped speaking, there was a long moment of silence; then Westfall put away his notepad.

"I think that gives us all we need."

"That's it?" Sean sounded a bit amazed. And a lot relieved.

"That's it." Nick rose and so did Coleman.

"I can't believe it's over. Or is it? What about Jesse's other plans, to blow up the nuclear reactor?"

Westfall paused, as though considering how much to say. "One of Rose's top men was in fact one of ours, undercover. Rose killed the agent's partner, but never found out about him. He gave us what we needed to ferret out the men involved in trying to detonate the facility. Some were working on the inside of the plant, with Red Badge clearance."

"Shit, that's scary," Sean said.

"Yeah. But the thing is, taking out a nuclear power plant is a lot harder to accomplish than we believe Rose's group truly had the ability to pull off. Thankfully, we'll never know. Our agents have rounded up most of Rose's men."

"Thank God," Eve said with a shudder.

"Tanner, Miss Marshall, it's been . . . well, *a pleasure* isn't exactly right under the circumstances. But it's good to know you, and I wish you both the best."

"Thanks. Same to you." Sean looked lighter than he had in days.

Now they could truly begin their lives together.

* * *

Working on Thanksgiving wasn't so bad. Especially when a man was lucky enough to have everyone who meant the most to him in the entire world right there, surrounding him.

Sean eyed the piles of food spread out on every surface of the station's kitchen. More than enough for their own shift and the other firefighters who would drop by. Some of the men on B- and C-shifts were single, didn't have families or couldn't get home to see them. Kat, Cori, and Grace would be here, and even Tommy and Shea planned to stop by, too. Soon the station would be bustling with people, eating, laughing, talking. As it should be.

Spotting Eve in an animated conversation with Jules and Zack, he strolled over and inserted himself into the group. They moved aside to make room for him.

"Man, I don't know where you get that shit," Jules ribbed Zack. "The Titans are *so* going to win the Super Bowl."

"Nope, my money's on Dallas."

Eve shook her head. "It's too early to speculate. But as long as we are, I favor New Orleans again."

After more friendly debate, Eve smiled at Sean. "You're standing there looking like the proverbial cat that ate the canary. What gives?"

"Oh, nothing." His grin refuted the claim.

"Come on, man." Julian nudged him. Six-Pack and Clay walked over to see what was going on.

Six-Pack spoke first. "What's up?"

Zack gestured to Sean. "The man has something going on, but he's not talking."

"You know we're not going to let you get away with that," Clay put in. "Out with it."

"Okay, I have two surprises to share," he said, barely

able to contain his excitement. "Well, really three. But two of them will have to wait until the first is revealed."

Clay wrinkled his nose. "Huh?" Thank God the guy was pretty, because sometimes he wasn't the brightest bulb.

"One surprise first, then the others will follow."

"Okay, so where's the first?"

"Should be here any minute."

They were exasperated with being put off, but if he had to deal, so did they. More men arrived along with Kat, Cori, Grace, Tommy, and Shea, and began to pick at the food, eyeing the spread like a pack of wolves. If his surprise didn't get here soon, he wouldn't be able to hold them off.

He was happy it didn't come to that.

"Someone told me there was a whole station full of hunky firefighters here to share my Thanksgiving with me. Lord have mercy, I'm feeling really thankful right about now!"

Eve swung her attention toward the door to the bay, and gasped. "Mama!" Rushing to her mother, she squeezed her tightly. Drew back, her happy voice warming Sean's soul. "I thought you were going to stay in California with Aunt Felicia this year!"

Amelia's brown eyes sparkled. "My plans changed when a really good man who loves my daughter gave me a call and told me how much my baby needed me home. So here I am."

Eve hugged her mother again, wiped her eyes. "I'm so glad you're here. Now we can really celebrate."

Sean walked over to them, took his turn hugging his future mother-in-law. "Thank you for coming home. You've made us both very happy."

"There's nowhere else I'd rather be." She kissed his cheek. "Thank you."

"This is touching and all, but we want to know what the other surprises are." This from Zack.

Sean let go of Amelia and addressed the gang. "Gather around, guys. I have a couple of announcements." He waited until they'd moved in closer before he continued. "It's not a secret anymore that Eve and I are together now. What you all don't know, that we've kept to ourselves, is that I've asked her to marry me."

"Hot damn!"

"You sly dog!"

After the cheers and whistles quieted, he went on. "I can't think of anyone I'd rather share this with than all of you, my family."

He'd be lying if he said he wasn't nervous as he pulled a velvet box from the pocket of his pants. Turned to Eve and held it out. Her hand went over her mouth, her love evident for all to see. "I want to do this again, and do it right. Here, in the place I love most, with the people I love most. Eve Marshall, will you marry me?"

With trembling fingers, she took the box. Opened it, and gazed at the big marquise diamond set in the gold band. "Oh, Sean, it's beautiful." Beaming, she launched herself into his arms. "Yes!"

More cheers ensued as his lady held him close. And kissed him, quite unprofessionally, in front of most of Station Five.

He'd never been happier.

"Put it on me?" She held out the box, and he removed the ring.

Placing it on her finger, he marveled at his good fortune. "Gorgeous ring for a stunning woman."

"Hey, Cap," someone called. "What's the third surprise?"

Now would be the tough part. An exciting new chapter, but bittersweet. Letting go of his future wife, he gave her a reassuring wink, and addressed the group again.

"As you all know, Chief Mitchell is retiring at the end of next month, and a number of promotions have resulted." A murmur rose, the men shifting. They knew what was coming. "I'm excited, but also sad, to tell you all that I've accepted the position of battalion chief, effective January first."

This time there were no cheers, but the faces looking back at him were smiling wistfully, and some of the guys uttered heartfelt congratulations.

"We're not surprised," one man from C-shift said. "You're the best, Cap, and everyone knows it."

His throat threatened to close, but he went on. "I'm not so sure I deserved it, but rest assured I'm going to do my damnedest to fulfill that role to the best of my ability. Never forget you're still my men, my friends, and my brothers. I'll just have a hell of a lot more of you to keep in line, that's all."

This earned some laughs and a lot of agreement.

"Of course you're wondering how my leaving will affect the station. Everyone involved said it was okay that I gave the news of their new positions, so here goes. Effective January first, Howard Paxton will be your new captain, Zack Knight your new lieutenant, and Julian Salvatore the new FAO for A-shift. Let's show these guys the recognition they deserve."

A round of applause met the completion of his announcement and he grinned. Before he could yell for everyone to eat, however, Howard stepped up.

"Before we chow down, Zack and I have a couple of surprises of our own, and our lovely wives said we could share the news." The lieutenant, beaming, gestured for Kat. "My beautiful wife and I decided we'd tell you guys that our baby is going to be a boy!"

His news was met with a loud, happy cheer. When it finally died down, all eyes turned to Zack and Cori.

"And ours is a girl!" Zack shouted.

Sean joined the guys in slapping Howard and Zack on their backs and handing out manly hugs, and kissing the moms-to-be. Then he turned and yelled at the crowd.

"Okay, guys, what do you say let's eat?!" he called over the hoopla.

That got everyone moving and a line formed at the food. Amelia was swept into the throng and gently pushed to the front of the line by his gallant men. The pretty woman soaked up the attention like a sponge.

Eve hooked her arm through his. "Thank you, for all of this. I'm so incredibly happy, I could burst."

"Me, too, baby."

After everyone was stuffed, he called the men together and they hung their stockings on the wall of the living room to kick off the holiday, a tradition they enjoyed. They also hung the ones for the men who weren't present, with Amelia's enthusiastic help.

There were three strings of stockings, one for each shift, and each stocking had the firefighter's name on it in glitter. Well, a bunch of stockings and two felt menorahs, but the sentiment was the same.

Peace, love, and joy.

Sean's stocking hung above the others, for the last time.

"They're going to miss you," Eve said softly, watching the men get into the holiday spirit. "At least I get to have you to myself at home."

Home was her apartment, while they shopped for land to build a new one, together.

"I'm not going far. I'll always be here for them. And for you."

"I'm going to hold you to that, handsome."

"See that you do."

And then he swept her into his arms and kissed her thoroughly, regardless of who was watching. He figured, perhaps, they'd turn the other cheek.

After all, he was a man who'd lost everything.

And found redemption in the arms of a very special woman.